Striking the Match

REDWOOD BAY FIRE
BOOK THREE

HJ WELCH

Arlo: A Daddy for Summer

Bears-4-U (Daddies and bears multi-author shared universe)
Keep Me

————

BY HELEN JULIET

Standalone contemporary Fairy & Folk Tale and Classic Literature Adaptations set in the UK

The Fairy Tale Collection Box Set (Beauty and the Beast, Cinderella, Rapunzel)

Daddy's Fairy Tales Box Set (Daddies and kink – Goldilocks, Little Red Riding Hood, The Three Little Pigs, Puss in Boots)

In Good Spirits (Daddies and kink, Christmas, MMMM – A Christmas Carol)

Sweet Tooth (Christmas – Hansel and Gretel)

Jacked Up (D/s – Jack and the Beanstalk)

Rise and Shine (Novella – Sleeping Beauty)

We're All Mad Here (Novella – Alice in Wonderland)

CHAPTER 1

Teddy

MY DAD ALWAYS SAYS, 'CAREFUL WHAT YOU WISH FOR.' Usually, I just roll my eyes at him.

Right now, I'm thinking I probably should have paid more attention to his warnings.

All summer, it's been as dry as a tinderbox with wildfires sweeping through the whole of SoCal, so you can bet I prayed my ass off for a little rain to help us out.

I think I prayed too hard.

The heavens opened when I was smack bang in the middle of my run, literally at the farthest point away from my house. They've been forecasting thunderstorms for days, but nothing ever materialized.

Until now.

Within seconds, I'm absolutely drenched. "Motherfucker!" I cry. It's like standing under a shower at full blast, and I gasp as I uselessly try to wipe the warm water from my eyes and spit it out of my mouth. My chest was already heaving from the cardio, but now I splutter as I stumble to a slower jog, blinking and looking up at the overcast sky.

The air already feels cooler, which I am grateful for. But

the earth is so parched and rock-hard, I know that most of this water is going to just run off the ground, fast. I might not be on duty, but that doesn't mean I ever stop thinking like a firefighter.

Sorry, a *probationary* firefighter. The One-Thirteen never lets me forget for long that I'm still not fully qualified. They also like to constantly remind me that I'm by far the youngest on the squad.

It won't last forever, though.

One day, I'll be a real member of the team, and somebody fresh will come up from the academy.

Then they'll be the baby, not me.

Which is one of the reasons my fitness is so important to me. I have to prove every single shift that I'm good enough to be there, that I can keep up. It's not even as if I'm young for a probie, as people frequently start training fresh out of high school and I went to community college first. But at twenty-three, I'm still a few years behind anyone else, and having such a round, baby face doesn't help matters. Truth be told, I actually like the way I look. But it drives me nuts how everyone always treats me with kid gloves, both at home and at work.

And don't even get me started on dating. None of the guys I'm attracted to ever think I'm mature enough for them, so I've basically stopped trying. At least for now. Maybe when I'm qualified and grow into my face a bit more, they'll start taking me seriously. And get my own place, god. Living at home makes financial sense, but it doesn't exactly scream 'I'm a grown-ass man.'

Having my workout disrupted is incredibly frustrating, but I don't need to be dwelling on those things right now. After balling my fists up for a few seconds and letting the rain wash over me, I take a couple of slow deep breaths and remind myself that I was basically heading home anyway.

Yeah, it'll be uncomfortable, but so is running drills in full turnouts, and I manage that regularly enough. So I kick up my heels and get going once more.

If I knew this downpour was doing any good, I'd probably be less annoyed. But it's going to take a while before the ground softens enough to absorb anything again. My route happens to currently be taking me alongside the river as I head toward the freeway looming overhead. I'm not sure what direction the storm rolled in from, but I can see that that water has already swollen, suggesting there's most likely already been rain upstream to cause the surge.

Like I said, everything's just rolling right off the ground and racing to get back into the ocean.

I'm just grateful I paid attention to the weather warnings, even if I didn't believe them after so many days of inaccuracy. But it meant that I left my phone and earbuds back at home. It might have been a boring run until now, but at least I'm not worrying about my electronics getting damaged. They're supposed to be water resistant, but at the rate this is coming down, I wouldn't want to risk it.

The rain is so loud all around me that I can barely hear my feet slapping against the pathway. There's no one else dumb enough to be out here. There wasn't ten minutes ago, either, but now it feels kind of creepy with the ominous darkened sky overhead. I know I should keep going, but when I stumble under the overpass, I slow to a halt to catch my breath and shake the water out of my ears for a sec.

I'm torn on whether or not it's a good thing I don't have my phone on me to summon an Uber. On the one hand, I need to finish this run. On the other...I'd really like to be home and dry as soon as possible.

That's not an option, though, so I roll my shoulders and stretch my calves, deciding that once I get going this time, I'm not going to stop until I get to my front door. Whatever my mom's cooking us for dinner, I'm going to earn it. Especially as she was making zucchini chocolate chip muffins when I left. I'll be having one or three of them, too.

I puff out my cheeks and crack my neck from side to side, my gaze drifting to the rushing water as I prepare to set off… then I stop.

A flash of orange catches my eye that looks out of place in the fast-moving river. It's bobbing around by a clump of reeds right on the edge of where the freeway above is blocking the rain, giving me slightly better visibility. Still, I frown and jog closer to the bank, my heart rate picking up, telling me something is wrong.

It could just be some trash. A scrap of plastic or a discarded high-vis jacket that's been blown into the current. But after all the calls I've been on with the One-Thirteen, I know not to ignore my gut. I'd rather double check everything's okay than make a mistake that might haunt me.

The loose soil of the sloping bank is already turning to mud before I even try scrambling down it. There's a small tree I can use for support, though, so I edge closer to the river, squinting my eyes at the patch of weeds, wondering if I imagined the whole thing.

That's when something thrashes just below the surface. I freeze, not blinking despite the water still running from my hair into my eyes. I make out a triangular ear. A paw. The tip of a tail. It snaps back and forth, like a rescue beacon screaming for help.

The struggling blur has broken free of the reeds and is being swept down the river. I gasp as my gaze meets a wide and terrified bright blue pair of eyes surrounded by matted ginger hair.

It's a cat.

And it's going to drown.

I don't even pause to think as I dive into the frigid water, the current immediately dragging me along, fast. But I don't spend all my free time training my ass off for nothing. Every day I set foot into the firehouse, I'm making a commitment to battle against nature, and I very rarely lose.

Today is not going to be one of those days. If it's me verses this deluge, I'm the one coming out victorious.

Within seconds, I'm powering through the water, back out in the rain, keeping my head up just enough to track where the cat is up ahead of me. The poor thing keeps being pulled under and I'm frantic thinking every time they submerge, they're not going to come back up again.

My body was already aching from the run, but now my arms and legs are burning. That's not going to stop me, though. If anything, it focuses my determination, pushing me to move faster so I can close the distance between me and the panicked creature.

Luck is on my side. The cat manages to dig their claws into a protruding root, granting me a few precious seconds to catch up.

"I've got you, baby!" I tell the little thing as the current slams me into the tangle of roots and reeds.

But I'm a *lot* bigger than a kitty, and the dry, crumbling ground was unstable before the downpour started. Everything breaks loose against my body, and the cat's makeshift life raft dislodges.

"No!" I splutter, automatically reaching out to grab the scruff of their neck. That only makes the drenched orange fluffball hiss and slash out with their claws. What brief grip I had on them is lost as we're both yanked back into the current. We're moving away from the freeway now, getting closer to where the river widens as it begins to merge with the ocean.

A flutter of fear graces my chest. I'm not coward, but that doesn't mean I don't appreciate a dangerous situation when I see one. In fact, that's one of the most fundamentally important things about being a firefighter. Understanding the peril but charging headlong into it anyway.

If we get caught in a riptide, however, it won't necessarily matter how strong of a swimmer I am. Nature could win this one.

Then I lock eyes again with the exhausted, pissed off cat bobbing just a few feet away from me, and decide that if this little thing still has fight in them after who knows how long battling against the water, then I can muster up plenty more energy still.

"C'mere!" I cry, lunging forward and sweeping my arm around the squirming bundle of fury. My reward is more hissing and slashes from their claws, but I'm not letting them go this time.

While the cat thrashes as I try and hug them under my arm, I manage to yank my hoodie zipper down a few inches. We both drop under the surging water while both my arms are momentarily out of commission, but if anything, the shock works to my advantage, making the kitty still and cling to me in panic. I thrust the little one inside my top like a baby's papoose.

Gasping, we resurface and I switch around so I'm on my back. I can't see shit now, and that's less than ideal. But if I stay on my front, the cat will be under the water. The rain pounds onto my face, making it harder to breathe. But I've got them. I realize they're not as small as I assumed. For a cat, they're actually quite a beast.

"It's okay, it's okay," I gasp as the cat wails in my face, their belly pressed against my chest. I wince, trying to ignore the sting of their claws through my T-shirt. It's worth it, though, as I hug them against me and realize they've stopped trying to resist. Do they understand I'm trying to help? I hope so.

With the not-so-small kitty safely anchored to me, I twist my head, trying to see what's coming up ahead of us. The banks have gotten much steeper here so even if the rain hadn't made them slippery, it would be hard for me to get us out. I don't fancy our chances any better farther down the river, though, so when I see another large clump of reeds, I kick my legs and aim us in that direction.

They only slow us down, however, not stopping us moving completely. I curse as my free hand flails around, hoping to chance on another root or anything sturdier that I can cling to. I'm not sure if I would call it luck, but I do wrap my hand around something solid but also sharp and rusty. I yelp as it cuts into my skin, but we're suddenly anchored.

Breathing heavily, I peer through the rushing water and just make out the shape of an old, contorted bike frame. "It'll have to do," I tell my new companion, glad that thanks to work, my shots are up to date.

Those bright blue eyes stare up at me, surrounded by bedraggled orange fur, and they let out a pitiful meow that sounds more like a howl.

"I know, baby, I know," I tell them, looking frantically around for anything to help us out of this predicament.

Being stationary isn't good enough. I need to haul us out of the damn water so we can get warm and dry. We're both probably going to need some medical attention as well, but one thing at a time.

First things first—how do we scale the bank?

I blink against the rain and suddenly realize we're not as alone as I previously assumed. There are people on the side of the freeway looking down at us and some more at the top of the bank on both sides. Some are waving at us. Some are shouting things I can't hear—I assume they're speaking as their mouths are moving, or they have their hands cupped either side of their faces. Quite a few people are filming us, because that's the age we live in now. And a couple are talking on their phones.

A siren blasts through the air.

I grimace, not sure if I'm happy they called for help or not. The last thing I want to do is make a fuss. I can handle myself. But even as I glance around me again, I appreciate that's not exactly true. Unless we get a hand, we're not going to be escaping this torrent any time soon.

Obviously, my team isn't on shift, but I know a few of the guys on the second and third watches, so maybe it'll be okay. However, when the engine screeches to a halt at the top of the bank, I can see by the One-Two-Two plastered on the side that it's one of the San Clemente rigs, not the One-Thirteen from Redwood Bay.

"Hold on, son!" the first firefighter yells down at me. "We're coming!"

"Yeah, I'm okay," I try and tell them, frustrated I need help at all. I should have been able to do this by myself. But another few guys have appeared, already throwing ropes down to reach me and the orange kitty.

"Don't panic, kid!" the next one yells as he prepares to scale the bank.

I sigh. "I'm a firefighter, too, I'm—"

"If you struggle, you might get loose, and the current will pull you under!" the man I assume to be their captain calls out to me. "Just stay there and wait for us!"

I grit my teeth, wondering if my team are this thoughtlessly patronizing to the folks we usually rescue. To be fair, without training, I wouldn't blame anyone for freaking out in this situation. But I'm mostly just cold, wet, and my hand is hurting like a bitch.

Then I glance down at my new friend and remember why I jumped into a swollen river in the first place.

"I've got a cat here," I tell the team as they approach. "It was drowning."

"You saved it?" one of the other guys asks, craning his neck as he gets closer. "Aw! Good job, buddy!"

"It's best to leave these sort of things to the professionals, though," the captain says sternly as they start throwing webbing around me to haul my drenched ass out of here.

"No, I'm also a—" I start to bite out, then I deflate.

What's the point? I *did* jump in here without backup and got both myself and this poor cat stuck. I'm always so determined to prove I can do everything on my own that I didn't stop to think. It could have gotten me into real trouble if those passersby hadn't called 911.

"Thank you," I say meekly. Now I'm more secure, I peel my hand off the bicycle, wincing at the gash across my palm.

"Our medics will get that seen to, don't worry," another firefighter assures me like I'm a frightened little kid.

I'm too tired to even get riled up about it, much like the ginger beast that's curled up inside my hoodie still, wide blue eyes darting around as we begin our ascent. I hope someone has a box or something up there I can use to keep my new friend contained. I don't know if they're a stray or someone's pet, but I know I'm personally going to get them to a vet before I go anywhere to get my hand seen to.

A cheer goes up as we make it back onto stable ground, and my fractious mood softens as I appreciate that all these people stuck around to make sure we were okay. Well, that *I* was okay, I guess. They almost certainly wouldn't have been able to see the cat from how far away they were.

It's important to me they know how valuable them calling for help was. Also…okay, yeah, there's a part of me that needs to prove I'm not a dumbass who got himself in trouble for no reason.

So as soon as I'm steady on my feet, I wave at the nearby gaggle of onlookers who have stayed out in the rain to make sure this little saga had a happy ending. I hug the ginger cat to my chest, praying they won't bolt, then use my bloody hand to peel back the hoodie so the small crowd can see my new friend.

One of the people recording on her phone gasps. "The firefighters saved that cat!" she cries. The gaggle cheers again and a couple of the One-Two-Two guys wave and bow in appreciation.

"Just doing our jobs, folks," one of them says, not sounding humble at all.

I look down at the kitty and chuckle ruefully. "Typical," I tell them.

The cat hisses at me and wriggles, apparently trying to make a run for it.

I'm not sure why I expected anything less.

CHAPTER 2

Cassius

"A̲ʀᴇ ʏᴏᴜ sᴜʀᴇ ʏᴏᴜ ᴡᴀɴᴛ ᴛᴏ ᴅᴏ ᴛʜɪs *ʀɪɢʜᴛ* ɴᴏᴡ," ᴍʏ PA asks, half incredulous, half irritable. But I'm already sliding into the driver's seat of my Ram Longhorn, so he sighs in resignation and yanks open the passenger side door.

"Yes, Bryan," I tell him firmly. He's only been with me six months, and I think he's great. Honestly, I'd have been totally lost without him since my retirement. But we are wildly different people, and sometimes I have to put my foot down before the sass overwhelms us both.

Secretly, the fact he takes zero shit from me is the reason I hired him in the first place and pay him a ridiculous salary. But I'd never tell him that. His ego is already outrageous enough.

The garage door is automatically rising, and I back out into the California sunshine. Usually, the weather would be a guarantee. But after a bone-dry summer, there have been some torrential downpours over the past week that have wreaked havoc across my little hometown of Redwood Bay.

Luckily, the land where I had my new place constructed is

"

a very low-risk flood zone. But I still picked a hell of a week to move in.

I can see why Bryan is confused why I had to jump in the car and get out of here so fast. The movers barely put down the last box. I bet if we hurry, we might even catch up with their trucks.

The truth is that although I'm happy to be back after a couple of decades away and closer to my family once more, the second my front door closed, the silence was deafening and the overwhelming thought of 'What the hell do I do now?' threatened to take my knees out like a linebacker. After spending most of my waking (and often not waking) hours of my adult life with my teammates, I'm more than a little afraid of the solitary life I'm now facing.

Not just that. Once I get used to it, I could probably do with a little peace and quiet after my high-flying career with the Seattle Seahawks. The problem is I have zero clue what to do with all my newfound free time. I went straight from school to football. My days have been carefully structured since I was a little kid. Now I'm at a loss, just bobbing along like driftwood in the middle of the ocean with no land in sight.

The thought of rattling around that enormous house all by myself is too horrifying to entertain for even a moment.

I'd already looked up the local animal shelter weeks ago, figuring I'd probably want to adopt a pet at some point. My schedule never allowed for it before, but we always had cats and dogs at home when I was growing up. I've missed having a four-legged friend around.

It became immediately clear to me, however, once I was actually standing in my new, empty home, that finding some company was more of a priority than I realized it would be. Sure, Bryan's going to be hanging around a lot while I get settled in. But he has his own place in town to get sorted, his own life to live.

He hates when I change plans on a whim, though, and I can feel his haughtiness beside me even with my eyes on the unfamiliar road. "Perhaps you should call ahead and let them know we're coming?" I suggest by way of an olive branch. He's always more content when he's busy.

Sure enough, when I glance over at him, his phone is already pressed to his ear. It probably was before I even asked him. "What do you think you pay me for?" he quips with an arched eyebrow, making me snort. He has a point. "Hi! Yes," he says suddenly to whoever has obviously just answered on the other end of the line. "Could I please speak with the manager? No, nothing's wrong. My boss is just interested in coming in today. In fact, we're driving down now, and well…I just wanted to make sure that was convenient for you guys and go over a couple of things."

I tune out as he begins the delicate matter of explaining who I am. I don't need to worry about security for things like this, thank fuck. After being the team's star player for so long, it'll take a few years for the cloud of fame to stop hovering over me quite so persistently. I used to hate that I couldn't even go grocery shopping back in Seattle without someone wanting a selfie.

Don't get me wrong, I adore my fans and understand the responsibility I have to them, not to mention what a privileged position I've been in. But some people can be real jerks with no concept of boundaries. They act like they know you, that because 'they made you famous' they somehow now own you. People like that don't understand someone like me can have a bad day and not want to perform on demand like a monkey in a circus.

But without the fame and the fans…who am I anymore?

Without the game consuming my life, what direction do I point myself in? Sure, Bryan has built on the sponsorship deals I already had, and it's been fun shooting a couple of different campaigns over the summer. But I can hardly say that selling cologne or vodka is my passion.

The boundary-challenged fans were an annoying but unavoidable side effect of getting to live my dream. Is it reasonable to hope that I find a new dream? Or have I already had my fair share?

I puff out my cheeks and shake my head. Bryan's still talking on the phone, so hopefully he hasn't picked up on my little existential crisis. I have to cut myself some slack or else I'm going to lose it. Moving house and potentially adopting a new pet is enough for one day. Maybe tomorrow I can ponder on who the hell I am and what the hell I'm doing in this new chapter of my life.

I remind myself that a little anonymity is going to be very refreshing. Outside of the football bubble, I'm genuinely not that famous. To be fair, a *lot* of people like football. But I'm hoping plenty of small-town folks will just treat me like an ordinary guy.

However, Bryan and I both know that as a celebrity, showing up somewhere unannounced where I'm going to need some customer assistance could be a real dick move. Luckily, it sounds like from his side of the conversation that the shelter currently doesn't have anyone else visiting the animals and they're going to do their best to keep it that way for me to have some privacy. It also seems like the woman Bryan is talking with knows who I am from the couple of high-pitched squeaks I caught down the line. I'm glad we didn't just walk in. She might have had a heart attack.

"All good?" I ask once Bryan ends the call.

He narrows his perfectly lined glittery eyes at me from behind his frameless glasses. "I'd much rather be back at the house coordinating with the interior decorator, but yes, the puppy people are expecting you." He sniffs and taps his phone on his thigh. "If I get anything unsavory on these shoes or anything else, I'm going to sue you."

I grin. He threatens to sue me at least twice a week. "It's a shelter, not a farm. But in the unlikely scenario that you get a spec of dirt on your designer-clad ass, I promise I will pay for the dry cleaning, okay?"

He harrumphs, pretending to still be mad as he stares out the window, but I catch the smile that tugs at the corner of his mouth. I'm fully aware that he lives for all the shit that I put him through, figuratively and literally.

My new pad is out of town, but Redwood Bay isn't all that big. It only takes us around fifteen minutes to get where we're going, and the lot is half empty as I park up my car.

I've barely killed the ignition when the front door flies open and a young white woman spills out, almost tripping over her own feet and clutching her hands to her chest, her eyes as big as saucers.

"I'm guessing that's my new friend, Paisley," Bryan says dryly, but I chuckle.

As much as fame can be exhausting, I do still get a kick out of seeing unbridled joy on strangers' faces like that. Knowing that me throwing a ball around a field was the highlight of some people's week or the thing that got them out of bed or kept them going when they felt like giving up… it was everything to me.

And now it's gone.

Nope. Stop that. Game face on.

"Come on, grumpy cat," I tell my PA with a wink. "If you behave, I'll give you a nice fishy as a treat after."

He wrinkles his nose as we close the car doors, and he comes around to my side of the car. "If you mean you'll get me takeout sushi from that Japanese place that just re-opened, then I promise to keep my claws away."

"Deal," I say enthusiastically, already planning dinner from there for myself as well. That way, I won't even have to bother digging out and washing any plates.

We looked it up earlier, knowing we'd probably need to order in after the move. If the reviews are anything to go by, the food there has only improved since an earthquake tore through the restaurant. The fact that the owners got back up on their feet so quickly after a disaster like that only makes me want to support them even more. Who knows? Maybe it'll become my new go-to place.

The young woman has been joined by an older Black man. He's placed his hand on her shoulder and seems to be gently anchoring her in place as she vibrates. He has a warm smile as we approach. The way his thumb is looped into the belt around his ample waist and how he rocks slightly on the balls of his feet make him seem relaxed and friendly.

"Mr. Garda," he says once we're close enough so he can unhook his thumb and reach out to grip my hand. "It's a real pleasure to have you here."

"A real pleasure," the woman, echoes.

"Please, call me Cassius," I insist as we shake.

The man chuckles. "Gus, and this little firecracker here is Paisley."

"I just think you're awesome, Mr. Garda," she gushes, her cheeks pink, and she vigorously pumps my hand with both her much smaller ones. "I went to Redwood Bay High, too. I was on the cheerleading squad!"

"No way," I say kindly, even though the options for schools around here are pretty much either the high school or one of the fancy private academies out of town. If she's a local, the chances of us having that in common were almost guaranteed. But I can tell the connection is important to her. "I was always a big Sirens fan," I tell her with a wink.

"Oh, actually, we changed the name to Krakens a little while back," she says, still shaking my hand. "It felt more inclusive."

"More badass, too," I admit.

She nods enthusiastically. "But the football team hasn't changed from the Buccaneers. If you're back in town now, you should come check out the homecoming game in a few weeks!" She looks down, apparently realizing she hasn't let me go yet, and jerks her hand away sheepishly. "You know, if you have time, um…"

I chuckle and glance at Bryan who is determinedly glued to his phone, no doubt trying to hurry this encounter along through sheer force of will. While some fans get under my skin if they're not respectful, I do enjoy moments like this. But I'm certain if Bryan had his way, he'd fend every single one of them off with a squirt bottle.

"Oh, I have plenty of time these days," I say to Paisley ruefully.

That is apparently enough to snap Bryan back to us. "Well, not *unlimited* time. We do have plenty to be getting on with today, so perhaps we should—"

"Yes, of course," Gus says, hopping back and indicating the front door with an extended arm. "Please, come inside. Did you have an idea of what you were looking for today?"

We cross the threshold into the air conditioning, and I hum. Paisley grabs a clipboard from the desk. "We've just got a couple of forms we'll need you to—"

"I'll do that," Bryan cries eagerly, launching forward, desperate for the chance to distract himself from the chit chat with admin. I don't want anyone thinking that doing that sort of thing is beneath me. However, I know how much he'd rather cross Ts and dot Is than deal with human beings. So as a kindness, I allow him to knock himself out.

"Honestly, I'm not sure," I reply to Gus's question. "You've got plenty of cats and dogs here, right?"

"And a few other slightly more exotic critters," Gus says with another easy laugh.

An image of owning a pet alligator flashes through my mind, and I repress a shudder. I'm guessing he means goats or hamsters or something, but I'd rather stick with what I know.

"Maybe we could take a look at the cats to start with?" I suggest.

I'm sure I'll be longing for a dog's high energy soon enough. But after everything over the past year, starting with a mostly self-sufficient pet might not be the worst idea. We can both adjust to the new house together in a slightly calmer fashion.

That's if I feel a connection. I'm sure the temptation to adopt every animal in the building will be strong. Whatever happens, I'll be giving a large but quiet donation to the shelter so I can feel like I'm helping all the little souls I don't take home today. But I have to have a spark with whoever I do pick. If I don't feel that today—whether that's with a cat or a dog or a god-damned baby kaiju—I'll just have to come back another day.

The truth is I'm not entirely sure what I'm looking for. But I'm hoping I'll know it when I see it.

"Oh, we have plenty of kitties who'll be delighted to meet you, I'm sure," Gus says as Bryan apparently finishes up the paperwork. While he looks like he wants to escape to the car, Paisley looks like she wants to grab my hand again and drag me through the doors to start our visit properly. Instead, she skips ahead and pushes them open, leading us into a clean and bright area with a few dozen cages, almost all of them home to a skittish looking cat.

"We let them out as much as we can," she explains to us as we follow her inside. I start peering at the faces as we pass. "Especially in the evening when we don't have any visitors. But it's easier to keep track of them like this and they spend so much of their time sleeping anyway."

I sigh, wishing for them to all find the happy forever homes of their dreams.

"Every animal here is chipped," Gus tells us. Well...me. Bryan doesn't look like he's listening as he practically tiptoes down the aisle, looking more apprehensive of the felines than they are of him. "If they're not fixed by the time they're adopted, we organize for that to happen with their new owners." Gus continues. "We do our best to profile our guests all on our socials to attract people from farther afield, but it's difficult."

"When we get litters of kittens, they always go fast," Paisley says, sounding less than bubbly for the first time since we arrived. "But the older cats..."

I shake my head, not needing her to finish her sentence. "I don't think I want a kitten or a puppy. I want to give someone a chance that might not have had one yet."

"We have plenty of those," Gus says, his voice warm but also a little sad as well.

They take their time as they show me along the row of cats. As predicted, I could easily take every single one of them. Who knows? If I don't work out what else to do with my time, perhaps I'll just turn my home into an animal sanctuary. But I'm not feeling that pull I was hoping for with any of them in particular.

Maybe I was wrong and I actually do need a higher energy pet right now to keep me on my toes. Rather than a calming presence, I might need a little crazy to get me out of bed in the mornings. Am I really going to find that here? Should I change tactics now and go look at the—?

"Holy shit!" I yelp as the cage to my left suddenly rattles and hisses. Okay, so obviously it's not the *cage* that hisses. It's the raging ball of orange fluff inside it. I grab my chest and laugh at myself, taking a breath and peering at the retreating aggressor. "Is…is that a tiny *lion?*"

Gus and Paisley laugh at me, but not unkindly. "Oh, that's Flow," Gus says with an exasperated sigh. "We haven't had her long. She's a Maine Coon, but she was so matted when she arrived, we had to shave most of her body to start over again."

"She had to be sedated for that," Paisley half-whispers, keeping her distance.

"She was a stray?" I ask.

The cat in front of us might be naked aside from the puffs of floof around her head, paws, and the tip of her tail. But she also has these big blue eyes that are looking at me with such intensity that I can't help but see her beauty despite her fear.

Gus nods. "A cat like that needs grooming every single day. She would have been in a lot of discomfort—maybe even pain—from the matting."

My heartstrings tug in my chest. All cats should have access to shelter and regular food in my opinion. But breeds like this need extra special care, and she's just been left out in the wild to fend for herself.

"You know her name is Flow, though?" I ask, assuming she had a home once and was microchipped.

However, Gus shakes his head. "We know nothing about her other than she was rescued from a river during one of the recent downpours. No collar or chip until we gave her one, no one posting about missing her online that we could find. We guess that she's about a year old, and I don't think she's belonged to anyone her whole, short life."

I bite my lip, my gaze still locked with her blue one. That's so sad. "So you named her Flow because of the river, yeah?"

"Yep! A firefighter pulled her out!" Paisley tells me excitedly. "He literally jumped into the water to get her and then a bunch of *other* firefighters had to get them both back out again when they got stuck! I saw a video compilation on TikTok. Super dramatic. That first firefighter brought her into us himself. Wouldn't leave until he knew she was going to be okay."

I blink, looking between the staff and this miracle kitty. I already know she's the one, but I have to ask. "Didn't he want to keep her?"

Gus smiles and carefully extends his fingers through the wire loops. Flow creeps forward to sniff them. "I think he would have loved to. He said something about someone being allergic at home."

"His mom *and* one of his brothers, I think," Paisley adds. "But a cat like this is going to be a hell of a lot of work for whoever adopts her. Not for the faint of heart. I reckon she's probably going to be here a very long—"

"I'll take her," I say firmly, not taking my eyes off Flow's blue ones. I'm not sure about that name, I must admit. But hopefully she hasn't gotten attached to it yet.

"You will?" Gus asks in surprise.

"We will?" Bryan asks with far more urgency.

I snicker at him and pat his shoulder. "Don't worry. I promise this is all on me. No lion-taming duties will be added to your roster."

As if on cue, Flow swipes at us again before hunching down and hissing.

"You could pick literally any animal in here," Bryan mutters, sounding genuinely concerned. He eyes up my ginger menace warily in spite of my promise to him.

Gus laughs fondly. "We wouldn't blame you if you wanted to keep looking."

"Seriously," Paisley adds with a wince.

I shake my head. "It sounds like Flow's going through a dramatic life change," I explain to the three of them. "I can relate to that. Maybe we can help each other and build a home together."

"Oh…" Paisley said faintly. I glance to see her looking all melty at me. "That's beautiful."

"Not the adjective I'd pick," Bryan grumbles, squinting at Flow. "But you do like a challenge, don't you?"

I grin at him. He knows me well enough by now to tell when I've made up my mind.

"Yes, I do," I murmur.

Speaking of someone who likes a challenge…

"You said a local firefighter rescued her?" I prompt Gus.

He nods, but it's Paisley who answers. "During a flash flood! He was sooooo brave and sooooo hot and…" Gus quirks an eyebrow at her in a very fatherly manner, and she stops talking with a squeak.

"He does sound brave," I agree. "I'd love to meet him."

If I'm going to commit to taking Flow home with me, I want to make absolutely certain that her original savior isn't having any lingering second thoughts. I'll be disappointed if he changes his mind and wanted to adopt her himself, but I'd rather know for sure.

And—not that my dating life is anywhere close to a priority right now—but if he's sooooo hot…it might not be a chore to say hello and thank him for what he did, right?

"I bet he'd love to meet you," Gus says enthusiastically. "Let me go find his details. I'm sure we took down his number."

"If not, there's literally only one fire house in town," Paisley tells me helpfully, a sparkle in her eyes.

"I think we've disrupted quite enough businesses for one day," Bryan says in mild alarm.

As much as I want to get this over and done with as soon as possible, I have to agree with him. It's one thing to drop in on the shelter when no one else is around. It's quite another to potentially interrupt a working fire station.

But if I could arrange a one-on-one with this guy before officially taking Flow home, I know I'd feel a lot better. I'm ready to get on with this new phase of my life.

Hopefully, this firefighter can help me out with that.

CHAPTER 3

Teddy

"Uh, yeah, sure…I can come in," I say with a frown.

Lili Kwon glances at me briefly before returning her attention to the screen. She's currently trouncing our other friend from the One-Thirteen, Sawyer Nelson. Luckily, I was taking a turn out when my phone rang. No way either of them would have missed an opportunity to race ahead or even run my avatar's car off the track, no matter the circumstances. Not that I was doing all that well with my bandaged hand, anyway.

"Eat dust, Nelson!" Lili crows as I close the call, jamming her thumbs against her controller.

"You're such a cheat," Sawyer growls back, not giving up despite Lili's obvious lead.

"It's not cheating, it's skill," Lili says smugly. Whatever it is, the race is over shortly after that, leaving Sawyer groaning and Lili with her arms in the air like she's just scored a touchdown. By then, I've already got my sneakers back on.

"You're leaving?" Lili asks when she finally notices, dropping her hands and pouting. We're at her place for the afternoon and I know the plan was to order pizza, but my heart is in my throat.

"Yeah, sorry, guys," I say, genuinely apologetic as I grab my wallet and keys. "That was the shelter calling about that cat I rescued."

"You mean that cat the One-Two-Two rescued," Lili scoffs devilishly. It took about five minutes for the story of what happened at the underpass to fly around the station, and my colleagues have very much enjoyed teasing me mercilessly about it.

But Sawyer's eyebrows shoot up. "Oh, no. Is she okay?"

"Uh, yeah," I say with a nod. That was my first question as well. "She's fine. Great, actually. Someone wants to adopt her. Apparently, this person wants to meet me to say thank you."

"Couldn't they just write you a note?" Lili asks dubiously.

"Or bake cookies for the house!" Sawyer suggests.

"Like we have a shortage of baked goods every shift," I say with a laugh.

The truth is I was thinking the same as them, though. The guy from the shelter, Gus, was clear I didn't have to come in if I was busy. It does seem a little presumptuous of whoever this person is to summon me there. I got the impression they really wanted a face-to-face before going through with the adoption after hearing their new cat's rescue had been all over TikTok. Perhaps they're feeling star struck or want to have a viral moment of their own.

Or maybe they just want to laugh at me for getting my ass stuck and having to be rescued by another fire house. My guys have certainly gotten endless torment out of it. Who knows?

Well, I guess I will once I show up. Because no matter the reason, you bet I'm jumping at the opportunity to see Miss Kitty one last time.

It broke my heart to hand her over to the shelter. Their onsite veterinarian gave the orange terror an examination right there and then and assured me that aside from being underweight and a couple of other minor health issues, she was in pretty good shape.

Then the staff asked me if I was interested in taking her home.

The hope in their eyes broke my fucking heart almost more than having to say I couldn't. Allergies run in my family, so there are several people that either live in my house or who visit regularly enough that would suffer horribly if any cat were to live there, let alone such a fluffy one as Miss Kitty. My brother Nate, especially, would kick up a shit storm if I even suggested it.

It was on the tip of my tongue to tell the staff that I could take my house deposit savings and start renting my own place as soon as possible just so I could keep her. *I'm* not allergic, after all, and I love the fire house's resident feline, Smokey. In fact, I usually bring treats on shift with me to bribe some affection out of her. Because of everyone's allergies, we obviously never had pets when I was growing up. However, I always hoped when I got my own place, I'd be able to change that.

So, yeah. Miss Kitty might be a handful. But we went through something together and it didn't feel right to dump her when she obviously didn't have anyone giving a crap about her for a long time, if ever.

Pledging to move house on a whim for a cat I just met would have been irresponsible and impulsive, though. Things I'm trying so hard not to be now I'm an adult. Miss Kitty deserves someone stable and secure in life, not someone like me who's still trying to get their shit together. Not someone who, despite having a good job, is still living at home with his parents.

So hopefully, whoever this person is who's interested in her right now can provide that for her. I'd feel better if I met them and knew for sure, so that's how I find myself making hasty excuses to my friends before high-tailing it to my car. It's a short drive to the rescue shelter, but it feels like plenty of time to get my nerves up.

What if I don't like this person? It isn't as if I have any right to put my foot down and stop the adoption. What if this only leaves me feeling worse?

I grit my teeth as I pull into the parking lot, trying to convince myself that I'm way, seriously overthinking this. I'm sure my first instinct is right, and they simply want to make another video to follow up after all the initial ones from the rescue. People will like that. It'll give them comfort if they know that the river cat landed on her feet.

Still unsure of what to expect, I kill my ignition and get out of my car, surprised at how deserted the place is. There are only a couple of other vehicles around, including an extremely swish-looking Ram Longhorn pickup truck. Wow. I'm pretty sure those things cost upwards of seventy grand.

"Mr. Foster?"

I drag my gaze over to the person who's just exited the shelter's front door. He isn't anyone I spoke to the last time I was here. I would have remembered someone so distinctive.

He's white and slim with frameless glasses that seem to highlight rather than hide his expertly made-up face. The SoCal sun catches the subtle glitter around his eyes, even from several feet away. He's gripping his phone tightly to his chest as he walks swiftly over to me like he's balancing on a tightrope but also has a rocket up his ass. I'm pretty much a jeans and T-shirt kind of guy, but even I can tell this dude knows fashion. His chinos are turned up to reveal bare ankles, accentuating the bright yellow shoes that perfectly match the shade of the vest he has on under a gray hoodie and navy tailored blazer. I want to ask how he's not melting in all those layers, but his blond hair doesn't even look damp.

His style and body temperature might be cool, but the intensity rolling off him as he comes to a stop in front of me reminds me of a blazing housefire. I'm stressed out just standing near him.

"Bryan Kallis," he says, sounding like the crack of a rifle. He stabs his hand toward me for a single but extremely firm shake. "Nice to meet you."

I'm not sure he means that, but I smile anyway. "You, too. Are you the one adopting the cat?"

"Am I…? No." His mouth twitches more than smiles. "I'm here representing my boss, who's inside. It was his idea to meet you."

I can tell Bryan doesn't agree, giving me an uneasy feeling. Just what exactly is going on here?

"Okay," I say slowly. "Does he want to film me? Are you here to get me to sign something? Because I might have to check with my captain if—"

"What? No," Bryan says, somewhat urgently. "Absolutely no filming. We shouldn't need an NDA, but would you mind shutting your phone off before we go inside? It would just make sure everyone's protected."

I blink slowly at him. An *NDA?* Who the hell is adopting this cat? The mafia?

"So…you didn't want to meet me to make a follow-up TikTok?"

Bryan's jaw clicks. "Oh, I'm sure there will be plenty of TikToketry. My boss loves that sort of thing. But at least he lets me review the footage before he posts. Look, I'm sorry for the cloak and dagger. The last few days have been…well, the last few weeks…months…"

He exhales, and I see a flash of tiredness and vulnerability that makes me think Bryan isn't completely the prickly asshole he presents himself to be.

"If privacy is your concern, I promise to be discreet," I tell him truthfully. To prove my point, I pull my phone from my back pocket and show him as I power it off. The guy's shoulders creep down a fraction from his ears.

"Thank you," he says softly. "I love the man, I do. But some days, it's like trying to keep a toddler from sticking his fingers into a socket."

The second the words leave his mouth, his panicked eyes flick toward me, like that inner thought was never, ever meant to be an outer one.

I mimic zipping my mouth shut, locking it, then throwing away the key.

Bryan gives me a weak laugh.

"Let's get this show on the road, shall we?" he says, shaking his head and walking back toward the front door, apparently trusting that I'll follow. Which I do, because not only do I want to see Miss Kitty, but now I'm also intrigued as to who this mysterious boss of his is. Some eccentric tech bro? A cute grandpa from old money? A movie star? Whoever he is, the fact that he's hired a clearly queer assistant makes me feel the chances of him being a total douche are less.

But this is still a million miles from how I imagined my afternoon from going, and it's all highly unusual. I keep my wits about me as I follow Bryan inside the building, then through another set of doors into the cat enclosure. And then...

And then I see Cassius Garda.

Former Seattle Seahawks quarterback.

Redwood Bay legend.

And my personal hero and longtime crush.

He's just…sitting cross-legged on the floor, holing his fingers out for a miniature lion on a leash to sniff.

I freeze. It isn't even a conscious decision. My feet and everything above them just quit working without handing in notice or anything. The electrons in my brain all fizzle out. There's nothing but sand where my tongue should be and my bones are suddenly and inexplicably made of Jell-O.

Then he looks from the cat directly at me with his warm, hazel eyes, and I think time itself comes screeching to a halt.

"You must be Theodore," he says with that dazzling smile I've been mesmerized by for over a decade. I know every line of his perfect face. Hell, it's plastered all over my locker at work. The guys give me crap about it constantly.

Am I even going to be able to tell them this happened?

"T-Teddy," I manage to stutter. "Everyone calls me…um…"

In a flash, I'm wondering if I should have just stuck with Theodore. No one calls me that, not even when I was little. I was named after my great grandfather, but my mom said as soon as I was born, it was clear I was a Teddy.

But Theodore is so much more sophisticated. Everyone in my whole damn life treats me like a kid, and now Cassius Garda is going to as well.

Shit.

"Hi, Teddy," he says without missing a beat. "Paisley's been showing me the videos of how you saved little Flow here. It's an honor to meet you."

The words simply don't make sense. Did I eat too much sugar at Lili's and fall asleep? This has to be a glucose-induced hallucination. Because Cassius Garda did not just say that it was an honor to meet *me*.

That would be ridiculous.

"Uhh…hi," I finally manage to croak.

"You're a real-life superhero!" the young blonde girl cries. I remember her from when I brought Miss Kitty in.

"Oh, it was a team effort," I say lamely, thinking about how the One-Two-Two is going to hold that incident over the One-Thirteen for the rest of time, I'm sure.

She waves her phone in my direction. "Nuh-uh. You were the one who jumped in first. If you hadn't seen Flow, who knows what would have happened."

My stomach tightens as I look at the freshly shaved cat—now apparently called Flow. I have a very good idea of what would have happened, and I don't want to dwell on it.

"I'm just glad she's safe now and, um, someone wants to adopt her."

It's almost comical how I try and avoid making eye contact with Cassius Garda. But it's as if when his eyes meet mine, they find the off switch to my brain. I'd rather come across as rude or shy than a drooling idiot.

Except he's unfazed by my awkwardness and just keeps trying to pull me in with the warmth that feels like it's radiating from him.

"You're a part of her origin story," he says reverently. It breaks through my fog of embarrassment, and I gape slightly at him.

"See...superhero," Paisley whispers loudly.

Why...why is Cassius Garda talking to me this way? I know for a fact that there are plenty of fanfictions about celebrities all over the internet that sound like this, and they get slammed as cringy self-insert fantasies. But judging from the fact I'm still not waking up despite subtly pinching my thigh several times...this is actually real life.

"Is that from the rescue?" Cassius asks. It takes me a second to realize he's pointing at my bandaged hand. "One of the videos mentioned it looked like you got injured."

Embarrassment makes my cheeks heat up. I'm so

ashamed that I couldn't even rescue one damn cat without needing help, but I hurt myself doing so. "Oh, it's nothing," I mumble. "There was an old bike in the river and, um, anyway, I'm fine now."

"Are you sure? Does it hurt?"

The way he asks…it's like he actually cares and isn't just trying to be polite. Obviously, my captain and the rest of the team care that I can still do my job, but I'd never admit to any of them that it still stings, because that would make me look weak. And my mom fussed because that's what mom's do, but all my dad cared about was that my insurance covered the hospital bill.

It would be really weird if Cassius Garda was the most concerned of them all about how *I* was feeling, right?

"Um, yeah, it hurts a little," I find myself admitting. "But—"

"Sorry about that!" the shelter's manager, Gus, interrupts as he comes ambling over to us, a docile fluffy white and gray cat lying belly up in his arms. "I wanted to start letting our residents out to roam free for a while, seeing as we won't have any more guests after you guys. How is Flow getting along?"

I grimace internally. Miss Kitty wasn't the best name, I know. And Flow is clever, seeing as she was plucked from a river. But I'm not sure it suits the tiny terror currently flicking her tail dangerously, looking like she wants to maul a man who's literally made lists titled 'The World's Top One Hundred Sexiest Men.'

"She's doing recon on me," Cassius quips. "Initial reports are sketchy at best."

I bark out a laugh before I know what's happening. But he always seemed like he had a goofy sense of humor in his interviews. I can't believe I just witnessed it for myself.

No one else heard that silly joke, though. There are no cameras here. It was just for the people in this room.

I feel like I've been given a precious gift that I'm going to treasure forever.

The shelter staff are smiling, and Bryan is engrossed in his phone, so I'm the only dork acting like a hyena at the idea of a shaved orange cat with binoculars. Heat flames across my cheeks, but when Cassius grins at me, my mouth seems to operate of its own accord.

"She's not a very stealthy scout. She needs some camo gear."

That's when Cassius Garda laughs at *my* lame joke, and I realize this isn't a dream.

It's a whole parallel universe.

I don't know if it's because the thought is so ridiculous that it unlocks something inside me. But in that moment, I don't tear my gaze away from my teenage hero's, and I keep talking. Like we know each other. Like we're friends.

"Are you really going to adopt her?" He nods, and so do I. "Good. That's good. She deserves to be spoiled. I wish I could have given her a home, but it's just not possible. Thank you for making sure I knew she got a happily ever after."

"Of course," he murmurs, hazel eyes still blazing into mine. "You can come visit her any time you like, though. I could get your number."

Get my...what? He didn't seriously just ask for my number, did he?

Whoever's writing this fanfic needs to calm the fuck down.

"Oh! Jesus!"

I spin around to see that Bryan's frozen as if he's been caught in the sights of a T-rex. His eyes are bugging from his skull, his back is hunched over, and his arms are up like he's about to start flapping them any second now. Except what's pinned him to the spot isn't a prehistoric predator.

It's a tiny black cat.

This creature is half the size of Miss Kitty-Flow, even after she's been shaved. I'm not sure if they jumped on Bryan from above our heads or scaled him like King Kong on the Empire State Building. However they managed it, they're now perched across the fussy assistant's shoulders, their claws extended enough into his well-tailored navy blazer to keep them steady but not to scratch him, or so it looks.

"It's…vibrating…" Bryan whispers, as if they're secretly a bomb that will detonate if he speaks above a certain decibel.

"Aww, that means she likes you," Paisley says, clasping her hands in front of her chest.

Gus sighs. "Come on, Twelve. Get down from there."

"Twelve?" I question. That's an even worse name than Flow.

But Gus just shrugs apologetically at me. "We get so many black cats through here, we gave up naming them. Now we just number them."

"So…you have twelve black cats alone?" Cassius asks, looking crestfallen.

"Oh no," Paisley scoffs. "If one gets adopted, that number is up for grabs again. This is probably our third Twelve, right, Gus?"

A lump forms in my throat. All these cats who need homes, and I can't adopt any of them.

It's as if the crazy bubble with Cassius pops. I've just stepped into his world for a brief moment. This isn't real life. I don't belong here. It was a nice fantasy while it lasted, but I have to pull the plug on this fanfic before I do something mortifying that I'll regret for the rest of my life.

"Uh, thank you so much for, uh, but I have to go. Yeah. Things to, um…thanks…"

"Hold on a second," Cassius says from where he's still sitting on the floor, his eyebrows shooting up. But I just smile and nod at everyone—even the cat on Bryan's shoulders—and hurry out the door so fast, I'm practically running.

When I get outside, I really do run. All the way to my car, turning the ignition as fast as I can before peeling it back onto the street, leaving a cloud of churned up gravel in my wake.

Luckily, home isn't far. Because I'm hardly watching the road at all as I replay every excruciating detail of what just happened on repeat in my mind.

Yeah, it was all pretty awkward. But I don't think I said anything truly offensive or dumb.

And I did make my celebrity crush laugh. Once. It was most likely out of pity, but I'll take it.

I think it's best for all concerned if nobody ever finds out about this. Maybe with time and some rose-tinted glasses, I'll be able to laugh about such a bizarre encounter one day.

But for now, I'm going to pretend like it never happened.

Fanfiction deleted.

CHAPTER 4
Cassius

"WHY DOES NOTHING IN THIS KITCHEN LOOK LIKE IT'S BEEN used?" my mom asks in a disapproving tone as she bangs her way through my cupboards.

I sigh fondly from where I'm lying on my side. I'm grateful for the shag pile rug I had imported, otherwise I'd be pretty uncomfortable on the wooden panels. "Because I've been here a day and a half, Mom. I'm still unpacking. I can't even find the forks."

"So you've been living off takeout, hmm?" She kisses her teeth. "That stuff will rot your guts."

I laugh and shake my head. "After two decades working with some of the best nutritionists on the West Coast, I am perfectly aware of how to feed myself. Some maki rolls and burgers aren't going to hurt for once."

"You're going to let me cook us dinner now, though, right?"

If she'd allow me to spoil her, I would. But her idea of a good time will be pottering around making us something ten times more delicious than I could ever order. I lean up and wink at her. "I wouldn't dare try and stop you."

"Good boy," she says approvingly.

I lean back down to continue my staring contest with the angry cat currently camped out under my sofa. But the angle is awkward, and my shoulder fires a jolt of pain down my arm as I do. I can't help but hiss and jerk my whole body with it.

Of course that spooks Kiki, who hisses in retaliation and backs another few feet away from me.

"Damn it," I mutter. So much for building trust with her. I know it's barely been twenty-four hours, but I feel like I'm failing her already.

"Are you quite all right down there?"

I blink and look up at Bryan's upside-down face. "Yeah, Kiki's under here."

"Kiki?"

I give up and wiggle around until I'm standing in front of him, brushing my hands on my thighs to get rid of any lingering debris left by the movers. The pain is already fading, thankfully. "Her new name. I thought she looked like a tequila sunrise, so 'Kiki' for short."

"Ahh," my PA says approvingly with a nod, tilting his head to peer in the gap between the floor and the sofa, but Kiki is far too well hidden to be seen from this vantage point.

I squint at him. "Are you okay?" He returns his attention to me, and I gesture toward the scratches on his arms and hands.

"Oh, yeah, fine," he says hastily. "Just…you know…putting furniture together. Hi, Mrs. Garda!"

I'm not sure why he's being skittish with me, but my mom is already barreling over to throw her arms around my usually touch-averse PA.

"Bryan! You're too skinny. You'll stay for dinner, yes?"

"Oh, I couldn't…" My mom narrows her eyes at him. "…

say no to that!" he pivots fast. Sensible man. "You got the grocery delivery I organized, then?" he asks me.

"Yeah, dude. You're a life saver. Thank you."

He preens. "I know."

For the time being, I concede defeat and leave Kiki to her hiding spot. The staff at the shelter warned me it could take a good while to gain her trust and see any improvement. She's used to roaming wild and fighting her own battles. I hope one day soon she'll understand she doesn't have to do that anymore.

She's definitely confused by why she's not allowed outside anymore. My plan is to build her one of those catio things out back, and I want lots of bridges and perches on the walls inside so she can roam around her own private urban jungle. However, she's currently unimpressed at my attempts to protect both her and the local wildlife by keeping her indoors.

Sometimes doing what's right makes us sad. Or in her case, cranky as hell. But I think about how Teddy Foster did the right thing by allowing me to adopt her, even though he clearly cares about her after their river adventure together.

My mom is chatting with Bryan, telling him all about what my younger sister and brother are up to at the moment. He settles on one of the breakfast barstools, and I find myself wandering over to the coffeemaker to fix us some drinks. If my mind is going to drag me back to thoughts of Teddy, it'll be good to have something physical to do with my hands so I don't end up daydreaming into space with other people around.

It's crazy, I know. We barely spent ten minutes together yesterday at the shelter. And yet I find myself mesmerized by the memory of him. When a guy's that cute, it's not surprising, really. His round face was almost cherub-like, complete with a dimple on his left cheek when he smiled.

I liked making him smile.

I liked making him blush even more, and with his pale complexion, it was quite easy. Last night I couldn't stop myself from imagining what I'd whisper in his ear to make him flush even harder. How I'd run my hands through his thick blond hair and grip his broad shoulders and...

The coffeemaker pings, saving me from my filthy thoughts. I clear my throat and set about fixing cups for my mom and Bryan the way I know they like it. But it doesn't stop my mind from wandering, still, musing on the past.

In many ways, I was incredibly lucky and privileged during my time with the Seahawks. Being their golden boy gave me the security to come out while I was still playing. It was fucking terrifying, nonetheless, and some fans and pundits had some truly vile things to say about me.

But the team's owner had my back and so did our coach. I knew how incredibly important it would be for queer representation in the game, and if I didn't have the guts to do it, how could I expect anyone else to?

So I made an Instagram post. Simple as that. I had to do two shots of vodka before jabbing the send button, then immediately wanted to throw up. But I had several guys from the team with me, cheering me on. They wouldn't let me chicken out after I explained how much coming out meant to me, and I'm grateful they didn't.

Yeah, the 'tight end' jokes came flying in thick and fast in the comments section. Some people tried to drag our center into the drama, saying I had no right being between his legs despite that being where—you know—the ball was I had to throw down the field. So many women took it as a challenge to try and 'turn me straight again.' There were countless memes and comedians talking about me on TV and sport journalists trying to trash my reputation retrospectively.

But then there was my team, who were cooler about it

than I ever could have hoped for. Countless fans who flooded me with support. LGBT organizations from all over the world heralding me as a hero. A couple of companies dropped me from their campaigns, but others jumped in to take their places, and I much preferred knowing I was working with people who weren't bigoted.

Ultimately, none of it mattered. Because when all was said and done, I was still the absolute shit. No one could throw like me, and I helped Seattle reach unfathomable heights. I was their shining star for a decade, and once I came out, I was going to keep on doing all of that, but also proving football can be a space for the queer kids, too.

Then I blew my rotator cuff and dislocated my shoulder, and everything was gone in an instant.

Nowadays, I understand I didn't lose 'everything.' But it damn well felt it at the time. My gay, Black ass was supposed to spend the next few years changing hearts and minds, one victory on the field at a time. But my spotlight was snatched away, just when I'd finally convinced myself to be vulnerable and set an example. In my mind, it felt like a punishment. I didn't get to go out on my terms with a Super Bowl ring on my finger, confetti falling from the sky.

Instead, I was stretchered off the grass in blinding pain, saying goodbye to my career with a whimper rather than a bang.

However…I wasn't even out of hospital before my agent got an email from an uppity, determined PA claiming that if I didn't want to fade into obscurity, I needed him more than I knew to get my life back on track.

As I sip my coffee, I grin fondly at Bryan from behind the mug, grateful every day for his outrageous audacity.

Gradually, my shoulder healed as best it could, and the pain faded. I'll probably have to do physical therapy the rest of my life, and it'll catch me out like it just did more times than I'll ever know.

But with Bryan working with my agent, thrusting me into shooting a series of commercials and doing interviews left, right and center, I wasn't allowed to wallow in self-pity. I was able to remind myself that I still had my family, my friends, and my reputation.

Oh, and I was still a millionaire. Kind of hard to get too down on life when I have the freedom and security to do pretty much whatever the hell I want.

While I was on this journey of self-discovery, though, it left little time to try and date now that I was finally out of the closet. As soon as I went pro, I was far too afraid to ever try and hook up with anyone in secret. I really don't want to think about how long it's been since I had sex with another human being.

So perhaps that's why my brain is stuck on a fixated loop of thoughts of Teddy Foster. I'm like a parched man finding an oasis in the desert.

Except, he's hardly the first gay man I've come into contact with over the past several months. Bryan certainly didn't elicit this response in me. I shudder at the mere idea, then laugh to myself. I love him, sure. But in a completely platonic way.

The feelings that have stirred around Teddy have been anything other than platonic.

Since coming out, the percentage of gay men in my everyday life probably quadrupled, yet Teddy has been the only one to turn my head.

And when I suggested swapping numbers, he ran a mile.

I lean against my kitchen counter and chew on my lip, grateful that Bryan and my mom are entertaining themselves, chatting and chopping veggies while I brood.

Teddy could be straight, but I'm absolutely positive I got a vibe. And it could be that he wasn't interested in getting to know each other, but his breathless laughs and starry eyes said otherwise.

The more I turn it over in my mind, the more I come back to the fame factor cock-blocking me again. Of course a young guy like that is going to be intimidated. In fact, I probably wouldn't be attracted to him the way I am if he was a rabid fan, enamored by my celebrity. If he sees that as a downside rather than a bonus to pursuing anything, that says a lot about his character.

But it still leaves me besotted and frustrated. Something that hasn't gone unnoticed by my eagle-eyed PA, apparently.

"Come on, spit it out," Bryan says, as if I'm a puppy chewing on the TV remote.

I arch an eyebrow at him. "Huh?"

"Don't play dumb with me, mister," he huffs. "You've had your head in the clouds since I arrived. No…" He looks slyly at my mom. "You've been distracted since about halfway through our visit to the animal shelter yesterday. Have you got a certain baby-faced firefighter on the brain?"

"No! I…" My argument dies before it can even form, and my mom's face has lit up like the Fourth of July.

"A boy?" she cries, abandoning the shallots she was crushing to give me her full attention. "You deserve to meet someone nice, Cassius!"

I wave my hands at them both before they can get the wrong impression. "We met for all of ten minutes," I say firmly. "He was the guy that rescued Kiki. But then he left, and that's it."

"It was clearly long enough to leave an impression," Bryan quips smugly.

I sigh and head for the fridge. "I need a beer," I mutter.

"Ooh, get me a glass of the chardonnay in that case," Bryan calls after me. "Rosie, you'll join me?"

"Naughty boy," she says with a laugh, lightly smacking him with a dish towel. "Oh…go on then."

I'm not sure if I want my mom getting tipsy and trying to fix my love life. But then I deflate and realize there's probably no stopping either of them…and actually…I don't want to. I don't have to hide this stuff anymore. It's about time I started discussing it openly and maybe asking for advice. Because apparently, I'm not getting anywhere on my own.

"So…" I say tentatively as I re-approach with our drinks. "What if I *was* interested in Teddy? Would that be a terrible idea?"

"His name's Teddy?" my mom practically squeals. "Oh, I adore him already."

Bryan, on the other hand, has his game face on. "Assuming he likes you back?"

I shrug, thinking about how fast Teddy left yesterday. "Yeah, it's entirely possible I imagined the vibe between us at the shelter."

Bryan scoffs, making me blink in surprise. "Bitch, please," he says, shaking his head. "Sorry for my language, Mrs. Garda. Cassius, that boy wanted to climb you like a tree. Again, sorry for being inappropriate, Mrs. Garda. But the big man clearly needs some help with this."

"With what?" I ask defensively despite absolutely knowing the answer.

Bryan flutters his eyelashes at me. "The pretty boys," he says slyly. "And that one was pretty for days, also, definitely interested. You just scared him off with…"

"With what?" I ask again, slightly pathetically this time.

He snaps his fingers then waves them around to encompass my house. "With all of *this*, honey. You. You're an international sporting legend. He's a small-town firefighter. I'm sure his brain short-circuited, and his survival instincts told him to flee. But trust me, the sparks were flying."

I take a sip of my beer and mull over his words. "Okay, that's cool," I say slowly, not wanting to get my hopes up. "But that brings me back to my original question. Is it a terrible idea?"

"You mean because he's definitely at least a decade younger than you with absolutely zero media training and clearly worships the ground you walk on?" Bryan crooks an eyebrow at me as he sips his white wine. "No, I can't see why any of that would be an issue."

I groan, but my mom sighs and gently swats Bryan's arm. "Sweetie," she says to me. "If you felt something special with this young man, you'll regret it if you don't give it a try. Let's say you ask him out on a date, what's the worst that could happen?"

One of the best things about my mom is that she still just sees me as her baby boy, her firstborn, her little prince.

It's Bryan who laughs before I can respond. "The worst that can happen? Hmm…he could lure Cassius into a honey-trap, swindle millions from him, gather compromising screenshots and photos, then go running to TMZ to earn even more millions in a devastating tell-all interview."

"No?" my mom gasps. "Surely no one would do that? Would they?"

I groan once more. "I'm never having sex again," I mutter, shaking my head. "I'm going to become a nun and go live in the mountains with my cat."

"Orrrr," Bryan says pointedly. "He could simply be a sweet, shy boy who would love nothing more than to hear from you again. You could live happily ever after together with a hundred angry cat babies."

I chuckle but something warm stirs in my chest. I like that option a lot better.

"He didn't give me his number, though," I say. "Even if I did want to reach out to him, how—"

"Got it," Bryan interrupts triumphantly. I'm not even sure when he picked up his phone, but he's grinning at it, then at me.

"You found his cell number?" I ask dubiously. That doesn't sound ethical.

Bryan rolls his glittery eyes at me. "Our new friend, Paisley, said yesterday that there's only one fire station in town. I've got *their* phone number in front of me."

"That's right!" my mom agrees cheerfully. "Such lovely boys. And they have a lady firefighter, too! Whenever the church has a fundraiser, they're always happy to bring their truck along for the kids to play on. And they do fire safety talks all around town!"

"Hi, there," Bryan's perky voice pipes up, and I realize with mild horror that his phone is pressed to his ear. "I don't know if you're able to tell me if Teddy Foster is on shift at the moment? It's only that he saved my friend's cat, and my friend would really love to say thank you." *Again,* he mouths silently at me.

I'm going to kill him.

He just smiles sweetly, though. "Yeah, I know people just show up in person, but my friend would rather not do that. He doesn't want to make a fuss. Of course, I understand if you can't divulge that information for security—oh! We can talk to the captain? Tomorrow? Yes, that would be amazing! What was your name? Nancy! Thank you so much, Nancy. My friend is going to really appreciate your help. You have a good evening, now."

With a devilish grin, my PA hangs up and sips his wine, ignoring my incredulous stare despite keeping his eyes locked with mine.

"You *are* a naughty boy," my mom titters, waving her veggie knife in his direction.

"I can't believe you just did that," I croak.

"You can call any time after eight tomorrow morning," Bryan informs me, then shrugs. "Or not. It's up to you. If you're thinking about dating and want someone who understands living in the limelight, I'm sure I can line up twenty adorable actors and pop stars before the end of the week. But if you don't want the boy next door to slip through your fingers, now you have a chance to speak to him again."

I glare at him, swirling the beer in my bottle. Honestly, I don't know what I want. Bryan reckons Teddy ran away because he was scared. Well, he's not the only one. It doesn't matter right now that I'm famous and rich. I feel like an awkward teenager trying to ask a boy out for the first time.

But is my mom right? Will I regret it if I don't at least *try*?

I think I know the answer to that from the way I physically recoiled at the idea of Bryan setting me up with someone from 'my world.' I'm not interested in a hypothetical also-famous boyfriend so we can parade for the tabloids together.

I want something *real*. And there's a chance I could find that with Teddy.

If I'm brave enough to come out to the nation, I can be brave enough to risk being rejected by a sweet and kind firefighter.

Like my mom said: what's the worst that could happen?

Ignoring Bryan's response to that particular question, I take a deep breath and nod. "I could just see if he wants to hang out, right? Show the new kid around town. No pressure."

"That sounds like a nice plan," my mom says, reaching out and patting my cheek.

"No pressure," Bryan scoffs, finishing his glass of wine. "Sure, big guy. If that gets you to stop moping and get proactive, I'll take it."

He winks at me as he slides off his barstool to fetch the

chardonnay bottle, showing me that despite his snarky tone, he is genuinely supportive. I'm certain he understands just what a huge leap this is for me.

But if Teddy can jump into that river like he did to save Kiki, then I can take this metaphorical step forward. I'm never going to date anyone if I'm too afraid to try. I get the feeling that Teddy is going to be worth trying for.

Maybe I won't have to become a nun after all.

CHAPTER 5

Teddy

IT'S ALWAYS A GAMBLE TO SHOWER BETWEEN CALLS ON SHIFT. I guess it's a gamble to do anything when the tones could go at any second. But you only need the alarm to sound once when you're buck naked with suds in your eyes to make you wish it never happens again.

After a call like the one we took first thing this morning, everyone's scrambling to get rinsed off as fast as possible so they're not left in a sticky situation…literally. Of all the trucks to jackknife and tip on the interstate, why did it have to be the one hauling crates of maple syrup? I've always been a fan, but now I feel like it's gotten into every crevice of my turnouts, not to mention my body. I'm not sure I'll be able to look at a bottle or stomach the smell for weeks.

"Don't use up all the hot water!" Lili warns, banging on my door.

There are four cubicles, so we have to take turns, and I intend on being as quick as I possibly can be. But as the probationary firefighter, I usually get last dibs on everything. It's just the way things are. However, today I caught a break and was able to sprint into the locker room and throw my clothes off just a little faster than everyone else.

"If you keep harassing me, I'll only take longer out of spite!" I fire back, just to yank her chain. I wouldn't really do that. But if there's one thing I've learned from being the baby of my family and then coming into this firehouse, it's that you won't last long if you show weakness.

"Unless you want to find a surprise in your bunk later, Probie, I suggest you—"

I yank open the door and grin at her. "All yours, Your Majesty."

She scowls at me and shoves past. "I might not be a girly girl," she grumbles. "But I sure as shit have way longer hair than any of you guys."

"Oh, please," one of the other firefighters, Anton Quick, chimes in. "Like you could possibly have a beauty regime more complicated than Sawyer's."

"I heard that!" his best friend yells from one of the other cubicles.

"You were meant to!" Anton shouts back, grinning at me.

It's times like these, when we're in it together, that I don't feel like I'm at the very bottom of the pecking order. We're all just running around in towels or nothing at all, desperately trying to de-syrup ourselves, laughing and giving each other a hard time. Even Lieutenant Flores is in the fray as well as our grumpy, older driver, Gene Haskell.

"No need to make a circus out of it," he says, towel wrapped around his thick belly, marching through to the lockers with his flip-flops smacking loudly on the tiles.

"You missed a spot," Rico Flores teases him, earning himself a flip of the bird. Gene tends to stay behind the wheel. Therefore, any maple syrup he managed to get on himself probably came from us, so I get why he's pissed. Still, I think he got off pretty lightly.

Unlike Lochlan Bell, whose red hair is practically vertical as he waits his turn to get under the water.

"Did you tip a bottle over your head or what, Beast?" I ask, looking at him in the reflection of the mirror I'm using to help me rub some moisturizer and sunscreen on my face.

He whimpers. "It's *sooo* sticky," he says, flicking his fingers like that might get more of it off his skin while he waits.

"Almost done!" our lead paramedic, Zahir Delacroix, assures him from the other side of the door.

"You sure picked a hell of a last shift before you leave for your honeymoon, Del," Lochlan says to him.

"Maybe it's a maplemoon!" Sawyer quips as he and Anton swap places in the end cubicle.

Anton shakes his head before he closes the door. "I'm pretty sure they're all about cherry flavored stuff in Japan, right?"

"I can assure you, the cuisine is just as diverse as the culture," Del says warmly as he too exits his shower, making way for Lochlan.

Unfortunately, Beast is too slow. Before he can set foot past the threshold, his young Dalmatian dog comes tearing out of nowhere, thundering through the puddles on the floor and straight into the cubicle.

"Rocky, no!" Lochlan cries, but it's too late.

So…Lili and I might have taught Rocky how to jump up and press the water button on the shower. It's not so funny when the wet dog then goes and lies on the sofas in the common area. But seeing the horror on Lochlan's face right now is absolutely hilarious.

The other guys join me in doubling up laughing as the now drenched Rocky slips back past Lochlan as he tries to grab his dog. The Dalmatian zooms around him with ease, though, leaving a still sticky, half-naked Lochlan to chase after him.

"Bets on how long his towel lasts," Sawyer says.

Our other paramedic, Yara Ortiz, frowns as she brushes her damp hair. "That's not very kind."

Sawyer shrugs. "You don't have to bet."

"Oh, no," Yara says with an even deeper frown. "Ten bucks says it's already off."

Sawyer meets her for a high five before running after Lochlan and his adolescent dog. "Ten bucks says they make it past the gym!"

Chuckling, I take a moment to focus on throwing fresh clothes on, then carefully bandage my stupid hand up once more. I'm sure we'd all appreciate it if we got a few more minutes before a call comes through, but at least I'm now decent and so are a couple of others.

I'm extremely grateful for the chaos of the house. It was nice to start with a job where no one was really in danger, too, so we could be busy without the stress of potentially losing any lives.

Busy is good right now.

I spent yesterday in a blur of chores so I wouldn't have to stop and think too hard about what happened at the animal shelter the day before. I'm sure my mom thought I was possessed as I went hunting for tasks that have needed doing for months but that no one ever seems to have time for. But I'd rather mend fences and paint skirting boards than dwell too long on…

Well, you know…

That time I met my idol, drooled all over him, and generally made a total idiot of myself.

I cringe even just thinking about it now, hoping none of my teammates notice anything's off with me during the rest of our shift. There's no way I want any of them to ever find out about my disastrous meet cute. They already tease me enough about the magazine cut outs I've got of Cassius

Garda in my locker. If they discover that I made a fool of myself face to face with him, I'll be hearing about it until my dying day.

My knee-jerk reaction is to take those pictures down. Looking at them first thing this morning made me want to pass out from humiliation and regret. But I think the crew will absolutely notice and realize something's up if I do, so I think I just have to suffer the constant reminder for now.

Hopefully, the shame will fade soon enough and it'll all just feel like some weird fever dream. I just need to make it to tomorrow without anyone calling me on my distracted mood. By the next shift, surely I'll have a handle on things again. I just pray that I can keep myself occupied enough so my wandering mind doesn't get the better of me. We've got most of the day and all night to go yet, and just because we started out with a bang is no indication of how the rest of the time will pan out.

If I hadn't just had a shower, I'd be tempted to try and burn off some of this nervous energy with a workout. Maybe later. Right now, I head to the kitchen in the hope of distracting myself with food for a bit.

It still doesn't seem possible that I actually met Cassius Garda, let alone that he was so nice and friendly toward me. If things like that happened in real life, they'd happen to someone like Lieutenant Rico Flores. He's handsome, in his thirties, accomplished, and can generally talk like an adult. Whereas I'm...well, I'm the probie.

But in the quiet moments yesterday I had to stop and confront the fact that the encounter *did* happen. To me. Cassius Garda smiled at *me*, laughed at *my* silly joke.

Maybe I shouldn't have run away.

What do I expect would have happened if I'd stayed, though? It would have just gotten awkward. That thing he said about getting my number—he didn't mean it and it would have been horrendously cringe if I'd actually tried to give it to him.

No, I saved everyone a lot of pain by leaving when I did. And in the moments where I stop beating myself up for long enough about being such a fanboy, I'm able to reflect on the fact that he was a genuinely nice guy, or at least he seemed to be during the brief time we had together.

They say you should never meet your heroes. But mine turned out to be even better in person than he appears on TV.

Should I have stayed longer? Tried to talk with him a little more? No, that would have been asking too much. I'm extremely lucky to have met him at all. He said my *name*, for crying out loud. I'm sure he'll forget it quickly enough. But for a brief, shining moment, Cassius Garda knew who baby Teddy Foster was.

That's got to count for something.

Lochlan is still running around the main open plan area of the fire house, dashing between the rigs in his attempt to corral Rocky. My sympathies get the better of me, so instead of heading to the kitchen, I jog over to them.

"I'll get him, Beast. You go rinse the syrup out of your hair before you start attracting wasps."

He gives me a goofy, grateful smile. "You sure?"

"Yeah," I tell him sincerely. He doesn't need to know how desperate I am for any distraction I can find.

"I owe you one," he calls over his shoulder, already running back toward the shower block.

I chuckle, doubting he means that. It's the probie's job to pick up the slack for everyone else. But it's still a nice thing to hear in the moment. I have a lot to learn and I'm eager to do it. I'd just rather not be taken for granted while I'm earning my place.

It takes a couple more minutes to finally grab Rocky by

the collar. I probably could have managed it sooner if I'd gotten serious and told him to heel the way Lochlan showed us from his puppy training classes. But I enjoyed playing chase with the excitable dog for a while and didn't want to spoil that. Hopefully I haven't derailed his training too much. But it seems worth it by the way his tail doesn't stop wagging the entire time I'm drying him off with a towel.

By the time we're done, most of the team is back in the common area, the TV is on, and Del and Yara are in the kitchen, preparing lunch and some kind of baked goods respectively. I'm on my way to offer any help if they need it, but before I can get there, Captain Valentine leans over the railing from the second floor where his office is.

"Foster," he calls down, getting my attention. "Telephone."

I stop and frown. "For me?"

"No, for Elvis," he replies, dead pan.

I laugh and jog toward the stairs. "Okay, okay," I say as Lili and Sawyer jeer at me.

But I've been here for over a year now and I don't think that I've ever had anyone call me on the landline. If they had, Nancy would have answered in her office then pulled me in there to take it. If Cap spoke to them first, I'm guessing it's official.

Oh…no. Am I about to speak to the chief or something? Have the One-Two-Two made a complaint about me interfering with their rescue of Miss Kitty-Flow?

Am I about to get canned before I've even qualified as a fully-fledged firefighter?

Shaking my head, I reach the captain's door and let myself inside where he's waiting by the phone. Why do I always let my imagination run off to the worst places like that? I haven't done anything to warrant a complaint or getting fired, I'm certain. But Valentine doesn't give me any clues as he passes over the handset, which makes my stomach tighten despite my best efforts to keep calm.

"Um, hello? This is Teddy Foster speaking."

"Teddy, hi!" the man's voice cries out from the other end of the line. Cap nods at me before slipping out of his office to give me some privacy.

I'm glad he did, because I am completely unprepared for the next words to hit my ear.

"It's Cassius Garda. We met at the animal shelter the other day."

I'm even more glad no one else is around to see my jaw go slack and my eyes bug out of my face. Wait—*what?* No...it can't be...

"Hello?" he asks uncertainly.

I clear my throat and scramble to collect my spiraling thoughts. "Uh...hi. Hello! I mean...uh..."

Why is he calling? This can't be happening, can it? Not again. I barely survived last time.

"I'm sorry, am I bothering you?" he says. "You're probably busy. It's just—"

"No!" I blurt out before I can stop myself.

As surreal and confusing as this is, there's a part of my brain that recognizes that it's also completely *awesome*. I never thought I'd get the chance to speak to him a second time. Whatever the reason, I'm grateful. And excited. And a little dizzy.

"I'm not busy, but I'll have to go if the alarm sounds," I explain.

"Of course," he says warmly.

"Is, um, everything okay with Flow?" I ask, thinking that's got to be the only reason he's calling.

He chuckles, sending delicious shivers down my spine. "Her name's Kiki now—short for Tequila Sunrise. And, yes.

She might be spicy and grumpy and an expert hide and seek champion, but she seems fine."

"Oh, good," I say, genuinely relieved. "And that's a much better name."

"I know, right?" he says happily, and something within me eases. If I can forget that he's a football legend, he becomes just a great guy that I'm chatting with. He makes me feel like I'm in on a secret with him, even though we're not really saying anything of much importance.

I really do prefer Kiki to Flow, however. Having that little tidbit of updated information actually does make me feel like I'm in on a secret with him.

"I hope you don't mind me contacting the station," he carries on. "I didn't want to come across like a weird stalker or anything, but I meant what I said about getting your number so you could visit Kiki if you wanted."

I blink, my heart immediately thumping harder in my chest. "Really?" I say in barely more than a whisper.

"Yeah," he replies. There's so much kindness held in just that one word. "In fact…if you're not busy, would you be able to head outside for a minute?"

It takes me a second to understand what he's just said. "Right now?" He hums in confirmation. "Uh, sure. I'd have to hang up, though."

"That's okay," he says, but doesn't elaborate further.

"Right, okay then," I say, still confused. "Um, bye then."

I put down the receiver and give myself a moment to process what's happening. Then I leave Captain Valentine's office and head downstairs, hoping no one stops me along the way.

Everyone's engrossed in their own business, so I manage to slip outside unbothered. When I shield my eyes from the sunshine, I realize the same fancy truck from the shelter is parked in front of me, just out of the way if the rigs need to tear out on a call.

That impresses me. Not everyone who visits the station is always that thoughtful.

But if that Ram Longhorn is here, then does that mean…?

Sure enough, the driver's door opens, and out steps Cassius Garda. Jesus Christ. He's even more gorgeous than I remember. Brown, glowing skin and defined muscles are on display in the shorts and tank he's wearing. His smile is full of perfect, white teeth, but it's the sparkle in his hazel eyes that really takes my breath away. His strong, square jaw has just a little stubble on it, and the way his hair is styled with a fade around the sides into short curls at the top makes his oval face seem a little longer.

For the briefest second, I imagine what it would be like to run my fingers along that jaw or against that hair. What it would be like to kiss those smiling lips.

Then I force my feet to start moving again, dragging me back to reality once more. He doesn't want me ogling him. I'm sure he gets more than enough of that. Just because I know *of* him doesn't mean I *know* him at all.

But what I *do* know is that he's here, in front of me, for a second time when the first seemed too impossible to begin with.

"Hello, again," he says cheerfully. I stop in front of him, unsure what to do with my hands. "I hope showing up like this is okay? Your receptionist said people do it all the time."

"Yeah," I croak, then clear my throat before speaking again. "We like to be a friendly point of contact for the community, day and night."

"I like that," Cassius says with a nod, looking the building over. "Well, I know you could get called away at any moment, so I just thought you'd like to say hi to someone?" He opens the backdoor of his truck where a cat carrier is sitting, wide blue eyes looking back at me from behind the wire mesh.

"Kitty!" I cry in delight, holding out my fingers for her to sniff if she wants. I'm surprised when she inches forward, putting her face closer to my hand. "I wonder if she remembers me."

"I bet she does," Cassius says. He's stepped closer to look at Kiki with me. That means he's also closer to *me*. Damn, he smells good. Sweet like vanilla but with something a little woodsy as well, so the scent isn't overly cloying.

I want an oversized hoodie drenched in it. I'd never take it off.

"We're actually on the way to a checkup at the vets," he explains. "She's having her spaying operation soon."

"Oh, we don't want any bad boys getting her in trouble, now, do we?" I joke. But I'm still amazed when he laughs. I did it again. That's crazy.

"Exactly," Cassius agrees. "As we were on our way, I thought I'd call ahead and see if you were in. I'm so glad you just got back. Apparently, there was an incident involving maple syrup?"

"Soooo much syrup," I inform him with a grimace, earning yet another laugh.

"But...yeah," Cassius continues. I glance back at him and see that he looks...well...nervous. How is that possible? He's Cassius Garda. "If you're not interested, I understand. But I'm sure she'd love a visit when she's in recovery from her hero Uncle Teddy."

I stand up and subtly shuffle back a bit to put some space between us so I can think straight. Because I'm finally starting to think that he really means it. He's inviting me to come see her. Maybe even at his *house*. It seems insane and utterly impossible and yet this is, what? The third time he's specifically mentioned it.

Would he really keep pushing the issue if he didn't mean it?

And then there's the fact that not only would I love to see her...I'd love to see *him*. I might have been able to talk myself into a rational interpretation of what happened when we met at the shelter, but there's only so much I can deny what's happening when he's right in front of me again.

For whatever reason, he seems to want to be friends. With me.

"I'd love that," I eventually manage to utter.

"Yeah?" Cassius says, his face lighting up like a Christmas tree. It makes my heart summersault in my chest.

"Yeah," I murmur.

He's already pulling out his phone, eager to get my digits. Mine's in my locker, but he shows me when he's sent a text.

And just like that, I have Cassius Garda's phone number.

Except, in my mind he's slowly becoming simply Cassius. A real man. Not a famous football star.

"Let me know when Kiki wants some company," I say, feeling lightheaded. "I'll come feed her some grapes."

He smiles and bites his lower lip. "If her human wanted some company, too, how would you feel about showing the new guy around town?"

"But you grew up here," I blurt out, then curse myself. He just asked to *hang out*. With me. Teddy Foster, the baby, the probie, the one always getting left behind and forgotten.

"Oh, yeah," Cassius agrees, looking unfazed by the foot I just shoved in my mouth. "But I left almost twenty years ago when I was a teenager. I've been home a lot for the holidays and stuff, but I haven't lived here as an adult. I've never even been to any of the local bars."

He's not...he didn't just ask me for a drink, did he? No. That would be ridiculous.

"There's lots of cool stuff around here," I say sincerely. I know some people prefer to move out to the big cities, but I really do think that Redwood Bay has a charm of its own. "I could, um, show you around a bit if you like?"

I want to snatch the words back as soon as they leave my mouth. A multimillionaire surely has all kinds of people that could help him out if he needed. But before I can cringe at myself, he's already nodding.

"I'd love that, Teddy."

Of course that's when the tones sound. "Shit," I cry, whipping my head around.

"Go!" he says with a laugh, shooing me off. "I'll message you, okay?"

"Okay," I say breathlessly, sharing one last look with him before sprinting back inside the station.

The crazy thing is...I believe him. I believe he wants to message me and wants to hang out. I might not understand why, but as I throw myself into clean turnouts, I can't find the will to care.

Cassius Garda doesn't just know who Teddy Foster is. He wants to be friends.

There's no way I'm running away from that a second time. If anything, I'm going to run toward it, just like this fire we're now on our way to tackle. There's a chance I could get burned by both.

But that's a chance I'm willing to take.

CHAPTER 6

Cassius

I SPENT EVERY SUNDAY FOR OVER A DECADE PLAYING IN FRONT of millions of people during football season. I've been interviewed by all the big talk show hosts. I've given speeches at universities and sporting associations. Hell, I've met royalty and presidents.

Yet I can't remember the last time I was this nervous as I park at the Redwood Walkway Experience.

The thing about fame is that it's a wonderful shield. As I was closeted for so long, I really did feel like there was a public Cassius and a private one that very, very few people truly knew. Only my immediate family were aware of the real reason why I never dated any women, but even then, we hardly spoke about it. I think they knew I couldn't do anything about the situation, and didn't want to hurt my feelings.

Except the situation is so totally different now, and it took my mom all of about three minutes to message the family group chat after dinner the other night, and now they're all gagging for updates about my 'sweet young man.'

Even my *dad* has instructed me to take a selfie of the two of us today.

I love that they're excited for me and it's clear they only want me to be happy. The sudden and brutal career change has rattled me, and they know it. So I get that they'd see a boyfriend as a completely different but equally huge life change, a positive one this time.

That isn't something I can will into being, though. My new career—if I ever decide what that could be—is at least relatively within my control. I can start a business or reach out to prospective collaborators or whatever.

A relationship takes two. Or hey, more than two works for some people. But the point is it's not a solo venture. That's literally the nature of the thing.

That other person needs to be interested to the same degree and want to put in the same kind of commitment, which is completely out of my hands. And it's not like I even know what the hell I'm doing, for crying out loud. I've barely dated, let alone been in a long-term relationship.

With all my accomplishments I've managed in this life, right now, I feel like a clueless kid on his first day of school.

All I can really trust is that when I saw Teddy Foster again the other day at the fire station, my heart leapt, my skin tingled, my breath hitched, and I just wanted to do anything to be closer to him. I feel like I could tell the moment when he realized I was serious about getting his number and hanging out together. It was as if his eyes got brighter and he stood up that bit taller. It was enough for hope to ignite in my chest that Bryan was right and I hadn't been imagining things.

There's a spark between Teddy and I.

Kiki and I genuinely were on our way to the veterinarian for a check-up. But given how scared she is of everyone, I honestly don't know if she'll enjoy having visitors post-op or not. But it did seem to me like she moved toward Teddy from the safety of her cage, not away. Maybe she really does remember him and they have a bond?

Whatever the case, the idea of Teddy in my house has been what's been getting me out of bed and throwing everything I've got into turning the place from a stark new-build into a welcoming home, much to Bryan's delight. Despite all the scratches and bruises he seems to be getting between setting up our two places up, he's absolutely in his element.

Seeing him happy makes me happy, even though he's refusing to let me come over and lend a hand with his pad yet. He keeps insisting that it's not ready, but isn't that the point? I want to help him get it ready the way he's been helping me. We've been in each other's lives long enough now that I'm fully aware when to stop pushing a subject, though, so I guess I'll visit when it's all pristine.

Wanting his home to be perfect before anyone visits does make sense, as that's exactly what I'm doing with Teddy in mind for myself. It would be way too soon to suggest him coming over today, so I was relieved when he asked if I've ever done the walkways in Redwood Bay's namesake forest. He was thrilled when I explained that I've walked our family dogs here for years, but I've never taken the time to book the walkway experience.

Even though we were only communicating via text, I could feel his excitement when I enthusiastically agreed to his idea. Yes, I'm extremely rich, and so are a lot of the people I've hung out with during my time playing for the NFL. And money can buy you some truly wild experiences that I'll treasure forever.

But there's also something even more special about having wealth and yet choosing to do something simple with a person whose company you're just really looking forward to. I'm fully aware that Teddy has a modest income, and I wouldn't expect him to pay for whatever we were going to do today, because this is definitely, absolutely not a date. Nuh-uh.

I don't want him to be intimidated, either, though. It's clear he knew exactly who I was when we met, and I have a sneaking suspicion he might even be a fan. But I don't want to sweep him off his feet by throwing dollar bills around. Luckily, the walkway is free. They just encourage you to donate at the end, which I will absolutely be doing.

If Teddy and I become friends, I want it to be because we click as regular human beings. Then if anything more develops, I'll be certain it came from honest, sturdy foundations.

"You're getting ahead of yourself again, Garda," I mutter to myself, drumming my fingers against the steering wheel of my stationary truck. "You like him, that's obvious. But don't go rushing into anything. Take your time. If you don't end up dating, there are plenty of other fish in the sea."

Literally. If I went down to the beach right now, I bet I could pick up a hot guy faster than an ice cream melting at midday. But I don't want a hook up. I mean, I don't think I could say no to some spontaneous sex right now, either. However, I'd much prefer a meaningful connection after all this time. Why spoil my appetite with snacks when dinner is going to be a sumptuous feast?

And there I go again, putting all this pressure on whatever fragile thing is blossoming between me and Teddy. That's the trouble with being an aggressively high achiever. I see something I want, then I work my ass off until I get it.

I just need to slow my roll for now and figure out if Teddy even wants to get got.

Nothing's going to happen at all if I never haul my ass out of this vehicle, so that's where I start. Since the storm that caused the river to swell, SoCal has gone back to blistering heat, and my skin immediately prickles with it. I might have complained about the rain in Seattle, but I did appreciate it was somewhere that had discernible seasons.

Still, I can't bring myself to actually grumble about the glorious sunshine, especially when there's a pleasant breeze at this altitude and plenty of shade from the trees all around me.

Of course these Redwoods aren't as gargantuan as the ones in Northern California or even those we had around Washington state. This forest was created artificially back in the seventies as an ecological experiment using some kind of irrigation system, and when it was successful, the town was built next to it.

That doesn't mean it isn't absolutely gorgeous and one of the town's biggest tourist attractions. Well, an attraction we share with San Clemente, and as they're the fancier, slightly bigger town, they get most of the hotel bookings. But Redwood Bay benefits, nonetheless.

Huh...it's funny how naturally I've slipped back into thinking of Redwood Bay as 'we' and 'us.' But I suppose feeling like San Clemente's underdog is ingrained into everyone who grew up here, so it's not surprising I've fallen straight back into that mindset. Sharing anything in the sort of no man's land between the two towns has always brought out competitive natures in people.

It's the same with the Critter Canyon amusement park, although that closed down completely last year after a major incident that my sister swore blind involved a runaway ice cream truck. I'm still not sure if I believe her.

At least the park has reopened now, although the disaster area is undergoing serious renovations still. Which is a shame, because that's where the Tunnel of Love is. I used to daydream about taking someone special there someday. It seems stupid, but it was like a teenage right of passage that I never got to join in with back in the day.

Who knows? Maybe by the time it's finally operational again, I'll have a boyfriend of my own.

"Hi."

I startle and spin around to find a nervous-looking Teddy Foster in front of me. But then he smiles, showing off that little dimple in his cheek, and all my apprehension melts away.

"You came," I say, probably sounding like an idiot. Because of course he came. He's standing right there. But I'm so thrilled, I don't care. He's here and he's gorgeous and we're going to go on a walk like normal people.

I'm more excited about that than any Hollywood premiere I've ever been to.

He looks bashful but happy. "I was worried I was going to be late," he says as we start heading toward the walkway entrance. "But the stoplight gods were kind to me."

I laugh easily. His whimsical sense of humor is one of the things I enjoy most about him, so far at least.

"It's cool," I assure him. "I only got here a couple of minutes before you."

I'm deliberately not going to count the several minutes I spent sitting in my car, being ridiculous.

We had to book tickets in advance for an hour-long slot so the organizers can make sure there aren't too many people out on the walkway at any given time. But it's all pretty laid back and although I can see people around us, we also have plenty of space to ourselves on the track that leads up to the several stories high wooden entrance tower. Once we get to the top, a bored employee checks our QR code on Teddy's phone.

The fact that neither he nor anyone else seems to recognize me thus far is an unexpected bonus. It goes a long way to making me feel like the private me, the real me, is getting a chance to come out to play for once.

"I can't believe I've never been up here before," I marvel as we begin traversing the rope bridges. They're suspended a few dozen feet in the air, connecting wooden observations platforms on the biggest and sturdiest redwood trees. I'm glad the bridges have netting along the sides to make us feel a little more enclosed. Heights don't bother me, but it's reassuring to know my foot can't just slip out into the empty air all the same.

"To be honest, neither have I," Teddy says sheepishly, looking over his shoulder at me. "It's one of those things I've always meant to do but never have."

If I'm being honest, I'm delighted he's in front of me so I can take my time drinking in his muscular frame. He might be wearing a loose-fitting T-shirt, but his shorts are clinging to his plump ass, taunting me and my dry spell.

"That's cool we're up here for the first time together, then," I say genuinely, keeping the conversation way more wholesome than my filthy thoughts.

We reach the observation deck, but rather than continue onto the next bridge, Teddy indicates he wants to walk around to the other side of the circular platform. We have a bit of privacy here as it seems like most people don't want to stop so soon after only just getting going. I'm happy to have him one on one, so I have no complaints as I join him in leaning my forearms against the wooden railing, looking out at the valley that leads back down to town and the ocean beyond. Geography has never been my strong suit, but I wonder if I could theoretically see my house from here.

"It's beautiful," I murmur.

Teddy hums, frowning slightly as he looks out over the vista. "Can I ask you something?" he says before glancing back at me.

"Shoot," I tell him genuinely.

Normally this would be the part when I'd groan inwardly,

dreading what invasive question someone was about to spring on me. But I don't feel that way with Teddy. Maybe that's naïve of me, but then he goes and proves me right.

"You could be up here with anyone. Why…"

I smile, my heart warming. "Why you?"

"Yeah," he confirms sheepishly.

Perhaps I should give him some space in this moment. But before I can overthink it, I nudge his shoulder with mine. I'm rewarded with a bashful grin and a gorgeous blush on his cheeks.

"Why not you?" I counter gently. "You're the first friend I've made since I moved back home. It seemed fitting to ask if you wanted to come explore the town with me as I get to know it again."

"You have a lot of friends, though, right?" he says, clearly not wanting to let it drop so easily. I nod, wanting to give him time to feel his way through this. To be honest, I'm glad the topic has come up sooner rather than later. "So why… what…you're Cassius Garda!" he finally cries. Then he whips his head around, wincing as he checks if anyone overheard him. Luckily, there's no one close by at present.

"I am," I agree cheerfully. "And you're Teddy Foster."

He rolls his eyes. "There are about two dozen people who know who I am," he says pointedly. "Whereas there are probably *two hundred million* who have heard of you. Probably two million of those would claim that you're their personal hero. I'm just confused why someone as awesome as you would be interested in hanging with some kid firefighter. I'm not even a real firefighter yet. I'm still in my probationary period."

He chews his lip and looks out over the forest again rather than meet my eye.

"How old are you?" I ask, realizing we should probably clear that matter up before anything else.

"Twenty-three," he mumbles, like it's something to be ashamed of.

Phew. Okay, so I thought maybe he was a few years older thanks to all the muscles, but that's fine.

"So not a kid at all," I tease him, bumping my shoulder against his once more. "Let me save us a little time, all right? I get the freak out. It's natural. I'm someone you've probably seen a lot on TV. And you're thinking you shouldn't even be breathing the same air as me, so why the hell would I want to be friends, right?"

"You forgot the part where you're fifteen years older and a billion dollars richer," he mumbles, but I can see the smile tugging at the corner of his mouth. Good. That means I'm getting through to him.

"Pfft. Age is just a number. And I hate to break it to you, but I'm *only* a millionaire."

He laughs and shakes his head. "Only a millionaire? What am I wasting my time for, then?"

I grin, already trusting that he's about as far from a gold digger than I'm ever likely to meet.

"You're forgetting something, too," I inform him kindly.

He crooks an eyebrow. "Yeah? What's that?"

I poke his chest. He blinks at me like that's the most unbelievable thing he's ever witnessed, which tickles me.

"You've forgotten that I also met you through a screen first. I saw half a dozen different videos of you rescuing my cat before you walked through that shelter door. *You* were already *my* personal hero. So that makes us a little bit more even, wouldn't you say?"

He stares at me for several seconds before scratching his fingers through his thick blond hair. "Huh."

I chuckle again. "Thought so. Those videos also showed me that you were brave, kind, and determined. Then we met and I found out you were sweet and funny as well. So, yeah.

Does it really seem so strange I'd want to get to know you better?"

He gives me a curious look. "I feel like you're talking about somebody else…but sure, I guess that makes sense."

I sigh happily and gaze out through the redwoods and down the valley for a minute. "I hope it's okay to say that making a new friend who isn't in the spotlight feels really great right about now. You might think it's crazy I'd want to spend time with somebody 'normal.' But I'm tired of all the fakeness celebrity culture brings. Being a regular Joe doesn't mean you aren't awesome, Teddy, because I think you are. It doesn't mean you can't be full of shit, either, but something tells me you're not."

He shrugs. However, I sense the pride glowing from him. "What you see is what you get," he says, peeking over at me.

This close, in the sunshine dappling through the trees, I can admire how his golden lashes fan his cheeks, and I want to tell him I think he's beautiful as well. But I can sense we've made a lot of progress already, and I don't want to freak him out by going overboard.

"I'm kind of hoping that you want to hang out with me today because I'm the goofball who adopted the cat you rescued," I prompt. "Not because you want to leech off an NFL star."

He nibbles his lip and considers me for a moment. Long enough for doubt to start creeping up inside me.

"If we're being honest…I am a fan of yours. A *big* fan." He blushes again, harder this time. "But if I ignore all that, it feels like I'm just meeting up with someone I met on an app or something. Which is crazy and cool and surreal, and I don't even know what else."

I nod, not exactly surprised that he's a fan. I guessed as much. I like what he said after that part a lot. Except…

"Have you got an, um, app friend at the moment?" I ask

clumsily. He creases his brow in confusion. I sigh, abandoning tact. "I'm trying to ascertain if you have a boyfriend, because I'm smooth like that."

"Oh!" he cries, then rubs his neck and grins as he glances away. "Uh, no. I haven't had a boyfriend for a couple of years now. I've been focusing on work."

"Same," I say, actually managing a teeny bit of smoothness. He doesn't say anything to that, but his rosy cheeks tell me he understands my meaning. "However, work isn't really an issue anymore," I follow up.

His expression changes immediately to concern. It doesn't rankle me the way it does with other people, though.

"I'm so fucking sorry about your shoulder," he tells me earnestly. "It was a shock to me, so I can't imagine what it's been like for you."

"Shit," I admit with a rueful laugh. "It's been shit. But things are getting better now." I move away from the railing and indicate the next bridge. We start walking without having to say a word about it. "I'm not really sure what to do with myself these days, but that's why Kiki was the right cat for me to adopt. We're going to figure out our new life together."

"I love that," Teddy says warmly. "I could, um, I mean, if you want, I could help you as well. If that's what you want? If you ever want to talk to someone with both their feet on the ground." He looks down at the drop between the swaying wooden slats we're currently traversing. "Well...not right *now*, obviously."

I throw my head back and laugh. When he says things like that, I genuinely don't believe he's trying to impress anyone. That's just the way his brain works.

"I'd love that, Teddy," I say sincerely.

He looks over his shoulder as we approach the next platform. There are other people lingering there, and I have a feeling some of them might have finally recognized me. Our little bubble is about to burst.

But only temporarily, if I have any say in the matter.

Teddy presses his lips together before replying to me. "I'd love that, too…Cassius."

It's like he's testing my name out on his tongue. I hope he likes the way it tastes.

Because I adore the way it sounds.

CHAPTER 7

Teddy

I THINK MY FANFIC WRITER IS DRUNK.

Today has been nothing short of a fever dream. But the truly craziest part of spending the afternoon with Cassius Garda has to be how *normal* it all feels. I meant what I said to him earlier. If I stop thinking about him as the sports hero from the Seahawks or the face from all the posters I once had on my bedroom wall, he's just…Cassius. The guy who asked me to do something fun with him on my day off.

I purposefully haven't mentioned how tough my last shift was. He said how he was grateful to have some time away from his fame and other celebrities. It's very different, but in some ways I feel exactly the same about needing to forget about work for a few hours with someone wholly unconnected to that world.

Sometimes, we can't save everyone, no matter how hard we try. Sometimes, I see things I know I'm going to remember for the rest of my life, whether I want to or not.

Usually, I force myself to shower off the horrors, then I crawl into bed and hope that my body is exhausted enough that I'll fall asleep and put some distance between myself and the rawness of it all. More often than not, though, I just end up staring at the ceiling, neither resting nor forgetting.

So I might be tired, but as we make our way through the forest, suspended mid-air, it feels as if I've literally left all my troubles on the ground. Like my new friend and I have stepped into our own universe where we can just be ourselves without all the baggage that otherwise might drag us down.

Then a fan will ask him for a selfie, and reality comes crashing back in again.

But every time it happens, it's less and less jarring to me. That's who he is, and I guess it's not so weird that humans want to feel connected with one another, even if it's with someone they've only seen on the TV.

People come to the firehouse all the time, after all, and most of them don't actually know us personally. Those we've saved who want to say thank you with cupcakes or other gifts. School kids on field trips. The mayor or the police captain to discuss policies and politics. Tourists asking for directions or members of the public in distress.

And of course, there are our neighbors, Mrs. Sylvia Bloom, and her Shih Tzu, Miss Margot Fonteyn. Seeing as she's widowed, extremely wealthy, and has no children of her own, I'm pretty certain Mrs. Bloom thinks of us all as her family. Primarily, that means feeding us and meddling in our love lives.

So, yeah. Perhaps it's not so surreal that I'm spending my afternoon with a guy who people feel like they know even though they've never met. Again, in a strange, parallel way I can sort of relate.

What is interesting is when someone notices me. Most of the fans we meet along the course of the walkway just glance at me curiously before getting their photo and respectfully continuing with their day. One girl excitedly asks if I'd like to get in the shot with them. I politely decline, but she's thrilled when I offered to take a picture of her and Cassius on her phone for her.

These people clearly all wonder who the hell I am and why I'm so special that I get to be the one hanging with Cassius Garda today. Don't worry, guys. I haven't stopped wondering that myself. But it's all pretty harmless and actually kind of flattering.

But then there's this one dude who goes out of his way to exclude me as he excitedly shouts at Cassius about what a super fan he is, physically putting himself between me and Cassius like he wants to cut me out and leave me behind.

It's kind of remarkable to watch Cassius maneuver himself away from the rabid fan without looking like that's what he's doing or pissing the guy off by rejecting him. But when he firmly tells the guy to have a nice day and slips around him to stand by me on the platform, the guy finally throws a look at me, something dark in his eyes.

The last thing I would ever want to do is anything to harm Cassius's reputation. I'm aware he came out not long before his injury forced him to quit the game. That announcement made a lot of people furious and disgusted. The way this dude sneers at me makes me think he was part of that camp but was just conveniently forgetting the facts when simping over a celebratory in real life.

All Cassius does is stand by me and smile at the guy, encouraging him to continue on his way without saying anything more. But it's like the fan flicks a switch and suddenly isn't interested anymore. Like my mere presence is enough to remind him that Cassius is actually out loud and proud as a gay man, and for someone like this jerk, that's enough to lose his respect.

The idea that if Cassius Garda were to finally start dating a man after all this time it would be me is so ridiculous I can't really take the rejection seriously. And if this dude is that prejudiced, I wouldn't want his respect in the first place, and I'm sure Cassius wouldn't, either.

But when he walks away, muttering, "Whatever, man. *Faggots,*" it suddenly feels like I've been slapped in the face.

He said that to Cassius purely because I was by his side.

"Are you okay?" I ask, my eyes trained on the asshole as he stalks off by himself.

Cassius curls his lip at the guy before turning his concerned face to me. "Oh, I'm fine. Are *you* okay? I should have stopped him bothering us way sooner. Fans like that are the worst. You don't deserve to be treated like that."

I open and close my mouth. The temptation to brush it off is strong, but my emotions are raw from the tough call the day before as well as not enough sleep at the station last night.

"It's a long time since anyone called me that word," I mumble, my throat and eyes burning.

"Hey, hey," he says kindly. Before I know what's happening, he's wrapping his arms around me.

Cassius Garda is hugging me.

And it feels fucking *amazing.*

It's not like I'm miraculously not still upset. But his woodsy, vanilla scent envelopes me as he presses his temple against mine and squeezes me with his mouth-wateringly hot, muscular arms. My whole world gets reduced to just him for a moment, and I feel completely safe, like nothing can affect me here.

Yeah, I'm obviously having a physical reaction to a gorgeous man touching me like this. But it's the emotional aspect that makes a little sob bubble out of my chest, so dazed and touched that my feelings have to spill out some way or another. We hardly know each other, yet he didn't think twice about protecting me and trying to ease my pain.

I'm the one who should be looking after everyone else. But it doesn't feel so bad to let my guard down and allow Cassius to care for me in this moment.

"Sorry," I say as I cling onto his back. "Work was kind of harrowing, and I'm not used to strangers in my personal space like that. The other people were fine but that guy—"

"Yeah, I know," he murmurs, his words rumbling from his chest against mine. He rubs my back and it's so good I can't help but shiver. "You don't have to apologize for anything. I'm the one who's sorry I put you through such a shitty encounter. And that work was bad. Do you want to talk about it?"

I shake my head and pull away, suddenly finding our closeness a little too overwhelming and confusing. He doesn't look like he minds, which I'm grateful for. It was exactly what I needed in the moment.

"I'm okay," I say truthfully. "The team always helps each other out when we get calls like that. Plus, our insurance covers a shrink that we can talk with any time we like. It's really important for us to let bad days go otherwise we'll go nuts. But thanks for asking anyway. Honestly, being up here —with you—was already really helping that."

He beams proudly at me. "Well, let's keep doing that, then. From the looks of it, we might even be the last ones in our time slot. If we get going again now, hopefully we can avoid anyone catching up from the next group and give ourselves a little peace and quiet."

Even before, it felt like he wasn't real just because he's famous. But now, it's as if he's maybe not real because he's just so damn kind and thoughtful. I might not have dated in a while, but I've hooked up with plenty of guys on the apps and so many of them are just selfish dicks.

So, yeah. I realize in that moment that my fanfic writer might be going off the rails with this too-good-too-be-true rich and famous hunk of a man. But what's the point in fighting it? I want to be here, I was having so much fun before that douche tried to ruin it, and like Cassius said… why *not* me? I can either continue to be baffled by this utterly unbelievable turn of events, or I can just enjoy one of the most incredible things that's ever happened to me.

Is still happening to me. I decide that I'm not going to allow one jealous homophobe spoil the rest of our afternoon.

"That sounds amazing," I tell him truthfully with a shaky grin.

"Hell, yeah," Cassius agrees with an even bigger smile that bolsters my own.

We take our time traversing the walkways now that we have them to ourselves, drinking in the scenery as we chat about all kinds of things. I hear stories about his siblings and the various pets the family had growing up. I tell him about being the youngest of five brothers and how I was always trying to keep up with them.

He talks about the moment he realized he could play football professionally after he saw a game on TV when he was seven years old, and how he never looked back. I tell him how I knew I wanted to be a firefighter since about the same age and some of the local crew came into our school to give a safety talk. He wanted to make people happy by playing for a team. I wanted to save people by joining one.

We compare fitness training regimes, debate favorite flavors of ice cream, and ponder how long these trees might last and what they might see in their lifetimes. I've read and seen and heard so many interviews with him over the years, but here we are, bantering back and forth about TV shows we've watched recently, the books we're currently reading, and the kind of music we jam to.

My pain from earlier today and the shift last night melts away. At some point, nothing else seems to matter except

Cassius's warm smile and the gently swaying forest around us.

When he worries that he's boring me by describing every tiny little detail about Kiki's new life with him, I immediately promise him it's not boring in the slightest. I want to hear about what kinds of wet foods are tempting her out from under the sofa, how she growls at herself in the mirror at 3am, and the time she managed to climb onto the top shelf of Cassius's trophy cabinet and started knocking down his awards one by one, maintaining eye contact with him the entire time.

"Luckily, the room was carpeted and only one of them was glass, but it was just the audacity of it," he tells me as we both laugh breathlessly.

It's only then do I look around and realize with a jolt that we're in the parking lot once more. I've been so mesmerized by Cassius that I barely registered coming back down the tower or walking along the pathway that brought us back to our cars.

Dread suddenly washes through me.

This whole scenario is so astronomically impossible. I don't want it to end, because what are the chances of anything like this ever happening again? The temptation to cling onto the moment with both hands, like I'm dangling from a building by my fingertips, is frighteningly strong.

"Oh, man," Cassius says with a sigh, glancing to his truck then back at me. "I swear we only just got here."

"Yeah," I say in a noncommittal way, not daring to get my hopes up. He's probably got plans with other friends. I do believe him when he said he's enjoyed having an escape with me, but it would make sense to get back to his real life and—

"You hungry?"

I blink, my heart doing a Simone Biles worthy flip in my chest. "Uh, yeah," I say nervously, not wanting my brain to jump to any conclusions along with the gymnastics happening inside my chest.

"Do you like Japanese food?" he continues easily, pulling his phone out of his pocket. "I've become obsessed with this place called Jiyu Sushi Bar."

"Oh," I blurt out. "We were first on scene when the earthquake tore a chunk of it down back in the spring! One of my friends—well, a colleague—no, a friend. Anyway, Del rescued his now husband that day and they literally just left a few days ago to have their honeymoon in Japan because the restaurant and the Japanese community around here became so important to them and..."

Oh dear lord, I'm rambling. It's not that I'm terrified what having dinner might mean for whatever it is that's developing between Cassius and I.

Nuh-uh.

"Um, yeah, I know it. The food's amazing. But I'm not really dressed for—"

He saves me from saying something totally mortifying like 'I'm not really dressed for a date with Cassius Garda at a fancy restaurant.' Mercifully, my fic writer apparently stopped to crack her knuckles at the right moment.

"Not to be the world's biggest jerk," he says with a grimace. "But I don't like to just drop into places without reserving a private area. It's no fun for me, nor who I'm with, and quite frankly, it can be pretty shit for the staff to have to deal with."

My heart squeezes. It's funny how people always think of the perks of fame and not things like that. "Damn, I'm sorry," I say genuinely.

The look he gives me is soft and I'm immensely grateful that there's no one else around in the parking lot right now. I don't want to share this feeling. Like I'm floating and melting all at the same time.

"I'd like to take you out to dinner sometime, though, Teddy," he murmurs.

My face flames and I try not to get too dizzy. But when he talks like that…it's like this could be a date we've been on, and I didn't even realize. The idea that he'd be interested in me like that is ten times harder to grasp than him wanting to be friends. But he just said he wanted to take me out to dinner sometime…and from what he explained a moment ago, that would involve a lot of effort and logistics. That would be a Big Deal.

Suddenly, it's like we both notice we've been gazing into each other's eyes. I laugh and he clears his throat with a grin, looking back down at his phone.

"For tonight, how does some takeout sound?" he asks. "There's this place I'd love to show you that I used to go to all the time when I was a teenager growing up here. We could get it delivered there and eat al fresco."

As if that doesn't sound even more special than the sushi bar. I don't care if it's a graffitied park bench. The fact he wants to share something from his childhood with me is such an honor.

"I'd love that," I manage to utter.

He bites his lip and grins, his eyes still on his phone. If his skin was lighter, I feel like I might even be witnessing a blush right now.

It's not even about him being a celebrity, not really. It's the fact that I can have that effect on a guy I really like. That he sees me and cares about me enough to hang onto my every word. The rush is more extreme than any burning building I've ever jumped off.

"I'm just ordering a bit of everything, if that's okay? Do you have any allergies or dislikes?"

"Not really," I admit. "But, um, have you tried the wagyu steak tartare? I've only had it once, but—"

"Yes, oh my god, it's incredible," he interrupts excitedly, pecking away with his thumb on his phone. "We have to get it with the caviar, though, right?"

Seeing as that triples the price, I can't say I've ever tried it that way. But rather than be crass and mention money, I just grin and say, "Oh, obviously."

"Okay, done," he says triumphantly a minute later before putting his phone away. "Do you want to follow me in your car, and I'll get us to the destination?"

This feels like another secret he's letting me in on. Imposter syndrome is still alive and well in the back of my mind. But it's also like I'm the hero of a kid's story, stepping through a magical portal into an unknown realm.

I guess we've upgraded from fanfiction now, huh?

"Lead the way," I tell him, accepting the call to adventure.

Redwood Bay isn't a big town. It doesn't take more than fifteen minutes to get from any point to another, even from the outskirts like where we are in the forest. But as I follow Cassius's Longhorn, it's still enough time for my nerves to creep up once more, like ivy growing extra fast in my chest, winding its way around my heart and lungs.

"This is fine," I whisper to myself as I drive. "You're fine. Actually, you're great. Don't sabotage yourself. Why shouldn't nice things happen to you? You might not be famous, but you're a good person. Don't overthink this. Just keep having fun with this cool guy you met. It's that simple, okay? No one is forcing him to hang out with you. He's doing it because he wants to. Just trust that and relax."

I keep up the pep talk until I pull up at a dirt lot by the beach. We're not near the main touristy area where the surfers congregate with the various little food stalls and trinket stands. In fact, it feels like there isn't much here aside from the sudden drop down to the sandy shore below. Not even a graffitied bench.

There *is* a guy waiting beside a motorcycle, though, and when Cassius gets out of the car before me, the driver smiles and turns to open his top box, removing a relatively large and full-looking brown paper carrier bag.

Holy crap. Is that our food? I guess Cassius ordered it a few minutes before we set off from the walkway experience and it probably took more like twenty minutes to drive here as we're basically past the opposite side of town. But still, that's impressive. As I kill my ignition and unbuckle my seat-belt, I see Cassius take the bag from the delivery guy and shake his hand. Except I swear he also presses several bills into the guy's hand, smooth as silk.

I know he's crazy rich. But the fact that I catch him discreetly tipping the delivery driver makes my heart ache with admiration. It's obvious I wasn't supposed to see that. He did it just to be kind to someone who rushed our food order, not because he wanted to impress me.

It makes me like him even more.

This feels dangerous, but apparently my fanfic-turned-YA-author is on a roll and doesn't seem to be slowing down any time soon. Could I actually allow myself to run away with the idea that Cassius and I might be friends going forward and this isn't just one unbelievable blip of an afternoon?

Could I actually allow myself to lean into these feelings pulsing through my veins of adoration and need and desire?

That's the dangerous part, the terrifying part. Because it seems like there truly is something simmering between us, and while that's absolutely thrilling, it's also bigger and more complicated than anything I've ever experienced before. He's not just a famous former football player. He's much older than me. Surely a sophisticated, worldly guy like him wouldn't be interested in a kid like me.

Then what are we doing here if he isn't?

Rather than tie myself up in knots, I get out of my car just as the delivery guy drives off, leaving Cassius and I alone again.

"Have you been here before?" he asks excitedly. I realize that as well as the food bag, he's also dangling a four pack of those Japanese lemonade bottles with the fun pop-tops from his fingers. I quickly take those from him so he doesn't drop them or our dinner. "Oh, careful of your hand," he says in concern.

I can't believe he remembered that. Yeah, I guess I'm still wearing a bandage, but most guys wouldn't notice that. "Thanks. I'm okay, though, I promise. Uh, no, I don't think I've been here before," I say, looking around, not entirely sure where 'here' is. I've probably driven down this road before, but I can't say I've ever noticed anything remarkable about it. There's a nice view out over the ocean, I guess, but the same could be said for several miles in either direction.

Cassius bounces on his toes like a big kid. "Ahh, excellent. This way!"

When he turns and leads me to the edge of the small cliff-side, I see he's wearing a backpack that he didn't have on when we were on the walkway. It makes me wonder if he was prepared to come here after that part of our day, or if he just happened to have it in his car with him, whatever it is.

To my surprise, there's a pathway I couldn't see from the road that leads us down to the rocky shore. I doubt this is a popular tourist spot as there are so many large boulders firmly planted in the sand it doesn't leave much room to sunbathe or play Frisbee. But Cassius doesn't lead us toward the waves lapping peacefully a couple of dozen feet away. Instead, he clings to the rockface, picking his way between the stones until he cries out in delight.

"It's still here!" he says triumphantly.

For a second, I lose sight of him. But after a few more

steps I see there's an opening in the rockface. It's big enough for Cassius to stand up in as he turns around with glee, and several feet deep. Almost like nature made us our own private awning.

"My buddies and I used to call this place 'Pirate's Cove,'" he tells me. "I don't even know who found it first. Maybe someone's older brother or sister. But we used to ride our bikes here all the time to hang out. I'm sure other people used it as well, but we never saw anyone else around. It was like our own private clubhouse!"

He's carefully placed the food bag down and now he's pulling a blanket out of his backpack, shaking it out and laying it on the dry sand. There's a lump in my throat and I'm not sure I trust myself to speak. He's showing me his secret childhood hang out?

At what point do I give in and admit this is a date?

I know he hasn't *said* it's a date and I really don't want to make any assumptions. But he specifically checked that I wasn't seeing anyone earlier, and this all feels incredibly intimate and special.

"I…" My voice cracks and he glances up at me, raising his eyebrows. I clear my throat and manage to give him a shaky smile. "Cassius, this is so cool. Thank you for sharing it with me."

Even just saying his name feels outrageous and daring of me. Like I'm claiming something of his as my own. But his dazzling smile in response lets me know I haven't overstepped in any way. In fact, he pats the smoothed-out blanket, inviting me to come sit beside him.

"Naw, Teddy. Thank *you* for sharing my first proper day re-exploring Redwood Bay with me. Annoying fan aside, it's been a blast. And getting to show someone new this piece of my past is such a thrill!"

I hum in agreement, not trusting myself to speak without

my voice betraying me again. He could have brought anyone in the whole world down here to his Pirate's Cove. Yet he chose me.

A sudden sharp breeze cuts through the little alcove, making me shiver involuntarily. Damn it. I always forget how the temperature can drop in the evening depending on what part of the beach you're at.

But apparently Cassius remembered.

"Oh, here. Take this."

He pauses where he'd been removing the various food cartons and placing them in front of us along with some chopsticks and napkins. From the same backpack where he got the blanket, he pulls out a couple of hoodies. Official Seahawk hoodies, one of which he thrusts at me with a grin.

It takes a moment to convince my fingers to curl around the soft material and take it from him. "I can wear this?" I ask uncertainly.

He shrugs like it's no big deal. "I have a bunch of them. You can keep it if you like?"

My heart is racing as my brain tries to cling to logic. He probably has several boxes of these that he gives out all the time.

Then why does it smell just like him when I slip it over my head?

Did Cassius Garda really just give me a boyfriend hoodie?

This is no longer a fanfic nor a YA novel. It's straight up fantasy and I, for one, can't wait to turn the next page.

CHAPTER 8

Cassius

"Bryan, I can tell you're home," I say with a sigh through the intercom. "If you want me to fuck off, just tell me. Otherwise, please let me in."

I'd never invade my PA's space unnecessarily. His time and his privacy are things I will always strive to protect. But he hasn't been answering my calls or texts, and I was genuinely getting worried.

The fact that I also need advice so desperately I might actually explode could be another factor in what pushed me into driving to his door tonight.

"Duuuude," I wheedle, pouting at the camera where—if he's watching—I know he can see me. "Come on. I don't care if the place is a mess. You've seen more than one of my homes at their worst. You know I won't judge you."

Still nothing. Fine. I'll bring out the big guns.

"I have goh-sip," I announce in a sing-song voice.

The door clicks open immediately.

I chuckle to myself as I head into the entrance foyer and go to push the second buzzer that will let me through to where the elevators are. My finger barely touches it before it also clicks open.

Lol. I knew I'd win him over eventually.

I opt to take the stairs as it's only a couple of flights up, and soon find myself in front of Bryan's apartment door. I knock and wait a few seconds before it cracks open. My PA narrows his glittery eyes at me through the slim gap.

"You swear you're not going to judge anything," he says dubiously.

I crook an eyebrow at him, truly curious what could be so bad it's got him this cagey. "Cross my heart and hope to die," I promise, swiping my finger over the left side of my chest.

He hums like he doesn't believe me but can't back out now. With a defeated huff, he swings the door all the way back to allow me into his entrance hall. The first thing I notice is that there are a lot of discarded cardboard boxes all over the place. He's so hot on the environment and recycling, I'm surprised he hasn't dealt with them immediately like he did in my place.

Due to his freaky ability to guess what I'm thinking, he sighs and shakes his head. "The boxes are apparently more valuable than what arrived in them. Come on. I'll show you."

Still confused, I follow him into the open plan living room-cum-kitchen area…then stop.

There's a five-foot-high roller wheel standing next to one of the windows. Shelving and little bridges are dotted across the walls. Several water and food bowls are on the floor as well as on the kitchen counters. Fluffy, crinkly, and feathered toys are littered everywhere.

And from the top of a six-foot cat tree peers a tiny fuzzy black face with green eyes.

"HA!" I crow, whipping my head around to see Bryan wincing. "What's all this, Mr. 'I Hate Anything Adorable,' hmm?"

"I...I couldn't leave her there," my PA mumbles, avoiding my gaze. Now the mysterious scratches he's had and the refusal to let me visit all make complete sense.

"You big softie," I gloat, dragging him into a hug and probably crumpling his pristinely ironed shirt. For once, though, he doesn't protest. "So this is Twelve, right?"

He glares at me. "Of course not. That name was the whole reason I couldn't just walk away after she chose me. She's far too elegant to be a fucking number on a list. Her name is now Noir."

"As in...the French for 'black'?" I tease him gently.

"As in Le Chat Noir, you philistine," he grumbles. But when he glances up at his new fur baby, I see something soften in his lined eyes that makes my heart melt. When Noir stretches and yawns at us, I see a pink diamanté collar sparkling back at us.

Yeahhh. This kitty is going to be even more spoiled than my one.

I'm still grinning like a proud cat guncle when Bryan folds his arms and huffs at me. "You promised me gossip. I'm getting us beer and wine, and then you are going to deliver. You are also not going to say another word about this recent development in my personal life."

I laugh as we both know I'm going to promise no such thing. But...

"Yeah, speaking of personal lives," I hedge as he pads over to the refrigerator to retrieve the drinks he promised.

That finally breaks his prickly spell, and he pauses with his hand on the open door, leaning back so I can see him arching a manicured eyebrow my way. "You asked the cute firefighter out," he guesses.

I wince and chuckle guiltily. "I didn't exactly ask him out on a *date*," I confess. "But we did spend all of yesterday after-noon and evening together."

"So it *was* a date," Bryan says as he pours his wine with a *glug glug glug* sound.

I shrug. "Maybe? But neither of us used that word."

Bryan scowls as he comes back over to thrust a cold beer bottle into my hand. "Did you fuck?"

"What?" I cry in horror. "No, absolutely not. Nothing like that happened. No kissing or handholding, and the only time I hugged him was because he got upset. It was all very chaste."

"Hmm," he says, apparently a little mollified. "Okay, then. So you really did just hang like bros."

He knows he's winding me up. I drop onto one side of his L-shaped sofa while he perches on the other. "Not like bros," I say firmly. "It was…really sweet. I've never spent time with anyone like that before."

Bryan bites his lip before letting out a long breath. But there's a smile playing on his lips, telling me he's not actually mad at me.

"So it was a date, but you were just too chicken shit to call it one."

"Bingo," I say ruefully, shaking my head before taking a swig of my drink. I love that even though he can't stand the stuff, he always has the brands of beer in that I like. He might act like he hates everyone and everything, but it's all a load of bullshit.

"So what's the problem?" he asks, getting straight to the heart of the matter. "You're not sure he feels the same?"

I pick at the corner of my bottle's label, considering how to answer. "I know I have to be careful that I don't put myself in a vulnerable situation with a gold digger or a psycho or anything like that. But from what I can tell, he seems incredibly genuine, and the chemistry is…" I whistle, unable to describe it better.

"For what it's worth," Bryan says, "my online investigation into him hasn't turned up any red flags so far."

I almost spit beer onto his couch. "Your what?" I demand.

But he just rolls his eyes at me from behind his glasses. "As *if* I wouldn't look into him," he says scornfully. "You're lucky I just gave myself the task and didn't hire an actual investigator. But this is a big deal, Big Man. I am not going to be caught off guard by the first guy you hop into bed with. This has to be treated with extreme caution."

"There's been no *hopping*," I remind him testily.

"Yet," he says like it's only a matter of time.

I puff out my cheeks, because isn't that exactly why I'm here?

He continues. "You're worried that *hopping* with the first guy you've been attracted to since you came out is going to end in a big fat mess," he observes accurately.

"I don't mean to whine about being an incredibly successful football star," I say as we both laugh appreciatively. "But it's been one hell of a cock block. I feel like I'm fumbling around in the dark, and I don't want to make a mistake that will hurt either of us." I glance over to see him watching me intently, glad he's taking my concerns seriously. "There was this one guy yesterday who got in my face and tried to push Teddy out of the way. I kept my cool, don't worry. But I swear he used the F-slur as he walked away from us. It really upset Teddy."

And me, but I think I was honestly more bothered by Teddy's reaction. Seeing him get choked up brought out something fucking primal in me, like a grizzly bear. It was probably best for everyone involved that the guy had already walked halfway across the next rope bridge by that point.

When I shake the memory off and look back at Bryan, there's something unnerving behind his glittery eyes. "He called you both what?" he asks darkly but doesn't make me repeat it. "Give me an hour. I'll have that failed condom's name and address good to go."

I bark out a laugh, releasing some of the tension I hadn't even been aware was so tight in my chest. "No, Bryan. We are not going to egg a homophobe's house."

"Who said anything about eggs?" he growls.

I point my bottle neck at him. "No. But this is my concern. How do I know if what I feel is strong enough to risk trying something official with Teddy and subjecting him to that kind of abuse on a global scale? The internet is a very cruel place. Not to mention people bothering him in real life. His job is *important.* He was trying to decompress from something genuinely traumatic yesterday when this guy pulled his crap. That could start happening all the time if people know Teddy's with me."

Bryan stares at me for a few more seconds before apparently realizing I'm serious about not retaliating against the asshole from yesterday. Because as tempting as the idea sounds, that would be highly *illegal.*

"You make a good argument," he concedes, sipping from his wine glass before tapping a polished nail against it. "I'm not going to claim to have all the answers, but here's my two cents. You can't control everything, and you can't protect everyone." He holds up a finger. "Ah! No. Don't pretend like that's not always your job in your mind. You bought your parents a house and put both your siblings through school. He might be the firefighter, but you have just as much of a hero complex. I hate to burst your bubble, but you are neither Superman nor Santa Claus. It's not your responsibility to save or care for everyone."

"Says the cat-hating twink," I grumble, turning around to see Noir watching us with a swishing tail.

"Fuck off," Bryan fires back with a smirk. "I adopted one cat. You didn't just adopt one cat. You donated enough money to feed a hundred cats for a year. I'm trying to tell you that it's healthy to accept that some things are out of your hands, and there comes a point where you just have to go with the flow and see what happens. I'm not saying you should be reckless," he adds quickly, looking alarmed.

"I know, I know," I assure him, meaning it. "But I have a really good feeling about this guy, and you said you haven't found anything worrying about him online, so…"

"So," he says, picking up my train of thought. "I'm suggesting that the next time you ask him on a date, you actually let him know that's what it is. The poor guy can't make an informed decision if he doesn't know the whole story. Put your cards on the table and tell him you're interested."

I rub my thumb against the bottle's lip. "And what about your worst-case scenario?" I ask, almost not wanting to hear the answer.

He sighs and wobbles his head from side to side a couple of times. "Yeah, it could happen. He could blab all your kinky secrets all over the internet. But I hope not. Seriously. And if it does, then you know I thrive at damage control."

"Oh, don't even joke about it," I say with a nervous laugh.

He simply shrugs, though. "In all seriousness, this was one of the reasons I was so keen to work with you, and it's why you were smart to hire me. I'm damn good at my job, and I would work with any number of celebrities if the opportunity came my way. But my main objective with bull-dozing my way into your life was to handle how you came out of the closet. As I know you understand now, it's not something you do once. You'll be doing it the rest of your life. But that means you're also going to be a role model to thousands—fuck it—*millions* of queer people across the world. Especially since you had to retire early from football —being gay is essentially your brand now. How you handle this first relationship matters. How your boyfriends behave *matters.*"

"No pressure, then," I mumble into my bottle neck. The way this conversation is going, I'm going to need another one soon.

"Of course there's pressure," he says glibly. "You know that. You thrive off it. I'm just reminding you that you'll need to think through big decisions like this. But it sounds like you already have. Now you just need to give this young man a chance to see how he feels about the reality of the situation. Put your cards on the table and let the chips fall where they may."

I frown. That sounds scary as fuck. But what's the alternative? Walking away from Teddy to 'protect' him and never giving the two of us a shot?

That sounds way scarier to me.

"So you don't think I'm jumping in too fast with the first guy I got a crush on?" I ask.

Bryan scoffs. Always a dangerous sign. "Oh, you're *absolutely* doing that," he tells me, dead pan. But then he smirks and shrugs. "Isn't that what love's supposed to do, though? Make fools of us all? Sweep us off our feet? It sounds like you've already dipped your toe in the water with this guy. Time to jump in with both feet and see if you can swim. And if he breaks your heart, it'll be character building."

Even though he's being dramatic, he's also kind of right. Part of why I'm so nervous about all this is because I'm inexperienced.

You know what the best cure for that is? Experience.

"A real date," I say, exhaling and nodding to myself.

"Yes, but you have to say the actual words," Bryan threatens me. "Don't dance around the issue because you're afraid. I know being vulnerable sucks. But instead of the worst-case scenario, you could try thinking about the *best-*

case scenario. If you're open and honest, that could encourage him to trust you, and this could be the start of something disgustingly happy for you both."

He pulls a face like he's just smelled something sour, making me laugh. But I'd never really thought about it that way round until this moment. Instead of wringing my hands over all the terrible ways this could go wrong, I could be imagining and manifesting all the ways it could go right. How amazing it could be.

Because Teddy Foster *is* amazing. And I don't want to let him slip through my fingers just because the situation is uncertain for both of us.

"A real date," I repeat, like a promise to myself.

"I'd say that deserves another drink to toast with," Bryan says, launching elegantly to his feet. "And perhaps some chicken treats for the mademoiselle?"

Noir meows loudly, sitting up with interest from the top of her tree.

"Oh, now it really is a party," I joke, but the truth is I genuinely feel light with relief.

It was almost as if I had to get Bryan's blessing before I could allow myself to move forward. Now I have that, it feels like the world is my oyster.

Expect I don't want any of the other fish in the sea. I just want Teddy.

Time to catch myself a firefighter.

CHAPTER 9

Teddy

THE CLOUDS OVERHEAD LOOK LIKE THEY'RE TEMPTED TO RAIN on my parade.

They better skedaddle, because I'm not having any of it.

If I was thinking with a clearer head, maybe I would have reconsidered going for a hike considering what happened last time I tried chancing it with the weather. To be fair, if I'd been sensible, I wouldn't have been able to save Kiki. I can't bear to think what might have happened to her if I hadn't been there. So it wasn't all bad.

But the sky above is looking eerily similar to that day, and that's the last thing I want while on a hike.

A hike with Cassius. Just the two of us. All alone.

When he messaged to say how much he enjoyed our walkway-and-sushi adventure the other day, he suggested we could do some more exploring. I was only thinking that he'd maybe like somewhere we were less likely to run into anyone like that homophobic fan again, and that's how we settled on a walk in the wilderness park to check out some of the falls there.

We're only about a half hour's drive north from Redwood

Bay. But as we start walking it feels like we're in the middle of nowhere and haven't seen a single other soul yet. They're probably smart enough to look at the weather forecast and stay at home.

But I was far too excited at the opportunity to spend more time with Cassius to think clearly and rearrange. Besides, being all alone was meant to be a bonus. After the way people kept asking for selfies last time, I thought he'd appreciate the solitude, not to mention we could avoid anyone else who might feel the need to one, speculate on the nature of our relationship or two, get weird and homophobic about it.

And…yeah. So maybe I wanted Cassius all to myself, just like when we were at the beach with our picnic in the Pirate's Cave. Most of the time, I'm desperate for people to stop treating me like the baby of the group when I'm a fully grown man. But right now, I'm very aware that I'm being extremely childish, acting like Cassius is my new favorite toy that I don't want to share with anyone else.

Which is why it felt like if I suggested anything else other than the hike we'd planned, he might turn around and say the day was ruined and he didn't want to ever see me again. Logically, I know how crazy that sounds. However, I've never felt this way before about anyone in my life, so logic isn't necessarily privy to all my decision making at the moment.

I've never had anyone so interested in me. I'm the 'kid brother' who everyone's gaze just slides over. The youngest in the conversation. The least experienced.

When Cassius messages me, when he has a conversation with me, I feel like the most important person in the whole world, let alone the room. Could anyone really blame me for wanting to cling onto that?

Which is how we end up an hour into this trail, I guess,

determinedly heading farther up the peak, neither of us mentioning the ominous clouds above as we determinedly try to outrun any rain that might be tempted to fall.

In my defense, it's not as if Cassius has mentioned anything about changing plans or heading back, either. As he's supposed to be older and wiser, this emboldens me that our plan might not be as foolish as a cool head would argue it is. All my wilderness training and health and safety protocols fly out of my brain whenever I hear Cassius laugh.

I know I'm also being reckless by putting myself in the middle of nowhere with a guy I've only connected with a handful of times. If he wasn't famous, I'm sure I'd be a lot more cautious of whether he was a predator. The trouble is I *do* think I know him, even though I've only just met him. The childish part of my brain is arguing that pro NFL quarterback Cassius Garda can't possibly be a serial killer because otherwise everyone would know about it.

Clearly, I should be watching less football and more true crime documentaries.

To be fair, I did have the common sense to tell Lili and Sawyer where I was heading this afternoon. Both of them sensed I wasn't going alone and after mentioning the walkway from the other day, I'm sure they're starting to suspect something's up.

Even if it was a regular guy I was tentatively seeing, I wouldn't say anything to them until I was sure. The fact that it's Cassius Garda who's been monopolizing my time means I'm going to have to be a hundred thousand percent sure before I utter a single word, and that will only be after I get his blessing to do so.

And that's another reason why I'm not going to abandon our tranquility, even if we're running a risk of getting drenched. If we're all alone, I'm hoping it'll mean more of a chance to talk openly. My gut's telling me there's something on Cassius's mind, and I'm dying to know what it is. Even if it's not necessarily the news I'd like to hear, I'd prefer that to the uncertainty I've been tying myself up in knots with.

Is this a second date? Is the chemistry I'm feeling real between us or just in my imagination? My fantasy author is dying to know. Maybe that's why she was so determined to set this scene in a forest. That's where the magic is most likely to happen, right?

"Man, this is gorgeous," Cassius comments, pausing to inhale deeply and look out over the terrain.

It's very different to the redwood forest. The flora is filled with scrubs and shrubs, craggy rocks, flowers in yellow, pink, orange and red, and twisted trees like a witch's gnarly hands. The peaks rise in the distance, beckoning us onward. The wind is stronger and cooler even when there aren't gray clouds overhead. Occasionally, the sun will peep out, though, fulling my delusion that this wasn't a terrible idea.

As he gazes out over the vista, I sneak a look at him, my knees going weak. He's dressed sensibly in jeans and a T-shirt with proper walking boots and a sizable backpack filled with more layers, food, and hiking gear. It's much bigger and newer than the one he had with him at the beach, and I wonder if he bought it especially for today.

The idea that he purchased it just to hike with me is so outrageous, but I can't help but hope it's true.

I can still see his incredible physique through the clothes. The way his muscles stretch and contract whenever he moves is like liquid beauty, stirring something fluttery in my belly. And his smile, his million-dollar, dazzling smile. How everyone who knows him isn't madly in love with him I'll never understand.

Not that I'm in love. That would be crazy.

But I can't deny I'm infatuated, spending all my time daydreaming about a boy like I'm hormone-riddled teenager.

Hey, I *was* one only a few years ago. I'm not sure if that's funny or embarrassing.

Cassius doesn't treat me like a kid, though. Perhaps worrying about people in my life thinking I'm not mature enough yet is actually encouraging them to keep infantilizing me. If I lead by example and just...*know* I'm a man now rather than waiting for permission from others to be considered one, their attitudes might change.

I want Cassius to see that man. In some ways, we come from different worlds. But in others, we're so alike and have so much in common. I don't want to focus on the negatives or what we don't have. Because what we do have is a warm, growing friendship, a lot of shared interests, and enough sparks flying between us to start a wildfire.

I've seen the way he's been ogling me when he thinks I'm not looking. Maybe a downpour will be needed later if we keep this up.

Whoa. That's an awful thing to contemplate. I'm tempting fate even just thinking about it. We spent the summer tackling some truly exhausting, terrifying wildfires. I tell my fantasy author to dial it down a notch with the metaphors.

"Hey, everything okay?" Cassius asks.

I blink and realize my internal chastising must have shown on my face. I'm tempted to cringe and mumble something about it being nothing. But for the first time in my life, I've found someone who doesn't make me want to hide myself away to try and fit in with the grown-ups.

Because I am a damn grown-up.

"Just some intrusive thoughts," I say with a sigh, shaking my head. Lochlan taught me that phrase when he got it from his boyfriend, Dario, who's done a lot of great work with his therapist. "Sometimes my subconscious decides I don't deserve to be happy, so it imagines disaster. I was remembering some of the wildfires we dealt with a few months back, and how if we get rained on, that'll be better than that alternative."

He frowns for a moment, apparently considering my words. "You don't think you deserve to be happy?"

I think about what I want to say as we start walking again, not wanting to come across like I'm throwing myself a pity party. We're not far from one of the waterfalls that I especially want to show him. I'd be so annoyed if we have to turn around before we reach it.

"That's not quite it," I try and explain. "It's more like... I'm not usually special. I don't normally get noticed or stand out. People don't look to me for advice. I'm never the smartest or fastest. So when something exceptional happens, I question it. Like when I graduated from the academy. For a second, I thought there'd been a mistake." I roll my eyes. "It doesn't help that one of my brothers has always been kind of a dick to me just because I'm the youngest. He looked at the screen over my shoulder and told me I'd read it wrong before laughing and saying he was just joking. But that seemed more plausible than me achieving my dream."

Cassius's frown deepens. "What a douche," he says, like he has half a mind to stomp back down to our cars to go beat my brother's ass right this minute.

I laugh and squeeze his arm without pausing to think about it. But it feels right, so I let my hand linger. The point of sharing that story wasn't to make him mad.

"Don't worry. My mom read him the riot act. She didn't give a shit that he's in his late twenties and has been taller than her for a decade. She told him to go mow the lawn and cool off while we celebrated." I grin, feeling a little emotional even though this happened a while ago now. "She's really proud of her baby boy."

"Good," Cassius says with a nod.

I let my hand drop, even though I don't want to. But it would be awkward to hold on to him any longer, I'm sure.

Cassius looks like he's still in thought. "So…when you were thinking about the wildfires, you were really second guessing being on this date and having a good time? At least, I really hope you're having a good time," he adds with a nervous chuckle.

However, my brain has ground to a halt and so do my feet again, despite feeling a drop of rain on my cheek. We're on a trail lined with those trees that have thick trunks and branches reaching over the path to create a sort of canopy overhead, so at least we have some shelter right now if the heavens are going to open.

It does seem like it's getting darker by the minute and there's an ominous rumbling in the distance. None of that really registers, though, as I stare at Cassius, my mouth hanging open like a goldfish.

"You're not having fun?" he slowly asks.

I shake my head, then realize how that could be interpreted. "No, I mean, yes! I'm having fun. Spending time with you is…I mean…did you just say *date?*"

He shifts uncomfortably, and I wonder for a horrifying second if I imagined it.

"Oh, shit," he says and pinches the bridge of his nose, not helping to ease my worries. "I promised Bryan I'd make it clear and use the right words, and I still don't think I did."

What's his slightly scary PA got to do with this?

Before I can spiral, he reaches out and takes my hands in his, and my heart stutters in my chest. "Yes, Teddy. This is supposed to be a date. The other day at Redwood Walkway and Pirate's Cove was a date, too. I was just too afraid of scaring you off to say it out loud, but that's not fair. I'm really sorry. I like you so much and hanging out together has been awesome. But I'm fully aware that I'm not an ordinary guy and this would be a complicated situation for you, even if you were interested in me, which I don't expect—"

"YES!" I blurt so loudly it startles a couple of nearby birds. Cassius blinks at me as a laugh bubbles out of my chest. But I feel lightheaded and giddy with joy, so I don't really care if I look like a dork right now. "Yes, Cassius. I'm very, very interested in this being a date. A *second* date, actually. And not because you're a football player. Or...were. Whatever. I like *you*. A lot."

His face splits into the most beautiful smile and his thumbs brush against my knuckles, sending shivers all over my body. I'm so consumed by him, I barely feel it as a couple more drops of rain fall on my head. The trees rustle discontentedly around us.

"Yeah?" he asks. "You'd want to...explore something between us?" He laughs and looks around. "Other than this big hill where we're about to get soaked."

He's probably right, but I don't care. I want to try and be as honest as I can be with him right now.

"I'd want to explore everything with you," I murmur, my heart thumping in my chest.

I'd say that I can't believe this is really happening. However, I think I'm so far beyond that point I'm just going to have to accept this is now my reality and move forward, otherwise I'm only going to annoy both of us.

"But?" he asks with a raised eyebrow.

I laugh. "But," I concede, "I can't promise not to second guess myself sometimes and have intrusive thoughts. I... Cassius, I wasn't just a fan of yours when I was growing up. I've still got photos of you in my locker at work *right now*. Getting to know you has been like something out of my wildest dreams, but better. Because you're not some athlete I've got on a pedestal anymore. You're a fun, caring, thoughtful, smart, *gorgeous* man that I've somehow accidentally gone on two dates with. I don't know how…I've never dated as an adult. This feels like I've jumped straight to the advanced level."

He throws his head back and laughs before beaming at me again. "Tell me about it. And I've had a bit more of an adult life than you."

I bite my lip, my pulse still throbbing in my ears. "You really never dated this whole time?" He shakes his head. "And you're sure you want to try…with me?"

"Yes, Teddy."

He squeezes our fingers and draws me closer so our hands are pressed against both of our chests. He's only a little taller than me, and I gaze into his eyes. They're so near that I can see little flecks of gold in the hazel. His breath is warm against my lips. The rain is getting heavier, making dark spots on our clothes.

"You could date any guy you wanted," I clarify, "and you're picking me?"

"Yes, Teddy." He grins. There's something sensual as his gaze travels over my face, lingering on my mouth. "They'd also have to want to date me. But I think you said you were open to that, right?"

"Yeah," I rasp, almost like I'm lost in a trance.

It seems he still has a little sense about him, though. "You're right that it will be complicated. There will be stupid rules we'll have to follow if we want to have any privacy. I don't ever want you to feel trapped or held back."

That sobers me up somewhat, and I frown. "You don't make me feel trapped," I tell him sincerely. "You make me feel free. Seen. Important. If you want to stay at home rather than going out where people might bother you, we can cook or order in. We can hike in the middle of nowhere or hang out with pirates."

He shakes his head and caresses my fingers some more.

"Not all the time, though. I'd want to show you off. I don't want to hide anymore. I'm done with the closet. But that would mean people probably getting in your face at times, digging into your life, leaving shitty comments online. It would be a lot, and I wouldn't want you to be unprepared."

Part of me—that childish part—wants to say none of that matters. But he's right. It's going to be really important to consider everything he's warning me about, and I shouldn't go into this blind. However...

"I think...I think I'd like to try," I whisper. "I've never felt like this about anyone before."

"Me neither," he says, and my heart explodes like the Fourth of July.

Except...the rumbling isn't just coming from my imagination. The rain is running down our faces now and splattering on the leaves all around us. Thunder booms over our heads and with a gasp I look around, realizing the gravity of the situation.

I'm still clinging to his hands, though.

"I think we might have to abandon the waterfall for today," I tell him ruefully. I'd say I was disappointed, but how can I be after the conversation we've just had? "We should probably..."

My words trail off as I frown. The rumbling sound changes. It's louder and lower. My training is screaming at me that something is very wrong. I turn around and squint through the rain and the tree branches, trying to discern what's causing the new noise and exactly which direction it's coming from.

Movement farther up the peak catches my eye, but I can't quite understand what I'm seeing. It's almost like the trees are waving or shivering in the cold.

Then one leans, like it's trying to reach for us from several dozen feet away...

Before it topples, rolling down the hill.

It's not the only one.

"LANDSLIDE!" I yell, grabbing Cassius's hand as we start to run.

It's moving faster than we can, though, and I already know it. I just have to pray that my author knows what she's doing.

Because this is *not* how mine and Cassius's story ends.

CHAPTER 10

Cassius

IT ALL HAPPENS SO FAST.

One minute, all I can see is Teddy, my heart racing with joy as I hold his hands and he tells me he wants to give this a try—give *us* a try. The rain falling around us actually felt romantic.

Then it was like the ground turned to liquid. I've never seen anything like it. For a natural disaster, it sure looked distinctly *un*-natural.

In a flash, Teddy is screaming at me to run.

It's like the landslide is aiming for us, which makes sense as the path we're on is in a sloping valley. Perfect for funneling the wave of earth, trees and other debris right on our heels.

I've never felt so terrified in my life as Teddy and I sprint as fast as we can. Our pace is evenly matched, which is just as well because I'm not fucking letting go of his hand until we're safe. But the adrenaline searing through my veins is making it incredibly difficult to think straight. Part of me knows that the chances of us outrunning this thing before it's on top of us aren't looking good. My brain is just yelling *GO GO GO* at me.

Teddy's the professional, though. So when he tugs me and cries, "This way!" I don't question it.

He darts right, dragging me with him. I look back to see the front of the landslide is heart-stoppingly close, probably only twenty feet behind us. Like me, it appears that Teddy's realized it's moving too fast for us to get ahead of.

So apparently, we're going to get above it instead.

He hurtles himself up the nearest tree, scaling it like a mountain goat in the blink of an eye. I waste no time following him, my hands trembling as I haul myself higher and higher. Even as the rubble cascades against the base, filling the valley we only just walked through, we don't stop until the tree gets too spindly to safely take our weight.

Teddy throws his arms around me, dragging me into a hug with the trunk between us. I do the same, clinging to him for dear life as the ground shakes below us. The volume of debris is staggering as the landslide grows, trees toppling over all around us.

It's not that surprising when our refuge starts to lean, but my stomach drops sickeningly all the same.

"HOLD ON!" Teddy bellows over the cacophony of sound. His eyes lock with mine. I can tell he's scared, just like me. But he's not giving up, so neither will I.

With a lurch, the roots break free from underneath us, and the world tilts. Grit flies into my mouth as I bellow incoherently, our tree slamming down. We find ourselves surfing the wave, thundering through the forest at breakneck speed.

The branches give us some shelter at least, but I'm still getting scratched to shit. I try and keep my eyes open to see where we're going, hoping that if something unexpected is up ahead that'll give me an extra second or two's warning to brace for it. But my instinct is to protect my eyes by closing them, especially as my arms are too busy gripping Teddy like a vise to shield my face.

So when our tree flips, it takes me completely by surprise. I cry out and almost lose my hold, but Teddy's strong arms aren't letting me go anywhere. Then we're rolling, being bashed about like we're on the inside of a washing machine. My teeth feel like they're getting jammed into my skull, and my skin is burning. We twist and turn, losing the few branches we had left that were desperately trying to protect us.

And then we slow.

As quickly as it happened, we suddenly grind to a halt. Dust and debris fly around us, but the rain is still gently falling, none the wiser of the carnage that just occurred. I gasp for air, blinking as the ground finally stops shifting.

"Is it over?" I rasp.

Teddy nods, looking ashen. Gingerly, we let go of each other. "I think so. Are you all right?"

I'm still trembling, but I take stock of my battered and bruised body with a wince. "Everything aches, but I think I'm basically still in one piece."

Teddy pushes himself into a seated position, then rolls his shoulders and cracks his neck. "Yeah, I think I'm good."

"What the fuck was that?" I ask as I sit up as well, shaking grit and muck from my arms before brushing off my torso. "Other than scary as shit, I mean. That didn't feel like enough rain to do so much damage."

Teddy shakes his head, still looking around at the aftermath. "No, it was probably an accumulation of all the bone-dry weather we've had over the past few months, and then the torrential rain a couple of weeks ago was what probably made the area unstable. The rain today was probably the last straw."

"So just a freak occurrence? Global warming?" I ask and he nods. "Lucky us."

I chuckle darkly, but he's still worriedly scanning the horizon as dark clouds continue rolling overhead, the rain washing everything clean around us. "I wouldn't be surprised if this happened elsewhere today. There's a strong chance we could see more landslides and flooding down the line if we get another big storm."

It strikes me how lucky we were…how lucky *I* was. What would have happened if Teddy hadn't been here with me? I don't think I'd be sitting here talking about weather patterns, that's for damn sure.

"I can't believe we didn't get flattened like pancakes," I say thickly. "Teddy, hey."

I reach out and snag his fingers with my own to get his attention and stop him fretting for a second. He blinks at me in surprise, but he's going to have to get used to that. If he's really now mine, it'll be impossible that I won't want to touch him all the time. He glances down at our intwined hands, then lets out a relieved little laugh before meeting my gaze again. My heart aches with pride as I look into his wide green eyes.

"You saved us," I say, not even embarrassed when my voice cracks. "You saved our lives, Teddy. Just like you saved Kiki. That's…fuck, that's so incredible. You know that, right? You're *incredible.*"

His throat bobs as he swallows, wet eyes flicking away briefly before he smiles sheepishly. "I was just doing my job," he says.

I laugh and shake my head. "I was told off recently for thinking it's *my* job to save and protect everyone. But that's not your job, Teddy. It's just who you are, isn't it? So thank you. I mean it."

He blushes, but he's still smiling as he nods at me. "It was my pleasure."

I'm still not convinced he's really listening to me, but I feel like we've made progress at least. I'm determined to make him see how exceptional he is. If anyone's unworthy of being in a relationship here, it's me.

Teddy squeezes my fingers, and that makes me look down at our intwined hands. "Oh, your cut?" I say in concern for his previous injury.

He laughs and shakes his head, though. "Nah. That's mostly healed. In fact, I bet thanks to that bandage my palm is now the least battered part of my body."

I laugh as well in relief. "Well, that's one bit of luck, I guess."

We're in a sea of rubble, but the park is huge, and not too far away there are plenty of trees that are still standing. "I think the rain might be letting up," Teddy comments, and it seems he's right. The storm is passing.

"What should we do now?" I ask. I pull my backpack off to get my phone out, but we didn't have any signal up here even before the landslide. Teddy has sensibly got a compass out instead of his cell.

"Okay. South is that way," he says, pointing. "I can't tell where we've ended up. But if we head that way, we'll eventually hit the highway, no matter what. We can either try and make it back to our cars from there, or if we find some service, we can call for help."

"Good plan," I say appreciatively. "Simple, but effective."

He looks skyward, then checks the time. "We're going to start losing the light soon."

I nod, understanding what he's saying. Trying to blunder through the forest in the dark doesn't sound like much fun. "We better get our hustle on, then."

With a groan, he gets to his feet, reaching out to help me do the same.

As soon as I try and put weight on my left foot, I know I've got a serious goddamned problem.

"Fuck!" I cry, crumpling straight back on my ass. Teddy immediately drops by my side, his expression concerned. I grimace apologetically at him. "I think it's sprained," I tell him.

"Not broken?" he asks, his hands flying to my ankle to start gently palpating it.

I wince and suck in a breath as his thumbs find the tender spots. "I don't think so. I'd have felt the snap. I didn't even notice this until now with all my other aches and scrapes. But still…"

Guilt and shame surge through me even though I know this isn't my fault. Facts are facts, however.

"You're not going to be able to walk very far or very fast, are you?" Teddy guesses. I shake my head, and he exhales, nodding and frowning at the same time. "Okay. New plan, then."

"You should go," I say in a rush. I'm not going to hold him back or put him in any more danger. "Get help. I'll be fine."

He stares at me like I've grown a second head. "Absolutely fucking not," he spits out, surprising me somewhat. He's usually so sweet, I wouldn't expect such vehemence from him.

It's kind of hot.

"Leave you here alone and injured as night falls? No, that's not happening, Cassius. This is the new plan. I'm going to slowly and carefully help you get away from this disaster zone. We're going to find some shelter, I'll build a fire, and we'll hunker down for the night. In the morning, we'll start slowly moving again, and maybe *then* I'll consider running for the highway to flag someone down. But only if I can leave you in a visible, easy to find location. Deal?"

"Yes, sir," I say a little breathlessly.

He seems to realize how bossy he's just been and blushes, but I'm more worried about calming my dick down right now than I am with my stupid sprained ankle.

"Right, um," he says. "Okay, then. Off we go."

He wraps his arm around me, and this time I'm prepared when I get to my feet to put as little weight as possible on the left one. Cautiously, I limp over the unsteady ground with him by my side. It's annoying, but it's by no means the worst pain I've ever experienced. As if to remind me, my shoulder starts to throb as well. Luckily, I always carry some regular anti-inflammatory meds with me that will help take the edge off once we get settled.

We're fortunate that it doesn't take long to find a large, unaffected tree to make camp under where the ground is mostly dry. The rain has totally stopped now. Teddy makes me sit and eat a protein bar while he pulls out an ice pack that he snaps and squeezes to activate. After he's forced it into a stretched sock so the coldness doesn't burn my hand, he gets me to press it to my injured ankle.

Then he ventures out to quickly find as much firewood he can before we completely lose the light. It's mesmerizing watching him collect branches and twigs, testing them to find the driest ones. After that, he uses a tote bag from his backpack to sweep up as many leaves and pine needles he can for tinder.

"It's a good thing a lot of these trees are oaks," he says as he starts constructing the base of the campfire. "Hardwood burns longer than softwood."

I hum, having been unaware of such a fact. I know he's trained in survival techniques, but it's still extremely attractive to see in action.

Bryan was right with his accusation the other night. I do see it as my responsibility to look after everyone in my life. If I was going to earn a stupid salary for throwing a ball around, it seemed the least I could do. Besides, it makes me feel good when I see other people's happiness, and I think being the oldest child in the family, it's just something in my genes.

Sure, on the Seahawks I had my teammates, our coach, the physical therapists, and everyone else around me who all worked together to ensure the very best for the players and the team as a whole. And when I busted my shoulder, my family were there fussing over me for every step of my recovery.

But I've never experienced a guy doing this for me, let alone a guy I'm seriously falling for. He refuses to let me lift a finger as he works meticulously to get the fire built. It's amazing how well prepared he is for emergencies and just how many things he's got tucked away in his reasonably sized backpack. He produces a waterproof tin, striking a match to ignite the flame, watching as the fire catches on the tinder and kindling, the comforting glow growing to keep us company.

He then organizes our little campsite so it's neat and tidy for us to brave out the night. If I wasn't injured or worrying faintly about attracting wildlife, it would actually be fun. Romantic, even. As night continues to fall, the stars come out. It's peaceful. Beautiful.

Teddy assures me that as long as we're vigilant about keeping all our food and the wrappers in his airtight box, we shouldn't attract any unwanted attention from the local inhabitants. He hasn't sat down once since we found this spot, barely pausing to shove a protein bar in his mouth while he works. Thankfully, our clothes have had time to dry off a fair bit from the earlier rain, helped now by the warmth of the fire. But as the light fades, the temperature drops, and a sudden shiver ripples through me, making him pause.

"Do you have any other layers?" he asks in concern. I'm already opening up my own backpack, though. I might not be as accomplished a boy scout as he is, but I'm not useless, either.

"Yeah. But I've just got the one hoodie this time," I say apologetically. However, my hope that he wouldn't have forgotten something like that is proven right immediately as he retrieves his own.

Except...it's not technically his.

It's mine.

My Seahawks hoodie that I gave him the other evening that looks so fucking sexy on him as he pulls it over his head. Seeing him in my clothes makes me want to growl with pride. I don't care if it's basic, like a dog peeing on a tree. As far as my primal brain is concerned, that marks him as mine.

Any other guys can fuck off. This gorgeous man is taken.

I discard the now lukewarm ice pack. "Teddy," I say firmly, catching his attention and stopping him from looking anxiously around our little space. "You've done enough. Everything's great."

"But..." he says, unsure.

"Come here," I tell him, reaching my hand out.

He looks at it, his confidence suddenly slipping, which is almost funny to me. It's okay, though. I'll show him he's got nothing to worry about.

I beckon him with my fingers, and he cautiously approaches until he's close enough for me to slip my hand against his and pull him down to the ground beside me. I wrap one arm around his shoulders and place my other hand on his chest.

"Thank you for taking care of us," I murmur.

He seems unsure of what to do with his own hands for a

second. But then he shifts so one slips against my lower back and the other covers mine where it's resting over his heart.

"Just doing my job," he says, but the twitch of his lips suggests he does so to deliberately get a rise out of me.

It works.

"Is that so, Mr. Firefighter?" He nods and I hum. "But who takes care of *you?* Is that my job now?"

"Maybe," he whispers.

"Definitely," I confirm, before leaning in and pressing my mouth softly against his.

CHAPTER 11

Teddy

Forget whatever book my author's been writing. She's going to have to skip to my obituary, because I've just died and gone to heaven.

If I had any wits about me, I might have been startled that Cassius Garda kissed me. But I'm far too busy kissing him back for anything as sensible as that.

It's also difficult to be startled when everything about this just feels so *right.* His lips are plump but strong as they claim mine over and over, and his tongue tastes a little like berries from the protein bar he ate not long ago. Despite the night air, his skin is warm against mine as he touches my face and slips his hand under my clothes to squeeze my hip.

We don't speak, but I move my leg a fraction to try and get closer to him than just sitting side by side. Before I know it, he's already hoisting me up to straddle his lap. What little common sense I have left is telling me I need to be careful of his sprained ankle and the injured shoulder that ended his football career, not to mention all our other cuts and bruises. But he doesn't seem particularly concerned about any of that as he moans and gasps against my mouth, his fingers digging into the damp skin of my back.

"Teddy," he utters between kisses.

If I thought wearing the hoodie he gave me made me feel claimed, it's nothing compared to hearing my name from his lips. I quiver in his grasp, taking a second to break away from the kiss and press our temples together, gulping down some air.

"Am I really yours?" I ask, feeling vaguely delirious.

He eases me away to meet my gaze with his beautiful hazel eyes. *"Mine,"* he growls possessively, an almost feral curl on his lip as he rolls us so I'm on my back with him looming above me. There's more than one twig or stone digging into me from the forest floor, but all those little twinges of pain do is electrify me, keeping me grounded in the present and all the delicious sensations flying through my body.

It's not like I've forgotten our conversation from earlier about this not being an ordinary relationship I'm embarking on. But that's the thing about almost dying. It often reminds you to do all the living you possibly can before it's too late. What's the point of waiting out of fear when Mother Nature can turn around and try and snatch it all away in the blink of an eye?

Besides, it's not like I haven't thought about what it would mean to be with Cassius. A lot. As incredible as this moment is, I have imagined it a thousand different ways already, most of them before I even *met* him.

None of those even come close to reality. Because reality isn't perfect. It's messy and slightly awkward, and that's what makes it real. I don't want a flawless Instagramable kiss.

I want to feel the grit on our skin and the slightly moist ground below me and the slightly chilly breeze. Even Cassius's injured foot adds a certain charm to it, so long as he's not in too much discomfort, because it's authentic.

When he winces for the second time, I huff and roll us over again so he's now the one underneath me.

"Better?" I ask with a crooked eyebrow.

He laughs and shrugs. "I suppose it's more elevated this way. Do you like being on top?"

"I like whatever," I tell him honestly, skimming my fingertips along his jaw and against the shorthairs at the back of his neck, just like I'd dreamed about. "Injury aside, what do you like?"

"Top, bottom, whatever," he agrees with me, grinning as he bites his lower lip and cards his fingers through my hair. "Fuck. I've wanted to do that since the moment I laid eyes on you."

Even though I promised myself I'd stop second guessing his attraction to me, those words do make my breath hitch. "The moment you...?"

He nods and pulls me down to kiss my mouth softly, which is somehow hotter than the desperate kisses we were trading before. I don't want it to end, but his next words are worth it.

"When you walked through that shelter door, Teddy Foster, I thought I'd been struck by lightning. I tried to fight it because I didn't want to scare you off. But holy hell, I just knew I had to get my hands on you someday if I could."

A laugh bubbles out of me, and we grin against each other's lips. "You can't just go around saying things like that to unsuspecting boys, sir," I tell him pointedly. "You'll give them all kinds of naughty ideas."

"Not a boy," he mumbles as the kisses intensify again. "A fucking gorgeous man. *My* man."

There doesn't seem to be any reason to keep talking after that. How could he possibly say anything better than he already has? Besides, kissing is a far superior use of our mouths.

The fire crackles and the crickets sing as we lose ourselves in each other. Hands cling and breaths mingle and hips grind until I don't know where I end and he begins.

But there's still too much between us. So when his hands fumble with my belt, I moan in relief.

"Is this okay?" he mutters against my tingling swollen lips.

"Yes, please, yes," I beg, copying him by reaching for his jeans. However, I have to keep one hand to prop me up, so I don't get very far. But Cassius just chuckles, such a warm sensual sound right by my ear, and as soon as he's done with my buckle, button and zipper, he makes short work of his own for me.

Then all that's between us both and a couple of hard, leaking cocks is a little damp cotton. I drink in the sight, suddenly apprehensive. With some random hook-up or any other guy I was considering dating, I'm sure I wouldn't be hesitating this way. But this feels momentous. Like if we cross this line, there's no going back.

Because if I share orgasms with Cassius Garda, I'm pretty sure I'm going to be ruined for all other men.

I'm broken from my trance when Cassius carefully touches my chin with his thumb and finger, encouraging me to look back into his eyes. "We can stop," he says quietly, kindly. There's no hint of irritation or disappointment, which helps me relax. I'm safe with him. He's going to take care of me, I know it. And if I really did want to pump the brakes, I'm certain we could try again some other time.

But I take a breath and shake my head. "I don't want to stop, it's just…"

"A lot?" he suggests. I nod gratefully. "Tell me, what's the worst that could happen? I'm not talking about social media or TMZ. What's the worst that could happen right now when it's just you and me and the stars?"

I blush and smile, ducking my head to have a moment of shyness. "That's stupidly romantic," I mumble.

"It was supposed to be," he says smugly. He rubs my back reassuringly. "I'm serious, though. If there's something you're not comfortable with or don't like, you have to tell me. That's a rule."

It's a good rule and I appreciate it. But it's not what's bothering me. I huff and roll my eyes. "What if...what if I'm not good enough," I manage to finally get out, my face flaming so hard I have to completely look away from him. Suddenly, I'm wishing we were still side by side. Being on top feels like a lot of pressure. Like I'm in charge when it's obvious he should be.

"Oh, baby, no. Please look at me."

If anything, that just makes things worse.

My brain short-circuits at the word 'baby.' I always thought pet names were kind of cringe. But hearing him call me that makes me feel something I've never really experienced with a partner before.

Cherished.

"Broke you a little bit, huh?" he asks, tilting my chin again until I can see him grinning. He's not laughing *at* me, though. That's very clear. "Am I okay to call you baby? I haven't tried it on anyone else before."

I blink and take a breath. Forget the hoodie and the way he said my name earlier.

This is what officially makes me feel like I'm now his.

"Really?" I ask in almost a whimper.

He cups the side of my face and rubs his thumb against my cheek. "Yes, Teddy. Really. Remember, you're probably a lot more experienced at this than I am." He frowns. "Although I really don't want to think about you being with other men right now."

The laugh that erupts from my throat is a little too loud

in the otherwise quiet forest. But I soon drop my face against Cassius's neck to muffle it. "I can't believe you'd ever be jealous over me," I say in delight, drawing back to grin at him.

"You bet your ass I am," he says with a fake glare. When he grabs my butt, though, he can't keep it up, and laughs with me. "This is the ass I'm referring to, by the way, and it should be an actual *crime* how good it looked in those booty shorts you had on at the walkway the other day."

I bite my lip, my nerves easing and my playfulness resurfacing. "Oh, you liked those, huh?"

"I'm going to buy you a pair in every color, baby," he rasps before planting his lips firmly back on mine, the kiss becoming heated within seconds.

I get lost in the embrace once more. But when his hand slides around my still half-hard cock, his fingers gliding over my briefs, I gasp and pull away just enough so I can look into his eyes.

"Is this okay?" he asks again.

What am I afraid of?

Slowly, I nod, purposefully lowering my shoulders and letting the tension seep from my body.

Wordlessly, he uses his free hand to caress my jaw with his knuckles then brush his thumb against my lower lip. He traces his fingers down my chest, and even though I'm wearing his hoodie, the touch feels so good. Then he takes the hand I'm not using to support myself and guides it between his legs.

He pauses just before I connect with anything, however, and raises his eyebrows, yet again asking for my consent.

What am I afraid of?

I bite my lip and drop my hand the last inch, skimming my fingers along his hard length, hot to my touch even through his underwear.

He lets out a truly filthy sound, sucking air through his teeth and arching his back.

It's not like I haven't believed him all the times he's told me he's spent the last however many years firmly in the closet. I got the impression he hasn't had sex in a long time. But for such a simple caress to have such an erotic reaction tells me I've greatly underestimated the situation.

I don't know if I'm an egotistical prick for feeling extremely honored to be the man he's trusting in this moment, but I can't help it.

He's rich beyond my wildest dreams. Yet I'd be a fool not to think I'm giving him something absolutely priceless right now.

The rest of my fears melt away as I slip my hand through the front opening of his briefs and wrap my fingers around his shaft, loving how the thick girth rests in my palm.

He snarls and surges forward, slamming his mouth against mine in a fierce, sloppy kiss. His hand is back on my cock again, although this time he copies me and fumbles until he can find his way through the opening.

With his rough palm on my sensitive length, I gnash my teeth and grunt as my whole world swims in front of my closed eyes. I'm gushing precum, and I'm ashamed to say that my own hand falters on his length, not able to keep up my rhythm as he pleasures me.

"It's okay, Teddy," he utters, nudging his nose against mine and pressing a kiss to the corner of my mouth. "Just let go, baby. It's okay, I've got you. Come for me. Come."

It only takes a few more jerks of his hand before I'm doing just that, spurting all over his hands and his clothes as I scream out, stars in my eyes.

That was embarrassingly fast.

"Shit…oh…shit…" I gasp for air as my climax slowly subsides, blinking my way back to reality. "Sorry, I…"

"Don't you dare apologize, gorgeous," he says cheerfully, apparently expanding his list of pet names. "That was so fucking beautiful."

Okay. If he's still having a good time, then I guess it doesn't matter how quickly I blew my load. Maybe he sees it as a compliment that he affected me that intensely?

I nod and manage a shy smile, but my thoughts are already turned to what I can do to make him feel amazing.

He's right. I probably have got a lot more experience than him, despite coming on a hair trigger just now. I want to use that to give him something else that costs nothing but I hope is worth its weight in gold.

I kiss his mouth and along his throat before moving down his body. I lift his T-shirt and hoodie enough so I can kiss his stomach and run my fingers along one of his deliciously defined cum gutters. Then I nip at the elastic of his briefs, looking up and raising my eyebrows in question at him.

He looks mesmerized, and he threads his fingers through my hair again and nods. My heart pounding in anticipation, I use my free hand to free his cock through his underwear and hold it steady as I slide my lips over the head.

"Holy fucking *fuck*," he cries, bucking into my mouth. I don't gag, though. I just suck him down, loving all the delicious sounds he's making as I take my time swallowing his stunning cock at the back of my throat.

Giving head is one of my favorite things to do during sex, and I'm suddenly really goddamned grateful that I've spent so long perfecting my technique.

I'm a little restricted by his briefs and jeans, but I still use all my best tricks on him. Working my tongue, twisting my hand, fondling his balls, stroking his shaft, humming as saliva and precum drip down my chin.

He's talking absolutely delicious nonsense as he squirms

and twitches under me. I pin his hip down, partly because I'm worried about him making his sprained ankle any worse, and partly because he seems to really enjoy it when I get bossy.

"Teddy, I...oh, I'm close...I'm gonna..."

I appreciate the warning, but if he thinks I'm going to pull back just when he's about to peak, he's got a lot to learn about me. I suck harder, taking him farther down my throat, breathing through my nose so I don't get dizzy and miss the best part.

"Teddy!" he shouts, bucking his hips.

And then he's shooting his load, and I drink it down eagerly, loving the way his cock is throbbing inside me. He's trembling as I drain every last drop from him, waiting until he starts to soften before gently sliding his length from my mouth.

"Fffuck," he stammers, still trembling from the aftermath. I snuggle up next to him and wait until he looks at me before smiling and brushing our noses together.

"Good?" I ask. We both know it was amazing and that I'm fishing, but I do it anyway.

He grins sleepily and grabs my face with weak fingers so he can press his lips against mine in a tired, satisfied kiss. "Baby," he sighs, hardly able to keep his eyes open. "Teddy. Baby. *Mine.*"

I think that means that yes, he thought it was good.

My protective instinct kicks in. As much as I don't want to let him go, I know that a little housekeeping now will mean a much more comfortable, cozy night for us. Well, as much as we can get out in the wilderness.

"Come on, Cassius," I say as I untangle myself from his sleepy form.

Luckily, I can reach my backpack without too much rolling and wriggling. I manage to find the packet of wet wipes that I'm sure we'll be using to 'shower' with in the morning. Christ, I've never been happier about being obsessively prepared for every situation in my life.

I use one of the wipes to clean both our cocks and what I can of my cum on his clothes before tucking us both away. Honestly, with all the other muck and stains from the landslide, it's not really noticeable at all, so I try not to worry about it.

My backpack might have an impressive number of resources stashed inside, but I unfortunately left my bedroll at home. Hopefully the ground won't be too hard and uncomfortable. But it's not like we were planning on camping out here, so I can't be annoyed at myself for not anticipating a natural disaster.

I move the bag itself so we can use it as a pillow and pull out an emergency foil blanket that only takes up a sliver of space in one of the pockets. I put it there a year ago and never gave it a second thought until now, but I'm extremely grateful for the little bit of warmth and protection it will give us.

Cassius is fast asleep, and I take a moment to appreciate what a privilege it is to get to see him in such a relaxed state. I'm obviously concerned that he's injured and pray it's going to heal up quick for him. But I hope it doesn't make me a terrible person that I'm also kind of thankful for it. If he'd been able to walk to the highway, we wouldn't have had to stay the night and share this incredible experience together.

Life isn't fiction. Things very rarely happen the way we expect they will or hope they might. But as I add some more wood to the fire and double check we haven't left anything out to tempt the local wildlife to come sniffing around, I know I'll treasure today so much more because of how it went completely FUBAR. It's already shown me how Cassius keeps his cool in a crisis and how kind and caring his nature is.

We've both been thrown in at the deep end and—so far at least—it seems we're swimming just fine.

Tomorrow will bring a different kind of reality, one that involves other people. They aren't something I can control, and that makes me a little nervous. For now, I find my power bank to charge my phone by my side. Not that we have any signal at all right now, but I want to be prepared whenever we do. That makes me feel less helpless.

Then I cuddle up to Cassius under the crinkly emergency blanket that's doing an impressive job of keeping the heat in, and rest my head on his chest to use as my pillow.

I know we could have died. I know we're currently stranded in the woods with Cassius's sprained ankle and very few supplies. But in this moment, I feel like the luckiest guy alive.

I'm just not sure how long I can expect that luck to last.

CHAPTER 12
Rico

I LIKE IT WHEN THINGS RUN SMOOTHLY.

As soon as I get to the station, I get the feeling that today is not going to be one of those days.

"Dray, seriously?" Sawyer Nelson cries in disbelief at our temporary team member, Drayton Hendrix. "You don't have a favorite dinosaur? Everyone has to have a favorite dinosaur!"

We've been on shift approximately three minutes.

Hendrix sighs and looks over at me across the locker room. "When does Zahir get back from Japan?" he asks wearily in his lilting Australian accent. Secretly, I think he quite likes getting ribbed on like a real team member. In fact, I think Hendrix needs a team of his own more than he'll ever admit, but it's not my place to speculate.

"Del doesn't return for another couple of weeks," I inform him apologetically.

"Lieutenant," Nelson shouts at me as he stuffs his duffle into his locker. "Tell me you're not totally lame and have a favorite dinosaur."

As much as I hate encouraging our spunky teammate

when he gets in one of these moods, *especially* at eight in the goddamned morning, I happen to have a firm favorite.

"Triceratops," I say as if that's completely obvious and should in fact be everyone's answer. "Living tank and vegan. Badass but kind."

Nelson blows a raspberry, making me want to put him on latrine duty. "Who picks an herbivore? Anton, tell him."

Nelson's best friend, Anton Quick, raises his eyebrows, having only just walked into the locker room.

"Favorite dinosaur," Hendrix supplies helpfully.

"Oh!" Quick says with a nod like this is a perfectly normal discussion topic that he hears all the time.

To be fair, he probably does.

"Stegosaurus," he answers confidently. "They're like living bulldozers and have these cool spines down their backs."

I raise my hand toward him in triumph as Nelson rolls his eyes. "No, Ant! Not you, too? Where are all my predators at?"

"We talking dinosaurs again?" Lili Kwon asks as she and Yara Ortiz, our other paramedic, enter together. "Because we all know I'm Team Velociraptor, right?" She makes a hissing noise and pretends to swipe at Nelson with her middle finger.

He jumps back just a little too enthusiastically, although I wouldn't blame anyone for being afraid of Kwon most of the time. If someone told me she had a secret retractable claw, I'd probably believe them.

"I like the cute little ones," Ortiz joins in cheerfully as she opens her locker, waving at her temporary partner, Hendrix.

He's a jack of all trades, so she's technically the lead paramedic for the next couple of weeks. But our Aussie is a mean driver and EMT trained like the rest of us, so while not a fully-fledged paramedic, I was still really glad to have him back for a longer stint than before. Rotating several different guys during someone's leave is a pain in the ass. But also…he simply fit with the One-Thirteen during the couple of shifts he did with us in the spring. It's a vibe. Sometimes you just need to roll with vibes.

"Psittacosaurus?" Nelson says.

"Gesundheit," Quick offers.

Nelson rolls his eyes. "No, that's a cute little dinosaur. Has a head kinda like a parrot."

Ortiz crinkles her nose. "Um, no, not that one. I mean the one that has a fan that appears around its neck when it gargles."

Kwon snorts. "You mean a Dilophosaurus? The one that spits *paralyzing venom* before it eats your face?"

Ortiz beams. "Yes, that's the one! They're so funny in the movies."

She wanders out happily as Bell comes running in with Rocky the Dalmatian on his leash. "Sorry! Sorry! Queenie got into the garbage and Dario had a meeting so I was elbow deep in vomit and…" He takes a deep breath and Rocky very sweetly sits at his feet. "I'm here now, reporting for duty, sir!"

I chuckle and shake my head. "You're fine, Lochlan. The third watch are still cleaning out some of their gear anyway. They had a couple of nasty calls yesterday with that rain."

When you've been on this job for any time at all, it doesn't take a genius to work out that after such an arid summer, these sudden heavy downpours are going to wreak havoc. Still, I hope the previous shift can finish up soon, and not just so we can have the peace of mind of being ready to go if the tones sound for us, which they could any second. Those guys need sleep. They look dead on their feet.

"Beast!" Kwon shouts at Bell. "Favorite dinosaur—go!"

Bell blinks then makes a little 'oh' noise implying, like Quick, that this is a perfectly normal conversation. "Well it's gotta be a T-rex, right?"

"Basic bitch," Kwon says, shaking her head at the same time as Nelson cries, "Thank you! Someone with taste."

I laugh in exasperation, loving every single one of these troublemakers.

It isn't always easy for me being a different rank, and I try and give them a little space so they can breathe. I miss the days when I could goof off more, but I'm proud to be their lieutenant. It means I have to hang back a lot of the time now, letting everyone else leave first so we can maintain some boundaries. So after I let Rocky sniff my fingers and give him some attention, I watch the others head out, planning on exiting the locker room in a minute or so.

Except Hendrix also lingers. "Pterodactyl," he says casually as he saunters past me.

"Huh?" I respond elegantly.

He snickers mischievously. "My favorite. It's a Pterodactyl by a mile. But it's not a *dinosaur*. It's a pterosaur." He flaps his wings and lifts a knee, like he's about to be shot in bullet time and makes a 'CAW!' noise. Then he returns his limbs to normal and winks at me before walking out the door, leaving me alone for a moment.

"Pterosaur," repeat and laugh to myself. "Asshole."

Yeah, Drayton Hendrix fits in well here, whether he wants to or not.

Our driver engineer, Gene Haskell, must have arrived before all of us because I didn't see him in the locker room and he's already busy whipping up a mountain of eggs and pancakes in the kitchen. He's offering breakfast to both our fresh-faced team as well as the dead-on-their feet previous shift.

I'm not sure how much longer our father-of-five, Haskell, will be able to stay with us. He's older than anyone else on the first watch, including Captain Valentine, who's no doubt currently tackling admin up in his office with a bucket of coffee. But Valentine's fitness is still as good as the rest of us. Haskell…not so much. He doesn't need it when he's behind the wheel most of the time, but the department still has regular assessments that I'm not sure Haskell is going to be able to pass for much longer.

The thought that the house dynamic could change in the not-too-distant future leaves a pang in my chest. If…when… Haskell decides to step down to a more desk-oriented role so he can spend more time with his family, I'm going to have my hands full finding someone who can drive like he can.

My thoughts drift to Hendrix again. It was Haskell who he covered for last time, and the Aussie did a mean job of tearing up the streets in and around Redwood Bay. But his whole deal is that he's a nomad, living out of his souped-up van with only his surfboard for company, going wherever the wind and the job take him.

I doubt he'd ever want to settle down. But if there was ever a group of ragtag misfits who could convince him, I bet it would be the One-Thirteen.

The station is going to be chaotic until the third watch have their fill of breakfast. That's going to take even longer after Bell puts on some bacon for everyone to go with the eggs and pancakes, as well as a couple of separate ones of kosher turkey sausages for Haskell and vegan ones for Hendrix. We're lucky not to get a call during it all. So while the two teams have a little rare time to mingle together, I set myself up to catch up on some paperwork on the sofa so I can at least be adjacent to the socializing.

It's not that I'm lonely. That would be ridiculous with my wonderful friends and family, and this exasperating but adorable team I get to affectionately lord over. But I think about when the third watch does head off, so many of them will be going home to their significant others, kids, parents, or even fur babies like Rocky.

One of the reasons I love work so much is because my apartment is always so empty and quiet. I guess I could get a dog like Bell did…except he pulled the Dalmatian puppy out of a burning building, defying direct orders from Captain Valentine. So maybe that's the not the best example. Besides, I don't have anyone to look after a pet when I'm here for twenty-four hours at a time. Bell brings Rocky with him most shifts, and our administrator, Nancy, or our neighbor, Mrs. Bloom, keep an eye on the dog when we go out.

If the whole team started doing that, it would be a zoo in no time. Absolute carnage.

It would be an irresponsible example to set if I got myself a dog and brought them with me to hang with Rocky, but then turned around and told the rest of the team that two's enough and they can't do the same. So for the umpteenth time, I push the empty apartment issue to the back of my mind, focusing on the house again.

It appears like the third watch are finally on their way out, thanking us for sending them off with full bellies and slightly less stress on their shoulders. Calmness washes through the building as people settle into morning chores… and I finally do a head count.

Shit.

It's no excuse, but with twice as many bodies milling around the common area for the past half an hour, I simply didn't notice.

But we're down a man.

"Hey, has anyone heard from Foster?" I ask, rising to my feet and sweeping the room again with my gaze in case I somehow missed him hiding in a potted plant or something.

The team collectively blink and also look around. "Teddy?" Bell calls out.

"Is he sick?" Ortiz asks in concern.

I shake my head. "The captain would have told me if he'd

heard that he was too ill to come in so we could try and organize cover."

"Unless he's *that* sick," Quick points out. "There's been a couple of nasty things going around my daughter's school after everyone came back from summer vacation."

Kwon shakes her head, though. "Nah, I don't think so. He told me he was going on a hike in the wilderness park with a *friend*."

She smirks as Bell's eyebrows jump up. "Oooh—a *friend* friend?"

"I reckon so," Nelson chimes in. "He told me that as well, and the text definitely had a 'if my date goes bad you know where to look for the body' type vibe to it." He laughs at his own joke, but almost immediately stops as his face falls. "Shit. Should we actually be looking for his body right now?"

I wave my hands and shake my head as people naturally gather around the dining table. "Let's not jump to any conclusions just yet," I warn them, although I've got a sense of uneasiness competing for space in my stomach with the eggs I just ate. "Has anyone tried reaching him?"

But even as I ask the question, I see that Kwon is already on her phone. She shakes her head and ends the call. "Straight to voicemail."

"Right," I say firmly, grabbing my tablet from my work bag. "Do you know whereabouts in the park he was headed?"

"He mentioned heading to one of the falls," Nelson says as I pull up a map. Kwon jabs her finger at the screen.

"Yeah, around there," she confirms. "Whether that's where he went, though, who knows?"

"He could just be at home with a hottie, sleeping off a hangover," Nelson crows.

Quick arches an eyebrow at him. "Not everyone is you, Sawyer. Besides, when have you ever known our probie to be anything less than punctual, respectful and eager to please?"

That makes Nelson hum in agreement.

I've already moved on to checking local reports, and my stomach drops. "Looks like there might have been some flooding around that area or...oh, no."

"What is it?" Hendrix asks as he and the others crane their necks to look my tablet as well.

I scan the text as fast as I can. "It looks like there might have been a disturbance in that area yesterday evening."

"Another earthquake?" Haskell asks with his brows furrowed. "We didn't get any phone alerts."

I shake my head, heaviness weighing on my chest. "No. It...it looks like a possible landslide. We should speak to Dispatch and see if they've had any distress calls."

"Um, Lieutenant," Kwon says with a wince. "If the signal is as bad out there as I suspect it is, nobody's going to be calling anyone."

"Should we alert the One-Two-Two?" Quick asks seriously. "That's their district. I don't want to send them on a wild goose chase, but maybe someone should inspect the area in person."

"Hang on," Nelson interjects, his eyes wide. "That's our boy who's possibly in trouble out there. If anyone's going on a wild goose chase, it should be us. Because what if it's not a false alarm? It's raining again this morning. What if Teddy's actually out there in a bad way?"

Ice slides down my spine. I can't deny that Foster is so dedicated that it probably would take a natural disaster to stop him arriving for his shift on time. He never thinks he can make any mistakes or show any weakness, like that might stop him from qualifying as a firefighter. Even slicing open his hand didn't slow him down. So him being this late and unreachable is definitely a red flag. But...

"We have a duty to our community," I point out.

Bell shakes his head. "We can inform Dispatch to put any

calls on divert. San Clemente has several houses that can cover for us. But Sawyer's right. Teddy's not just some probie. He's one of us and we never leave anyone behind, right?"

"Damn right," the captain's voice rings out behind me over the chorus of agreement. He approaches us, coffee mug in hand, and glances at my tablet. "You're concerned about Foster, did I hear?"

I nod and bring the map up again. "He hasn't shown up for work and his phone's going straight to voicemail. He told a couple of the guys he was going for a hike in this area yesterday, and there have since been reports of a landslide. However," I sigh, really hating to be the pragmatic one when all I want to do is gear up and charge out on a rescue mission. "This is well off the beaten track. Even if we do get permission for a search and rescue mission, we're never getting any of the rigs up there. Not even the ambulance."

"Um," Hendrix says, raising his hand like he's at school. "You might not want to send the One-Two-Two up there in our place, but they might be able to do us a favor anyway. I know a guy from my time working with them. I think he could help."

That's all the encouragement I needed, and I look at Valentine. "What do you say, boss? Permission to go look for our missing man?"

"No," Valentine says with a frown as he puts his mug on the table with a little more force than necessary. "Not without me, you're not."

"Yeehaw!" Kwon cries, punching the air and making Rocky bark in excitement.

Bell raises a finger and makes him calm down. "You're not coming with us," he tells the dog firmly.

Valentine hums. "*He* can't, no. But let me see if Captain Padilla can't spare someone from the K-9 unit. A sniffer dog might not be the worst idea if anyone's trapped under the rubble, not just our man."

"Do we have anything of Foster's we can use for a scent?" I ask the group.

Nelson grins. "We will if you let me pick my way into his locker," he says with far too much enthusiasm.

"I didn't hear a thing," I tell him, waving my hand by my ear.

"Say hi to the twenty-five Cassius Gardas he has in there," Kwon calls out as Nelson rushes gleefully off. Quick only pauses a second before following him, presumably to make sure he doesn't break into anyone else's locker while he's at it.

"To be fair," Ortiz says thoughtfully, "Teddy probably only has like four pictures of Garda hanging up there."

"Four too many for a grown man," Haskell grumbles before frowning at me. "The kid's probably fine, you know."

I chuckle as I look our driver engineer up and down. "Can't help but notice you're the first one dressed and ready to go, though."

He harrumphs and ambles off to sit behind the wheel of the rig.

"Okay," Valentine announces as he puts his phone down. "Dispatch has been notified and so has the One-Two-Two. Apparently, there's already a team combing the area, but they'll appreciate whatever help we can give them. I'll call Padilla on route and see if she can spare anyone to meet us there."

"My guy's on board!" Hendrix announces excitedly as everyone starts making their way to the truck to ride together.

I linger, giving Nancy a nod as she stays behind with Rocky. Our aloof station cat, Smokey, peers out with interest to see what all the fuss is about.

The One-Thirteen are rolling out on a different kind of call, that's what the fuss is, kitty. Because no matter how much I might feel apart from the group sometimes, when I jump on board and Haskell hits the siren and the gas, I know that every single one of these people would go to hell and back for anyone else on this team, including me.

If Teddy's in trouble, we'll find him.

Because that's just what we do.

CHAPTER 13

Teddy

WHEN A LARGE, COLD DROP OF WATER HITS MY FOREHEAD AND startles me awake, I'm completely disoriented for a good few seconds.

Then the events of yesterday come flooding back to me, and I can't help but feel a little dizzy. It's a lot to process, from the conversation with Cassius about our relationship that rocked my world, to surviving the landslide that *literally* rocked our world, to his sprained ankle, and then finally to making love out in the open air under a blanket of stars.

It might sound crazy, but I think it was the best day of my life, near-death experience included. Certainly the most memorable.

As I snuggle up against Cassius's sleeping form, watching the weak light of dawn get stronger through the rain clouds that have burst once again, I feel a shift in perspective.

It was a thought I had yesterday, but right now, I have the luxury of contemplating it in quiet solitude. I could have lost it all. What's worse than that? Skirting so close to losing our lives in a freak accident makes me repeat the question: what am I afraid of?

'The unknown' is probably the most obvious answer. I spend so much of my time trying to plan for every eventuality, whether that's at work to keep people safe or in everyday life to keep people happy. Therefore, the idea of having no control over a situation is understandably scary.

I know I compared Cassius's fame to the role the firehouse plays in the community. But when people are grateful to us or want to thank us for our help, they just know us as a unit, the team who came to their aid in one of the worst moments of their lives. It's rare they remember specific names or faces.

There are people out there who literally live and breathe Cassius Garda's every waking moment. His life is their fandom. I'm very aware I joked to myself about accidentally finding myself in someone else's highly implausible fanfiction, but there are *actually* stories about him online. I looked. And we're not talking about a couple of random fics. No. One site I checked numbered in the four digits.

The fire department being 'known' by people we've barely met isn't the same thing as people devoting their time to imagining what it's like to be Cassius Garda enough to generate millions of words about him living a secret life as a superhero, running a coffee shop, or falling in love with various former teammates. People have tattoos of his face on their bodies. There are questions about him on gameshows. The sitcom I was watching the other night referenced him by *name.*

There's being known by the small community of Redwood Bay…and then there's being worshiped by fans across the globe.

They are not the same thing.

So it's not exactly that I'm afraid. More like I have a sensible apprehension about what us trying to date would affect beyond the relationship itself. Which, by the way, is kind of a big deal in and of itself. Even if Cassius wasn't famous, I think I'd still be pausing to think about what I want from my first serious adult relationship before jumping in feet first.

But the fact remains that this could never be a regular situation because Cassius *is* famous, very famous. More than that, he's one of the few NFL players to ever come out while still playing. It doesn't matter so much that his injury forced an early retirement not long after that. He's still fresh in people's minds as a star player, and there are going to be a lot of folks out there like that jerk from the other day who will be really mad if Cassius 'rubs it in their face' by openly dating a guy.

That guy being me.

Would the public really care that much about some nobody Cassius is dating? We don't have to flaunt it, I guess, especially while we're getting into the rhythm of being in each other's lives. But I realized I was gay when I was thirteen and, even though it was kind of scary, once I came out, I knew I never wanted to go back in the closet again. I'm pretty certain Cassius feels the same way after making such a big deal out of his announcement.

So if we do this, we're really doing it out in the open for all to see, or at least some of it.

If I step into the public eye...that feels like a genie that can't be put back into its bottle. The media and the public could start rummaging around in not just my personal life, but my family's and my teammates' lives. I don't *think* I have anything to hide, but what if I have skeletons lurking in my closet that I'm not even aware of? Or what if the people I know and love have secrets I have no clue about that could be exposed just because I got swept up in a celebrity romance?

Would I be selfish if I throw caution to the wind and leap into a relationship like this?

"I can hear you thinking," Cassius grumbles sleepily. But before I can cringe too hard, he kisses the top of my head and hugs me tighter to him. "Everything okay?"

I'm not sure how to answer that, so I hum and look out over the park for a moment. The vista is still picturesque despite the damage from yesterday. Although the sky is gray and stormy again, the light behind the clouds makes me think it's later in the day than I first thought. I'd check my phone—as telling the time is basically all it's good for right now—but I don't want to move away from Cassius. Judging by his possessive grip, he wouldn't be keen on the idea either.

It occurs to me that I might not be the only one feeling insecure right now.

"Sorry for waking you," I tell him sincerely.

He shudders under the crinkly silver heat blanket as he fully rouses and yawns. The rain isn't that heavy, but it's still falling hard enough that some droplets are making their way through the tree canopy, like the one that hit my face and dragged me back into consciousness earlier. Every few seconds, one splats on the tin foil blanket, and the ground smells earthy around us. The sights and sounds are quite cozy, really. But dampness has seeped into my clothes just enough to make it uncomfortable.

However, Cassius looks content as he squirms against me. "S'okay," he says in reply to my apology. He blinks his eyes into focus, then smiles down at me where my temple is resting on his shoulder. "I think I like being woken up by you."

I bite my lip and try not to blush, but it's difficult. Will I ever get used to his easy praise and affection?

Am I going to give him the chance for that to happen?

My continuous hesitation is clearly affecting him, though. It's subtle, but I don't miss the flash of hurt in his eyes.

"I understand if you'd rather keep last night as a one-time thing," he says softly.

That certainly lights a rocket up my ass.

"What?" I squawk. "No! I mean…if that's what you want, then I guess…"

He huffs and presses his lips to mine. It's chaste compared to anything that happened yesterday, but seeing as neither of have a toothbrush at hand, that's probably for the best. Besides, it still sends a delicious thrill down my spine.

"Sorry," I mumble once he releases me from the kiss. "I don't mean to be weird."

"You're not," he assures me. "You're being sensible."

"Am I?" I ask, curious what he thinks I'm thinking.

He shifts on the uncomfortable ground, but his gaze never wavers from mine. "I assume you're considering the bigger picture. I know we talked about what this might mean for you yesterday in terms of people invading your privacy. And we spoke before about how the fame could create a pretty big power imbalance between us."

"And the money," I point out as it is a serious, practical point.

He laughs, though, and I hope that's because he knows by now that I'm so not interested in him for his riches. The way he regards me warmly and brushes his thumb against my cheek reassures me he does.

"But," he continues, "I feel like I'm getting to know you now, and I'd guess you're worrying if any scrutiny you might face will also affect others in your life. Loved ones you care deeply about."

I stare at him for a moment. "Yeah…" I say slowly. "That's *exactly* what I was thinking. How did you…?"

"I'm a mind reader," he says with a flick of his eyebrows,

but it only takes him a second to crack up. "Naw, seriously. I've been doing this a long time. There have been countless guys I've seen join the Seahawks or teams like them that came straight from college, and they were given zero fucking media training on how to handle being thrust into the spotlight."

His expression darkens, and I can't deny it's pretty hot seeing him getting protective and angry on his teammates' behalf. Obviously, it sucks those guys went through that, but it doesn't surprise me. Entertainment industries, be it sports, music, film or television, all love to chew up fresh young talent and spit them out without a second thought. In that moment, I wonder how many guys Cassius helped along the way to protect their privacy and keep their sanity.

God, how is he so fucking perfect?

"So are you going to tell me everything's going to be okay?" I ask.

He scoffs. "Sorry, baby, I'm not. But...anything worth having is worth fighting for, okay?"

I've heard that expression before, and it's always rung true for me. I nod and sigh, not sure I feel much better. But Cassius cups his palm against the side of my face, and I melt.

"If you still want to try this," he says, looking deep into my eyes with such sincerity it snatches my breath away, "I will be with you every step of the way. I'll prepare you and protect you any way I know how. And not just you, but your friends and family, too. It takes effort, but I promise you that with just a little consideration every day I live a pretty normal life." He pauses and purses his lips, seemingly deliberating something for a second. "But it's been a lonely life for a while now. Outside of my immediate family, it feels like nobody knows me at all, even if they think they do. I want you to know me, Teddy. I want to know you, too, in every way possible. I'll do whatever I can to help you with this transition because I believe you are absolutely worth fighting for. If...if you're reconsidering in the cold light of day, though, I will understand."

I try and swallow the lump in my throat and blink back the wetness collecting in the corner of my eyes. But when I can't hold back my smile any longer, a hiccup escapes and a couple of tears roll down my cheeks.

"Nobody has ever made me feel as seen as you do, Cassius," I tell him thickly, not caring that my emotions are getting the better of me. I think I want him to see what I'm really feeling, anyhow. "Being with you makes me feel like I'm finally in the right place in this world, not forgotten or overlooked for once. I'm scared it could change my life in ways I can't even anticipate right now. But I'm more scared of walking away from one of the best things that's ever happened to me just because I'm a bit afraid." I laugh and wipe my eyes as he beams at me. "Which is a lot of goddamned words to say I'm not reconsidering. In fact, having thought about it even more, I'm definitely, absolutely sure I want to try, um, whatever we want to call this."

"Yeah?" he asks excitedly with raised eyebrows. "I want to call you my boyfriend. How does that sound?"

I don't care about the toothbrush situation. There's nothing that can stop me from launching myself at his face and kissing his mouth senseless. Seeing as he reciprocates with just as much gusto, clinging to me the way I'm clinging to him, I'm going to go out on a limb and guess he feels the same way.

"That sounds amazing," I mumble against his lips. "So long as I can call you my boyfriend, too."

"I've never been anyone's boyfriend before," he says with a grin, slowing down and pressing sweet kisses against my cheek and temple. "I bet I'm a great one."

I laugh, loving his playful arrogance when he's happy. The

fact that I get to know things like that about him now is mind blowing. I promise myself never to take that for granted, and not just because there are millions of people around the world who'd love to know things like that. But because one person—the one special person I want to give my heart to—is trusting me enough to show me intimate details that no one else gets to see.

We trade a few more kisses and content gazes into each other's eyes, but eventually there's no holding reality off for any longer.

"Urgh, nature calls, I'm afraid," I inform him with a groan.

He chuckles and releases me. "Yeah, tell me about it. Shall we?"

I help him to stand and carefully limp to a nearby tree. Then I run off to find my own to relieve myself behind before hurrying back to rescue him.

"How's your ankle?" I ask as I sit him back down where we slept. From how little weight he was able to put on it just now, I think I know the answer, but his grimace confirms it.

"I just need fresh ice, stronger painkillers, a compression sock, and to properly elevate it for a day or two," he says with the confidence of a man that's dealt with a lot of injuries during his life. "But I don't know how fast I'm going to be going with you to the highway."

"Yeah," I agree reluctantly, chewing my lip for a minute. "Okay, here's what I think we should do. Let's pack up here, then very slowly start making our way until we can see the road or we find a distinctive landmark where I can set you up. If I'm going to make a run for help, I have to be able to find you again."

My heart squeezes painfully at the idea of abandoning him, accidentally or not. He's promised to protect me from the media, so it's absolutely my job to protect him from coming to any further harm.

I don't admit it out loud as I don't want to worry him unnecessarily, but with this continued rain, I'm more than a little worried about the possibility of another landslide or flooding from the falls. The drought all summer has left the ground so unstable that it's going to take a long time for it to settle down again.

But it seems he feels the same need for urgency just as I do. "Okay," he says with a nod. "Let's do this."

We didn't have much stuff, so it only takes me a few minutes to pack everything away and make sure we're ready before we hobble out into the inclement weather. The campfire was down to embers anyway, so I stomp it out with ease. A wildfire is unlikely under the current circumstances, but I'm still not taking any chances.

At least this is California, so as it's daytime once more, the temperature has risen again. It's unpleasant being warm and damp, but it's way better than freezing our asses off. I prop Cassius up with his arm slung over my shoulders, and I keep my compass at hand to make sure we stay headed south.

It's a struggle, but we slowly move away from the disaster area and find a path again. I don't recognize it, but the level ground makes it a lot easier for Cassius to walk. Still, he's already flagging, sweat pouring down his body with the effort of hopping along, and I know I'm not going to be able to push him much farther. When I see the first big tree that will offer decent shelter, I make the decision to set him up there.

"Now we're on a trail, I'll be able to retrace my steps much easier," I explain as we ease our way over to the spot and out of the rain once more. "Will you be all right?"

He smiles despite his obvious discomfort. "I'll be fine, baby. I promise."

"Someone might even walk this way, you never know. Do you have some water left?" We've had to ration it but at least with the rain we haven't been as dehydrated as we could have been.

He stops before I can sit him down and kisses my mouth. "I do have some water left, yes. I mean it, I'll be okay. You should probably get going…" His gaze shifts over my shoulder and he frowns. "Do you see that?"

I turn and look in the same direction as he is, squinting through the rain. I'm about to ask him what I'm supposed to be seeing, when a flash of color in the sky catches my attention.

"No way," I say, not allowing myself to feel hopeful until I know for sure. "That looks like—"

"A helicopter!" Cassius cries.

In an instant, I let him go, make sure he's steady enough on his feet, then rip my backpack from my shoulders. I don't have a flare, although after this incident, I'm tempted to pack one for the future. What I do have are a couple of orange hi-vis reflective strips that I usually clip onto my bag or clothes if I'm running in the dark. They also have LEDs inside that I can set to flash, which I do now with fumbling fingers.

"WE'RE HERE!" I bellow at the top of my lungs, stepping out from under the tree to wave the lights like I'm guiding a plane in for landing. I know whoever's in that helicopter absolutely can't hear me, but it makes me feel better all the same. "HEY!"

I continue waving my arms in the rain, hoping the fact I'm wearing a blue hoodie might help me stand out against the foliage as well as the LEDs and reflective strips. I know we're not exactly stranded in the middle of the Sahara Desert, but if there's a chance we could be rescued right here and now, I'm going to do everything I can to make that happen.

Anything so I don't have to leave Cassius all alone.

"I think they see you!" he cries happily from behind me,

and I have to agree. It seems like the blip in the sky is getting bigger, making me want to sag in relief. I don't stop waving my arms until I know for sure.

Once I can confidently make out the distinctive red tail and white front of the air operations chopper, I finally let my arms drop and stagger backward into Cassius. He wraps me in his arms and kisses my cheek.

"It's going to be okay," I assure him.

"I never doubted you for a moment, baby."

Recklessness takes over me, and I twist in his arms to kiss his mouth, regardless of whether the crew in the helicopter can see us or not. We break apart after only a few seconds, flushed and smiling at each other before reluctantly moving so I'm simply propping him up on his good leg once more.

"If this was our second date," I shout as the helicopter pilot carefully swings around to land, "I'm almost scared to think what the third date will be."

"Swimming with sharks," Cassius says without missing a beat. "No cage, of course."

"Oh, of course," I reply with a grin, turning off the LEDs now they're no longer needed and slipping the reflective strips into my hoodie pouch. I wonder absently if it's still going to smell like him after I've put it through such hell.

I guess after I wash it, I'll just have to make sure I cuddle him a lot more in it.

Because apparently, I'm going to get to do that.

The helicopter is settled, and the blades are slowing down. "Are you ready for this?" Cassius asks me, his tone more serious. "There are bound to be questions."

"Yeah," I say with a sigh. "At least this will be one of the San Clemente crews, or maybe even LA. We don't have a heli..."

The words die in my throat as the rescue team begin

disembarking. "Probie!" Lili screams in delight. "You're not dead! See, you guys, I told you he wasn't going to be dead."

My jaw drops and I watch in horror as the entire first watch of the One-Thirteen fire station pour out of the helicopter, as well as the police captain, Lucy Padilla, and another officer with a tracker dog. Everyone's talking at once.

"Teddy! Are you all right?"

"You had us worried there, Foster."

"We saw reports of a landslide in the area you said you were going hiking in and…"

The lieutenant slowly stops speaking as he approaches us, no prizes given for the reason why.

"Holy fucking shit," Sawyer blurts out, smacking Anton's arm. "Is that—?"

"Hi," Cassius says with a tired smile and a feeble wave.

"Uh, my friend sprained his ankle," I say, trying not to meet all the incredulous eyes trained on me in that moment.

"Of course," Lieutenant Flores says, hurriedly dashing over to help support Cassius from his other side. "Ortiz, over here!"

"Already on it, sir," Yara tells him cheerfully as she and Dray make their way through with a backbaord. "Don't you worry, Mr. Garda. We'll have you taken care of in no time."

She seems completely unphased, unlike the rest of my team who are still slack jawed and bug eyed. Well, except for Drayton. I'm not sure how long he's lived here in the US, but I'm guessing American football isn't as big in Australia as Australian football.

"There you go, sir," he says as he eases Cassius from my grip.

I meet Cassius's eyes, realizing that the last time he was carried out on a stretcher would have been when he ripped his rotator cuff and ended his NFL career. My stomach swoops, but he reaches out and gives my hand a squeeze as well as a little nod, letting me know he's okay. At least that's what I hope he's saying.

Suddenly, the sniffer dog starts barking and pulling on their leash, drawing the attention of everyone in the group. "Everything okay there, Officer?" Captain Padilla asks. "Our missing person is alive and well over there." I notice she gestures at me while pointedly not looking at Cassius, a blush on her cheeks. I guess even 49er fans know a Seahawks legend when they see one.

The dog's handler frowns as her partner starts dragging her toward a clump of bushes. "Not sure, Captain. What is it, Klaus? Have you got something?"

The German Shepard determinedly pulls her through the rain until they're practically running toward the bushes.

Then a couple of teenage girls run *out* of the bushes, squealing.

"Don't let it eat us!" one of them wails.

I blink in shock, completely thrown by their presence. Where did they come from? How long have they been there?

Oh...god. One of them is holding up her phone, despite the rain.

Captain Valentine pushes his way through the group with Padilla by his side. "Are you girls injured?" he asks in concern.

They huddle together, looking guilty and bedraggled in their raincoats. "Um, no, sir," the one with the phone says. "We heard there was a landslide, so we came out to film some content while it still looked cool. Then we heard that guy shouting," she says, pointing at me, "so we changed direction to see what that was all about instead. But then he *kissed* Cassius Garda! We didn't want to interrupt, so we hid in the bushes, but then you guys landed, and we were going to sneak away, but we wanted to see how it all ended. Mister!"

She addresses me again. "Are you Cassius Garda's boyfriend?"

"Duh," the other girl says to her friend with and eye roll. "He's wearing a Seahawks hoodie. It's probably Garda's." She clasps her hands in front of her chest and swoons at me. "You're *soooo* cute together!" she cries over the rain.

I feel like a trap door's opened up under my feet and I'm falling in slow motion.

"Uhh…" I croak, too afraid to look at Cassius.

"Hold up," Padilla snaps, making both girls jump. "Are you filming right now?"

Miss Cinematographer flicks her gaze from the screen back to the captain. "I started live streaming on TikTok as soon as we arrived," she admits sheepishly.

"She has over *two million* people tuned in!" her friend shrieks, dancing on her tiptoes as she looks at me. "Everyone is asking who the guy Cassius kissed is! Do you want to introduce yourself?"

My knees feel like they're going to give out. I want to run, to hide. But there's nowhere to go. My chest is heaving yet I can't seem to fill my lungs, and the edge of my vision is going dark.

Am I going to pass out in front of two million people who have probably already made up their minds that I'm not good enough to be Cassius's boyfriend?

Then our driver engineer, Gene, marches right in front of me to block me from the livestream and folds his arms with a harumph. "Kids these days got no respect," he grumbles. "Too busy filming every second to help anyone out."

Lili and Lochlan spring up to his right. Lochlan might be huge, but Lili is radiating fury. Anton and Sawyer mirror them on Gene's left, creating a human shield. The lieutenant joins both the captains who are still halfway between me and the girls, while Klaus starts barking again, his handler only just holding him a few feet back from the camera.

"Turn it off, *now*," Padilla growls.

I startle as something touches my hand, only to look down and realize Cassius has slipped his palm against mine, a sympathetic look in his eyes above the oxygen mask my guys have put on him. Yara and Dray are standing close to the gurney, doing their best to protect Cassius from view as well.

My heart aches with love for my friends, but dread is still pooled in my belly. They can hide us now and force the livestream to end, but it's too late.

Who knows how many millions of people saw me and Cassius kissing?

The genie is out of the bottle.

CHAPTER 14
Cassius

"It's getting worse," Bryan whispers frantically as he paces my private hospital room, his thumbs angrily jabbing at his phone. "How? *How* can it keep getting worse?"

"Bryan," I say wearily, sharing a look with my mom who's sitting beside my bed. I'm not ashamed to admit she's holding my hand, and I really fucking appreciate it right now.

"It's been less than six hours since the livestream," Bryan continues to hiss as he goes back and forth, glaring at the screen like it's the one who personally wronged me. "Six! And the internet has not only worked out that Teddy was the same guy that rescued the viral river cat, but that *you* adopted that same cat. Yet again, I ask: HOW? I knew I should have made the shelter staff sign NDAs. And the veterinarians."

"Is it really that bad, hon?" my mom asks, finally making Bryan rip his gaze up to look at us. "Think about it," she continues firmly. "Rescuing a cat and having a boyfriend are *good* things." She turns her head back to smile at me and kiss the backs of my fingers. "I'm so happy for you, sweetie! When do I get to meet him?"

Bryan sighs and drags himself over to slump in the other visitor's chair by her side, putting his phone away. We're just waiting on the MRI results to check what I'm certain I already know. It's just a light sprain on my ankle. It's already feeling a million times better after all the things I said I needed. Decent painkillers, a cold compress, elevation and rest.

My head and my heart aren't so easily soothed. Teddy rode with me in the helicopter, he and his colleagues eerily quiet as we flew to the hospital. But everyone agreed it would be better if only the paramedics escorted me in.

He looked so pale and worried as they unloaded me and closed the door between us.

Has our relationship ended before it's even begun?

Bryan rubs his forehead then looks kindly at my mom. "Of course those are wonderful things, Rosie," he says sincerely. "The slightly mind-blowing connection between Teddy, Kiki, and Cassius is making people rabid in their thirst for more information. It's not that we lost control of the narrative. It's that we never had it to begin with. Internet pundits are running away with the story and spinning it all kinds of ways, digging up whatever they can on Teddy before I've had even one minute to prepare him for what's to come. It's only a matter of time before they sniff out his former classmates from high school and the academy, looking for anything juicy they can find."

"I promised I'd protect him," I say ruefully, grinding my teeth.

"No," Bryan snaps at me with a frown, like I'm a bad puppy. "This is *not* your fault."

"Which part?" I ask with a rueful laugh, not really wanting to listen to logic right now. "When nature tried to kill us just as Teddy and I talked about dating? Or when my ankle decided to sabotage our attempt to leave the forest before dark? Or when those girls filmed us without our consent and outed our relationship to the whole world less than an hour after we used the B-word for the first time?"

"Which B-word?" my mom asks innocently.

"I can think of a B-word to call those morally-challenged proto-humans," Bryan says darkly, scowling at the hospital bed before shifting his sparkly eyes back to me. "None of those things are your fault and you know it, so stop being a drama llama. You're far too ruggedly handsome for that."

My mom pinches my cheek with a grin. "Now ain't that the truth?"

I sigh at both of them. "Yeah, okay, maybe I know I'm not to blame for those things. But the outcome is the same—a total mess."

Bryan puffs out his cheeks and shakes his head. "I might be livid, however, that will pass. And then I will rise like a phoenix from the ashes and do what I do best. Which is?"

He cups his hand behind his ear and raises an eyebrow at me.

"Damage control," I fill in dutifully.

"Damn right, damage control," he says with conviction. "Your lovely mom is absolutely correct that there isn't actually any kind of scandal here."

She preens, making me chuckle. He presses his splayed digits together, touching his thumbs to his chin and his index fingers to the bridge of his nose, closing his eyes. After taking a long, deep breath in and releasing it, he lowers his hands and looks at me once more.

"Are you guys serious about pursuing a relationship?" he asks.

I lick my lips and glance out of the window. It's still drizzling, which suits my mood just fine. "I mean, we were, but—"

"Nuh!" he interrupts. "No buts. Before the livestream, what had you both decided?"

"To try dating," I say, shifting in the slightly scratchy cotton sheets. Compared to the dirt we slept on last night, this single bed is heavenly. That doesn't mean I'm not desperate to get home to my own rainfall shower and memory foam mattress, though.

Christ. Am I ever going to bring Teddy home to that bed?

Bryan is waiting for me to elaborate with an arched eyebrow. So I clear my throat and make an effort not to think about sex again while my own *mother* is sitting beside me.

"We talked at length about what it would mean if we started a relationship," I say. "He understood it would almost certainly compromise his personal life and privacy, and he was worried about the effect it might have on his friends and family. But…" I bite my lip and try and hold onto the fleeting moment of joy that flutters through my chest like a hummingbird. "We have real feelings for each other. He thought about the risks overnight and was absolutely sure he wanted to…" Words fail me for a moment and I'm not quite sure how to capture how we felt this morning. "He wanted to be my boyfriend," I finish softly.

My very first boyfriend.

"Oh, pumpkin," my mom says, patting my hand.

Bryan rolls his eyes and huffs. "First rule: stop using the past tense. You've graduated from letting him know that you were already damn well dating to labelling it. Well done, you get an A-plus in boyfriending. Now I've had my tantrum, it's time for you to stop moping. I am…" His fingers twitch and his jaw clicks. *"Disappointed* I wasn't allowed to control the how and when that knowledge was made public. However, it's time to turn lemons into lemon drop martinis."

He cracks his knuckles.

"What do you have in mind?" I ask, a flicker of hope igniting in my heart.

I've been telling myself ever since we got on that helicopter that if Teddy was nervous before about committing to a relationship, he was almost certainly going to run for the hills after TikTok blew up. But there's a fire in Bryan's eyes that makes me think the ref hasn't called the final whistle on this game just yet.

"Surely they should just be honest," my mom says earnestly, sitting up straighter in her seat. "Hold a press conference and tell the world they're in love."

"Whoa, there, Mom," I say with a laugh. "Not to rain on your parade, but it's way too early to use that word just yet."

She narrows her eyes at me and hums. "If you say so, sweetie."

"Hmm, yes, honesty," Bryan says thoughtfully, nodding as he pulls his phone from his pocket once again, tapping it on his knee. "That works a treat for manipulating people's heartstrings."

"Manipulating—?" my poor mom cries in horror, but Bryan is right. This is what he's great at. Why I hired him. I know he'll never make me lie to the public.

But there are ways to...channel emotion into ways that work to your advantage.

Suddenly, Bryan snaps his fingers, flicking his slightly manic gaze toward me. "We're not going to change the narrative," he says, one side of his mouth curling into a grin. "We're going to build on it."

"Okay," I say tentatively.

He stands up and starts pacing again, but the energy is different now from earlier.

"Teddy saved your cat, then saved you...so now...you're going to save him right back."

I frown, not sure I'm following. "Are you talking about staging an emergency, because—"

"Oh, hell, no," Bryan cries, wrinkling his nose like his waiter just bought him burned soufflé. *"Honesty*, remember? No, no, nothing like that. I'm talking about *charity*. People will soon be charmed by the filthy rich football player—"

"Ex-football player," I remind him.

"Shh," he says with a wave of his hand, like he barely heard me anyway. "They'll be charmed by the rich football player dating the humble firefighter if we throw a *fundraiser* for the department. You said they borrowed that helicopter from a neighboring town's station, right? So what if they had their *own* chopper? I'm sure the coastguard would appreciate that as well, right? Oh, and what about the clean-up from this recent flooding, the landslide you got caught in, the wildfires from over the summer? So much money we can throw around."

I kind of love that he's too busy scheming to ask if I'm okay with him arbitrarily tossing my fortune around. But that sounds fine to me, so I just let him keep rolling. After all, I've made so many investments, but I still have hundreds of thousands just sitting in the bank, waiting for me to do something with it.

He snaps his fingers on both hands in quick succession, dancing his feet over the linoleum floor to music only he can hear. "We host it at your new place, so it has that intimate, humble vibe. Teddy and his crew are the guests of honor. We encourage everyone to get their glad rags out." He suddenly fixes his gaze on my mom. "You'll be there, won't you, Rosie?"

"Oh, I'd love to!" she cries excitedly, and my heart pangs with happiness that I was blessed with such a good woman as my mother.

Never mind how great the optics will be painting me as a

doting mama's boy. That's just a nice bonus that she never needs to consider. But I know what's on Bryan's mind.

He's still dancing at the same time as his thumbs animatedly tap on his phone screen. "Yes, we'll invite the firefighters, as well as the animal shelter staff and the vets—even if *someone* there has loose lips. Because that's what we want this time. We're not doing a press conference or even looking like we're trying to control the narrative at all. We'll just let our guests do that organically. There'll be a mix of local heroes and community leaders as well as some glittering stars whose wallets we intend on *gently* encouraging them to empty for a good cause or three."

He spins and clutches his phone to his chest as he grins devilishly at me.

"Thoughts?"

I rub my chin and turn it over in my mind. "So you want mine and Teddy's first official event as a couple to essentially be a party at my house with no press, just our guests' social media posts, and we'll be asking people to donate?"

Bryan taps his finger against his jugular. "Hmm...not quite. We'll be...encouraging the rich and famous to bid on... oh my *fucking* god! Bid on fucking puppies and kittens at the shelter where Kiki came from!" he punches the air and shimmies his shoulders. "We'll just have photos of the critters so the place doesn't get, you know, messy. Our affluent guests will bid to sponsor—adopt? No, sponsor, less pressure. But there will be the option to adopt as well! They'll sponsor each adorable fur baby's room and board for a year, and any excess just goes to the shelter itself for renovations or whatever they need it for. Oh! Veterinarian bills...they have debt, right? Maybe that's what people pledge towards. Hmm... Then for the fire department, if they want that helicopter...something separate...something more dramatic...let me brainstorm..."

"Bryan," I say in disbelief. "You're willing to make all this effort and raise all this cash for charity in our name? To launch our relationship?"

Finally, he stops his fancy footwork and lowers his phone, looking seriously between me and my mom.

"Cassius," he says seriously. "You've put love on hold your whole life because this world told you that men who play football—who play *any* sport professionally—aren't allowed to be like you. Aren't allowed to be authentic and follow their hearts. And yes, *yes*…it's probably too early to use the L-word for your B-word. But it's the *possibility* of love we're fighting for right now." He flares his nostrils, his eyes oddly glassy as he waves his hands like he's trying to get rid of that burned soufflé smell. "You *deserve* this, Big Man. You are *owed* this. And I am going to make sure I do everything I can to make it a success or *die* trying."

He takes a long breath in, his knuckles going white around the grip he has on his phone. Then his shoulders twitch, he nods once, then he clears his throat.

"Um, if you'll excuse me for one second," he says with a sniff. He marches out of the room, presumably to collect himself after his passionate outburst, leaving my heart thudding in my chest and my mom squeezing my hand with a triumphant grin on her face.

"You heard what the man said," she informs me. "You deserve this, sweetie. You've spent so much time making sure me and your pops and your brother and sister never wanted for nothing. It's time for you to let something amazing happen to you."

I allow myself a few shaky breaths, not really believing that to be true, but trusting my mom knows best pretty much all of the time.

"He *is* amazing, Mom," I say thickly. "I don't want to blow it. Do you think we're onto something with this fundraiser idea?"

She shrugs and smiles. "Like Bryan said. Those are all good things. Raising money for charity and stepping out into the world with your fella? If you do it from the *heart*." She leans forward and pats over mine. "What could go wrong?"

If I've learned anything over the past year, it's the old saying that if something *can* go wrong, it will. But...I'm also willing to put my faith in a power a little greater than myself. My mom is right. Our intentions are noble and good. Yes, yes, I remember what the road to hell is paved with.

But I also think I finally believe what Bryan was saying.

I sacrificed a really important part of myself for my career, and now it's time for the universe to pay its dues.

If I can't carve out some happiness with Teddy Foster, then who? He's the first person in my life who's truly stolen my heart.

Time to see if he's open to a stupidly big gesture to prove that.

CHAPTER 15

Teddy

I PROBABLY SHOULD HAVE JUST GONE HOME. I DOUBT THE situation would be any better, but I'm feeling awkward and useless here at the station. Still, Captain Valentine seemed pretty certain earlier when he said it would do me good to come back with the rest of the team, even if I just stuck to light duties. Seeing as I wasn't sure what else to do with myself, I allowed the decision to be taken out of my hands. That felt good, for a moment at least.

After we dropped Cassius off at San Clemente General, we only had to wait a few minutes before Yara and Dray returned to the helicopter and the pilot flew us all back to the One-Two-Two. Of course some of them had worked out that I was the same guy they'd had to save when I jumped in the river to rescue Kiki and tried to give me shit about it, but Cap shut that down real fast. I'm just grateful none of them had seen the TikTok.

Yet.

The drive back to Redwood Bay was filled with deliberately vague chatter, mostly kept up by Lili, Lochlan and Sawyer arguing passionately about which Fast and Furious is the worst. Captain Valentine let Dispatch know that the One-Thirteen was back open for calls, and the tones sounded not even ten minutes after we disembarked from the rig.

Cap told me to stay behind and take a shower. I was more than happy to comply.

Now I'm clean and dry in fresh clothes, sitting on the floor of the common area with my back against the sofa, eating sugary cereal with Rocky's head in my lap as he looks up at me with big sympathetic eyes.

"Yeah, it's been a day," I admit to him.

I lose my appetite for the fruity grains and marshmallows halfway through my bowl, so I set it down on the coffee table to let it go soggy. Rocky allows me to absently stroke his back, his tail wagging every now and again. When the station cat, Smokey, makes a rare appearance on the sofa behind my shoulder, Rocky whines for a second. But then the two of them cohabit the space peacefully with me, which tells me how bad my vibes must be if they've agreed on a détente just to make me feel better.

I appreciate it.

Since returning to civilization, my phone's been blowing up, mostly from my family. I guess people they know have been messaging them as news of the initial livestream spreads. Of course it's not just that one video now. People are reblogging, remixing and reacting to it across all social media platforms. I've received voicemails from news outlets looking to confirm the story. The first one I listened to sent a chill down my spine. I hate that someone I know is giving out my number to these vultures.

But there doesn't seem to be anything I can do right now except ignore them. I don't want to speak to anyone before touching base again with Cassius and his team.

Cassius. My heart aches. I desperately want to talk to him.

But as he's the one in hospital, we left it that he'd message when he could with an update. So I'm not going to bother him, no matter how much I want the reassurance that everything's okay between us.

A part of me has accepted that the genie is out of the bottle and there's no going back in terms of the public being aware of us. It scares the shit out of me even more so than before because we never got the chance to prepare. It's bizarre, knowing that all over the world people are losing their minds over this. But what can I really do except let them? I'll have to deal with the fallout—however horrendous it is—later.

Because the only way I can see to stop it is to deny that Cassius and I were ever a thing and say it's all a big misunderstanding.

I'm not doing that.

Right now, I just want to know if Cassius and I are okay. Does he still want to give us a chance? Or has it all been ruined before it could even begin? If I could believe that he still wants me, that he's going to stand by my side, then maybe I'll have the guts to look at my phone again. At the moment, it's staying on silent in my pocket until further notice.

My parents are worried about me, especially my mom. I think my dad's trying not to sound too excited until the dust settles. I imagine he'd love to brag to his buddies that his youngest is dating a legend. Finally, something original from his fifth son. My mom will want me to be happy, I know, whether that's with Cassius or the boy next door. Thinking of talking to them both later—with happy news if I have any luck at all—makes me smile. Rocky whimpers and smiles at me, picking up on a brief respite from the doom and gloom rolling off my body. Smokey is purring behind me.

"This will pass," I tell myself out loud.

My brothers seem curious and confused more than anything, judging from their messages asking what's going on and if I'm okay. All except Nate, naturally, who I seem to do nothing but irritate since the day I was born. His message was an absolute treat to read.

NATE: What the actual FUCK dude??? Why is everyone in my office asking if my kid brother is taking it up the ass from Cassius fucking Garda??? IS THIS TRUE???

I'll never be anything more than an embarrassment to him, and after all these years I'm still not really sure why. I learned very early on in life not to even try hanging out or playing with him and his friends. I wasn't cool enough, fast enough, smart enough—you name it. And when I came out, he acted like I'd done it deliberately to humiliate him, because of course he thinks that being gay is still something to be ashamed of in this day and age.

It's not surprising that would be his main concern in the wake of this disaster. Not worrying I almost *died.* He loves reminding me that I chose a meat-headed profession where 'that's part of the glory,' so if something harrowing happens, I was asking for it, as far as he cares. And I doubt he's going to lose a second of sleep over what that TikTok has done to my privacy.

No. He's just mad because strangers he'll never meet are picturing me getting fucked by a football player, and that's gross and mortifying for him. He's going to have people asking him about me when he'd rather pretend I don't exist. In fact, I'd bet he's already been on the phone whining to my mom how unfair this position I've put him in is.

Poor Nate. Thoughts and prayers.

And yeah, I know, *poor Teddy,* too. He's maybe (hopefully?) dating a gorgeous, rich sports star. How will he survive?

I blow out a long breath and scratch behind Rocky's ears. All these thoughts are bouncing around like ping-pong balls inside my skull. I need to distract myself before I go crazy. Crazier. There's got to be something around here that needs cleaning or organizing. Or perhaps I could cook something. It's sort of between lunch and dinner time, but I'm not sure when the guys would have last eaten before heading out to look for me.

That seems the best way to say thank you for dragging themselves out in the rain to beg the One-Two-Two for their helicopter so they could pick my ass up off the side of a mountain. I'm not sure what groceries we have, but I can start by looking.

However, before I can move, I realize that I'm no longer petting just one dog, but two. I blink at the ball of fluff that's appeared underneath my other hand, a little diamond brooch keeping her long hair out of the dark eyes currently looking up at me, a small pink tongue poking out between her lips.

"Oh, hello, Margot," I say in delight. "Where's your mom, hmm?"

"Here, here!" Mrs. Bloom calls out, coming into view over the sofa. She's got two enormous trays in her hands, balanced one on top of the other. They're covered in foil, but whatever it is it smells rich and spicy, and my stomach rumbles.

"Oh, you're a life saver, Mrs. Bloom," I say with a grin.

"You're assuming these are for you?" she says tartly with a raised eyebrow. As always, she's immaculately put together in a plum two-piece pencil skirt and blazer with white piping that makes me think of Jackie Kennedy. All she needs is a pillbox hat on her coiffured white hair to complete the look. Her pumps click on the floor as she laughs to herself and marches over to our kitchen. "They're for my *other* constantly ravenous neighbors."

"Sure they are," I drawl, already feeling lighter for her presence, even if she can be a little intimidating sometimes.

Most of the time.

"What's got you here all by yourself, young Mr. Foster?" she asks as she sets the trays of food down on the counter before flicking the oven on. "Where's everyone else?"

"On a call," I say simply, standing up so I feel a little more dignified talking with her. Smokey shoots off to perch on top of something high as usual, but Rocky and Miss Margot Fonteyn trot next to me as I move to sit at the breakfast bar. "They actually had to rescue me this morning. That's why I got left behind. So I could shower and get my head back on straight."

She clasps her hands together, large diamonds and other precious gemstones glinting on her fingers under the artificial lighting. "My goodness. Is everything all right?"

I shrug. "That's a complicated question," I tell her honestly with a laugh. "Physically, yeah, I'm fine. My friend and I got caught up in a landslide yesterday evening. He sprained his ankle, and we had to camp overnight. The guys found us this morning with a helicopter they borrowed from the One-Two-Two."

Mrs. Bloom sits opposite me on another high stool, automatically picking up Margot Fonteyn to perch in her lap. Rocky makes do by lying at my feet.

"Well, that does all sound dramatic," she says in concern. "That would rattle anyone."

I nibble my lip and drag my fingernail over a grain in the wood on the countertop. "I'm used to adrenaline and life-threatening situations," I admit without bravado. Not to sound like my brother, but it *is* part of the job here. "It's more…oh, there are several things bothering me," I spit out in frustration.

"Keep going," Mrs. Bloom says, sounding genuinely interested.

I don't want to explain the Cassius situation just yet, so I start with what else is eating at me.

"The One-Two-Two think I'm a joke," I grumble, trying not to feel like a petulant child. I'm not sure how successful I am. "That's the second time in as many weeks they've had to rescue me when I couldn't do the job myself."

"Forgive me, dear," she says with a flick of her perfectly penciled eyebrow. "But isn't *their* job equally rescuing people? Why do you believe they'd think less of you for needing them to do what they literally get paid for?"

I shrug, trying not to let the shame get the better of me. "Because I should have done better. Both times it was like I could only half finish the rescue. How am I ever going to graduate to being a proper firefighter if I have to keep getting bailed out?"

Mrs. Bloom tuts. "You are a proper firefighter. The others have just been at it longer. And it's not supposed to be a solo venture. That's why you're part of a team. If anyone thinks less of you for having the common sense to ask for help when it's necessary, they're the ones who need to step back and examine their own insecurities. Now, is that all that's troubling you?"

I sigh, knowing she's probably right, but still feeling like the little boy who had to ask the big kids to help him out of a jam. My brother's sneering looms at the back of my mind. But if she's offering to help with what's really on my mind, I'd be a fool to pass her up.

"No, there's something else," I admit. "It's the actual problem, really. Well, I don't know if 'problem' is the right word, but…"

Of course that's when the rigs come trundling back inside the station. The fire mustn't have been that bad for them to have made it back so quickly. I'm happy that it wasn't serious and grateful that the place will be busy again. But nervous that they're finally going to want to talk about…well, exactly what I was just going to mention to Mrs. Bloom.

She holds up a finger and places Miss Margot Fonteyn back down on the floor. "Hold that thought, Mr. Foster." She turns around and peels the foil off the two big food trays, revealing what looks like some kind of bean casserole that she puts into the now-heated oven.

"Oh, Mrs. Bloom!" Lochlan calls as he hops out of the engine and slips out of his turnouts, leaving them in a pool on the floor for the next call. Hopefully, I'll be able to join them for that one. Rocky sprints over to greet him as he walks to the kitchen area. "You angel. You've made us lunch?"

"Think nothing of it," she says, waving the oven mitt at him even as she preens in delight. "Allow me to get some rice on to go with it. Young Mr. Foster here was just telling me his woes."

"Ahh, dude," Lochlan says sympathetically, wrapping his big arms around me and resting his chin on the top of my head. "How you holding up?"

"Are you ready to spill all the juicy gossip yet?" Lili demands, skipping over and throwing her ass onto the stool beside me. "You know it was *killing* us not to ask earlier."

"Hey," Lieutenant Flores says firmly. "Go easy on him. He's been through a lot already."

"Well," Mrs. Bloom says with a hand on her hip as she gets a large pot of water boiling. "Now I simply *must* know what's eating you, Mr. Foster."

"Not what but who," Sawyer quips with a grin as he leans on the other end of the breakfast bar.

"Manners, Mr. Nelson," Mrs. Bloom tells him, and he has the grace to look sheepish.

"Sorry, ma'am."

"Teddy has a boyfriend, Mrs. Bloom," Yara says from the back of the ambulance where her and Dray are cataloguing their supplies after the call. "He's famous and someone took a video of them this morning, so now Teddy's getting attention, too. But honestly, I'm not sure why all that matters. Do you like him for *him*, Teddy?"

"And is he *actually* your boyfriend?" Sawyer asks with wide eyes, leaning closer in. Lili smacks his arm but he just smirks at her before winking at me.

I sigh, but the lieutenant sets a cup of coffee in front of me, and I didn't realize how much I needed it until I take the first sip. He knows exactly how everyone takes theirs, and I feel a flood of gratitude wash through me that I'm so blessed to have such amazing colleagues. For all the teasing, I know they only want what's best for me. It's about time that I share what's been going on in my life these past couple of weeks rather than bottling it all up and trying to deal with it alone.

Mrs. Bloom is right. We work as a team. That's the whole point.

"I like him so much," I tell Yara, my voice catching. It feels momentous to admit that out loud in a room full of people. "And not because he's Cassius Garda, former NFL pro. But because he's a kind, funny, generous guy who apparently likes me as much as I like him."

"Hot," Lili says, wagging a finger. "You forgot insanely hot."

"And rich," adds Sawyer, shaking his head.

The rest of the team collect their coffees from Lieutenant Flores at the machine. They find a place to sit or lean against while Mrs. Bloom stirs the vat of rice. Gene looks to be taking a call, no doubt from his wife needing to discuss one of their kids. But everyone else is looking expectantly at me.

Lochlan waves his hand at both Lili and Sawyer. "Never mind all that," he says, raising his eyebrows incredulously. "How the *hell* did you meet him, Teddy? Did you send him fan mail with dick pics inside?"

"What?" I splutter in horror. "No! Nothing like that, no. Do you remember the cat I saved from the river?"

"You mean the cat the One-Two-Two saved from the river?" Sawyer corrects with a smirk.

"Dude," Anton says with a frown. "Read the room. Not the vibe."

Sawyer looks genuinely contrite. "Sorry, man. Yeah, we remember the cat. The person who was going to adopt them wanted to meet you first, right?"

I wince and laugh. "Yeah…that person was Cassius Garda. I almost had a heart attack when I walked in and saw him."

"I bet," Dray says, sounding intrigued. "What did you do? Did you keep your cool?"

"Absolutely not," I say, making everyone laugh. I shake my head, grinning as I recall that moment. It's nice to finally share it with the guys, having vowed to take the experience to my grave. "I thought it was a disaster. But apparently, he thought I was cute." I blush, not quite believing I'm daring to admit that out loud.

"I *knew* I recognized that voice," Captain Valentine says with a shit-eating grin, wagging his finger at me. "So he called the station to get your number?"

I nod just as Mrs. Bloom shakes her head. "I'm sorry, who are we talking about?"

"Cassius Garda," Lili explains to our elderly neighbor. "Former Seattle Seahawks star quarterback and little Teddy's personal hero." She whistles and looks me up and down. "Damn, dude. This is like one of those Christmas movies where the baker somehow ends up catering the royal ball and falling in love with the prince."

"That sounds like an oddly specific reference," Lochlan says with a flick of his eyebrow.

Lili shoves him. "Oh, like you literally don't watch them with me every year," she fires back with an eyeroll.

"Ah," Mrs. Bloom says, steering the conversation back on

track. "I'm finally starting to see why the situation is complicated. So what happened specifically this morning?"

I take another sip of coffee to fortify myself. "Well, we've seen each other a couple of times since we met at the shelter," I start explaining.

"The day at the walkway?" Anton guesses, and I nod sheepishly.

"It was all so surreal, and I didn't really know *what* was going on, so that's why I didn't tell any of you guys. But, yeah, I found out yesterday that was actually a date and I didn't realize. Yesterday was a date, too, which he finally clued me in on." That gets a nice laugh from my avid listeners. "Then this morning...well, we officially agreed to try dating. I'm, um, he's my—"

"Boyfriends!" Yara squeals excitedly. "Aww, how romantic."

I huff. "The thing is, we'd talked a lot about the fame thing and how it would probably affect me, then those girls went and did what they did."

The lieutenant catches Mrs. Bloom's eye. "A couple of teenagers filmed Teddy and his boyfriend kissing without them knowing and put it on the internet."

"How rude," she says crossly with a furrowed brow. "But hopefully not many people saw it before you made them take it down, right?"

I share an awkward glance with Flores. "It was a live video, Mrs. Bloom, that other people have now copied and shared all over the place. It was everywhere before I could do anything about it."

"Like glitter," Yara adds with a slightly haunted look in her eyes.

"One of the videos I saw had over eight million views," I say glumly.

I stopped looking at TikTok after that.

"Eight million. I say. And you feel violated," Mrs. Bloom accurately assesses. I nod and sigh again.

"I thought I'd be more prepared," I tell them, feeling like I have to defend myself. "Cassius was going to train me, and he has this slightly scary but very efficient PA who was also going to help. But we didn't get the chance to do any of that. Now people I've never met all over the world are digging into my life, acting like they know what's best for Cassius, and are judging me. My family is worried and one of my brothers is being a real dick about how it's going to affect him, but he does have a point. I just…I really like Cassius so much. What if all this scrutiny is too much, though? For me and them and maybe even you guys."

The troubled faces of my colleagues don't exactly fill me with confidence. I can tell it's only just occurring to a couple of them that this could blow back on them and the One-Thirteen as well. Guilt and shame well up inside me.

It's the lieutenant who shrugs and speaks first. "Fame is a bitch, man. I won't lie. You're right to be worried, but it's not your fault. It's something that's been done *to* you. Fame gives people a false sense of entitlement, like they think they know someone because they act on TV or play for their favorite team. They love you one minute then love to see you fail even more the next. Public opinion is fickle as fu—" He glances at Mrs. Bloom, who raises her eyebrows. "Fudge. Fickle as fudge. Nothing's really changed since we made gladiators fight in the Colosseum."

Anton whistles and squeezes the lieutenant's shoulder. "You sound like you're talking from experience."

Flores shakes his head. "Nah, not me. But my best friend from high school has this younger brother who starred in a kids TV show when he was like ten years old. Once the program ended, he totally lost his way and nobody in Hollywood gave a shhh…shamrock." Mrs. Bloom nods in approval. "He was in rehab by fifteen, but he's never been able to make sobriety stick. Got himself a couple of DUIs that he only just scraped out of. The tabloids ate up every mistake he made, delighting in his antics despite how he was obviously suffering."

"Is he okay now?" I ask, my heart going out to this guy. He reminds me of the younger players on the team Cassius mentioned who he tried to take under his wing and protect.

Flores shrugs again, looking into his coffee cup. "He did a couple of reality TV shows and won back some hearts and minds, I think. Last I heard, he was dancing at a strip club in LA. His brother checks in on him when he can. I hope he is okay." He rallies himself once more and smiles at me. "Sorry, that was all meant to say that I agree with you. Garda's fame is something you should seriously consider, as illustrated by that video this morning."

"But..." Yara says firmly with a frown. "You said you really like him, right, Teddy? And he likes you. So you're not going to give up, are you?"

"Aww, you're such a romantic, baby girl," Lili says fondly.

"I don't want to," I admit honestly. "I'm just not sure where we stand right now. I'm waiting to hear from him."

"He hasn't messaged yet?" Lochlan asks.

"Well, he's probably still at the hospital," I begin saying, before I realize something. "Oh, hang on." I pull my phone out. I forgot I'd put it on silent.

Sure enough, there's a text from Cassius waiting for me, and my insides swoop like the first drop on a roller-coaster.

CASSIUS: Hey, baby. I hope you're doing okay. I'm fine, just waiting on my MRI results, but the foot is already feeling way better. I'm so sorry for what happened this morning, but if you're not reconsidering this whole boyfriend thing, Bryan and I already have a plan to smooth things out. Did you want to come over to my place tomorrow night to discuss? And also cuddle. And kiss. And other things. Oh, and Kiki wants to see you, too. Let me know, your *boyfriend.*

He ends with several emojis that include a devilish face and a kissing one. My heart flips in my chest and I can't stop the grin splitting my lips as I fire back a quick reply to say I'll see him tomorrow night.

I look up only to see the entire first watch staring at me with barely concealed glee.

"He wants to have dinner to talk it all through," I tell them shyly. "And, um, he signed the message calling himself my boyfriend."

"Hell yeah!" Lochlan cries as some of the others whoop and clap, making Rocky and Miss Margot Fonteyn bark.

"And on that happy note," Mrs. Bloom says. "Lunch is ready, so I suggest you all go sit at the table before that blasted bell goes off."

I feel lighter as the team starts to move, but the lieutenant makes a point of catching my arm and giving me a sad smile. "I didn't mean to be pessimistic," he says. "I think you're being very sensible about the whole thing."

I shake my head. "No, I get it. Thank you. I do hope your friend's brother lands on his feet in the end."

Flores tilts his head, his smile half-hearted still. "We'll see. You can't help someone unless they let you. But don't let that steal your sunshine right now. Kwon's right. Your story sounds like a movie script."

"Or a fanfiction," I joke, even though I'm not sure he knows what I mean. But as we sit at the table and dig in to Mrs. Bloom's delicious home cooking, I appreciate something.

No matter what happens with Cassius, I need to remember that I have a loving and supportive family here and at home, aside from my dickhead brother. But there are always going to be dickheads, or jealous fans trying to sabotage us, or homophobes, or whatever. Let them waste their energy like that if they want. The One-Thirteen has my back, and Cassius has invited me to his *home* where he wants to do 'other things' with me.

I can't control what other people think, whether that's strangers on the internet or family members. But I can own my happiness and enjoy it. Life's too short to let good things go just because you're scared.

And Cassius isn't just a good thing. He's one of the very *best* things to ever come my way.

I'm not giving him up without a fight.

CHAPTER 16

Cassius

"Now, how do we feel about maybe trying to be a little social, hmm?"

Kiki has been mad at me for various reasons since I brought her home, but right now, she has a very valid excuse. After her operation to get her spayed a few days ago, she's had to wear a cone around her neck to stop her licking her stitches, and that means most of her usual hiding spots are now inaccessible.

At least she was okay when Teddy and I got stranded overnight because her feeder is automated and I made sure her water fountain was filled to the brim before I left. Bryan dropped in to check on her before coming to the hospital as well, and apparently she was terrified, hissing and swiping at him as she tried desperately to get herself somewhere safe.

With true orange cat logic, that meant she just backed herself into a corner and seemingly hoped that made her invisible. Bryan sounded happy to get out of there before she could change her mind and go on the offense.

I know it's going to take time, but I just want her life to be as stress-free as possible. She should feel secure here and know that nothing's going to hurt her. It's difficult to explain that the cone isn't a punishment, though.

She's currently on the sofa, swishing her tail angrily back and forth as she glares at me with those big blue eyes of hers. "Teddy is our friend," I assure her. "We like Teddy very much. Teddy saved Kiki *and* Daddy's lives. So I know you're scared, sweetie. But it would be cool if we could keep the maiming to a minimum, hmm?"

For a moment, she considers me. Then she lets out a disgruntled howl and starts scratching at the upholstery.

"Ah, no!" I say firmly. I don't really care about the sofa. I can always buy a new one. It's more that I want to train her so she knows that the *thirty-seven* scratching posts—give or take—that I've put around the house for her are more suited to that purpose.

While she does stop digging her claws into my couch, her glare is still just as murderous. But when the bell for the front gate chimes, she bolts onto the floor and out of the door like she's trying to win an Olympic medal.

I chuckle and shake my head. "Baby steps," I remind myself.

I'm going to be using crutches for a week or two while my foot heals up, so it takes me a second to get to the intercom. They're more of a precaution than anything as the MRI confirmed it was just a mild sprain that felt worse under the extreme circumstances. I probably could have pushed myself and walked to the highway the evening it happened, but I'd have done more damage in the process. Not only am I looking at a faster recovery now due to taking preventative measures, but I wouldn't trade that night with Teddy under the stars for anything, even if we could have died.

Because we didn't. And now he's outside my door, waiting to come in and spend an evening with me and my only-slightly-deranged miniature lion-cat.

Nerves flutter through my belly as I make my way down a level to the garage. As the house is built on a slope, the front door is technically on the second floor. But I wanted Teddy to park his car safely out of sight with the rest of mine, so I opened those doors for him automatically and he knows to drive around the back of the house. I hope he doesn't feel like I'm sneaking in a dirty little secret. I just want this time to be completely ours, and I've had an annoying number of paparazzi hanging around outside my gate lately.

This is such a strange experience for me. I've never had a date come over to my home before. I'm excited but also anxious about being a good host, especially as I'm encumbered with these crutches. But as soon as I open the door and see Teddy's face light up, I know everything's going to be okay.

"Hello, gorgeous," I say breathlessly, like I haven't seen him for a couple of months instead of just a couple of days. In fact, it's only actually been a day and half. Yet my heart is pounding, and my blood is rushing.

"Hi," he says, stepping closer to hug me, tucking under my arms and expertly avoiding the crutches. "How are you feeling?"

"Better now you're here," I tell him truthfully, grinning as he blushes. I hope he never stops taking my compliments to heart like that, no matter how long we're together. "Come in. Make yourself at home."

I'm trying my best not to dwell too long on thoughts of the future. I know from personal experience how impossible it is to predict. But I do indulge myself a little bit as I close the door and appreciate Teddy in my lower entrance foyer. He toes off his shoes without needing to be prompted, and when he looks up and smiles at me, I ache with the sense of how *right* he looks in my home. It thrills me because since

I've only just moved in, all my memories of this place will also be tied to him.

Let's just hope that won't be something I'll regret one day.

Annnnd what did I tell myself about not fixating too much on the future? Good or bad, what will be will be. What matters right now is, well, *right now.* I want to savor having Teddy in my home for the first time, but also, we have an important conversation that I'd rather get out of the way sooner rather than later.

"Come on up to the kitchen," I say as I sail past him on my crutches and start scaling the stairs.

"You're good on those," he comments with a little laugh as he follows me.

I wait until I reach the landing to turn and face him with a grin. "Not my first rodeo, baby. I got paid to let grown men hurtle themselves at me for entertainment."

"That's true, I guess." He shakes his head as we head over to the kitchen area, and he drops his bag by the dining table. "But you're not feeling too bad, right?"

Warmth blossoms in my chest. I pause on my way to the fridge to turn and balance one of the crutches against the counter so I can hug him again. I've told him several times via text that for all the trouble it caused, it really is a minor injury, but his fussing is still appreciated. I don't want him to feel guilty or responsible. But having a *boyfriend* who cares so much is a novelty I'm not sure I'll ever get tired of.

"I'm feeling all kinds of things," I mumble against his throat as I trail kisses against his fluttering pulse point. "Bad definitely isn't one of them."

"Oh, um, good," he squeaks.

I love getting him all hot and bothered, but I did promise myself we'd talk first before having too much fun. So I sigh and pull away, pressing a final kiss against his lips with a grin.

"I'm so happy you're here," I tell him honestly.

"Yeah?" he asks breathlessly. "Even after all the fallout from yesterday?"

And this is precisely why we need to talk, because I hate the doubt in his voice. There's no point trying to straighten the situation out or plan our next move if we're not on the same page in this moment.

"*Especially* after all that bullshit," I say, trying not to frown too hard. I don't want him getting the mistaken impression any of my ire is directed his way. "Let me get us something to drink and we can go over everything, all right?"

"No, you sit, I can do that," he insists, steering me toward the nearest chair.

I chuckle. "Yes, sir, Mr. Bossy Pants," I tease him.

He falters. "Oh, sorry, I—"

Before he can apologize, I kiss it right off his lips. "I love it. Fridge is over there."

His smile is bashful. "Sorry. I think that's one of those things I'm going to have to get used to. Um, what can I get you?"

"I'll go for a beer," I tell him, sitting down. "My painkillers aren't that strong. Feel free to help yourself to one, too. Or there's wine, plenty of soft drinks, or spirits if you'd like something stronger."

"Beer's great," he assures me, fetching two from the top shelf. I point out the drawer where he'll find the bottle opener.

"Is it the teasing?" I ask, following on my previous train of thought. He cracks the first top off and looks at me with a quirked eyebrow. "That you'll need to get used to," I elaborate.

"Oh," he says with a nod. He opens the second bottle as well before coming and sitting next to me. The table is an oval, so he only has to angle his chair a little so we're facing each other. He feels too far away, but I know that's preferable while we talk.

I can't wait to get my hands on him again, though. This time in the comfort and privacy of my own home.

He nibbles his lower lip briefly, not helping my horniness. But I wait patiently for him to speak. "I think it's more that I need to get used to trusting that the teasing is flirting…at least I assume it is?"

Without hesitating, I squeeze his knee and smile. "It's absolutely flirting, baby. Cheers." I tap my bottle neck to his and he nods thoughtfully.

"Cheers," he murmurs warmly. "Good. Thank you. I guess…there's a part of me that knows that. But growing up, teasing was usually intended to be mean. My brothers are mostly okay, but being the youngest meant I caught a lot of shit from them. It's taken me a while to realize that at work, with the One-Thirteen, teasing is supposed to be fun. It creates bonds. My last boyfriend was pretty serious, though, and he'd never joke around with me like that. I thought if I wasn't being serious, it was childish, and I didn't want that."

"I can rein it in if you want," I offer sincerely. Between my family and my teammates, I've always shown affection by roughhousing and talking shit because to me that shows how comfortable I am around the people I care for. But I'd never want to make Teddy feel uncomfortable. I could adapt.

He shakes his head, however, and reaches out to entangle our fingers together. "No, I love it. It makes me feel seen. Like…um, like you're celebrating me being here. Like I'm allowed to be big and take up space. That's why I said I'll have to get used to it. Just because it's different doesn't mean it's not good. Great, even."

I beam at him and rub my thumb against his fingers. "I see you, Theodore Foster," I tell him. "You deserve to take up space. And if it keeps earning me all those delicious blushes, you bet your ass I'ma keep joshing with you."

He giggles and smiles around the lip of his beer bottle. Memories of his lips wrapped around another similarly shaped object send my pulse racing. I lick my lips, trying to recall what else we were supposed to discuss. That was enough serious talking for now, surely?

"So, um, about yesterday," he prompts.

Damn. That certainly pours a metaphorical bucket of cold water on the desires I had brewing. *Later,* I promise myself.

"Right, yeah," I say, taking a swig of beer before placing the bottle down on a coaster and giving him my full attention. "Are you all right?"

"Apart from logging out of all my social media accounts, I'm doing okay," he says with a rueful laugh.

I wince and squeeze his hand. "It'll calm down, I promise. People will move onto the new hot gossip by next week. Maybe even in a couple of days. In the meantime, I'd like to schedule some time for you to sit down with Bryan so he can update some security settings for you and give you some advice on how best to navigate being online moving forward."

"I don't want to ever do anything to embarrass you," he says urgently.

"Oh, no, baby," I say, my heart melting. "I mean, I appreciate that. But I'm talking about you protecting yourself. It's advice you might want to pass on to your friends and family as well if they're worried. This attention really shouldn't impact your life so much."

"It just takes a little forward planning," he says, echoing back words I've said to him before.

"Exactly," I say, proud of him. "So long as you're absolutely sure I'm worth all this effort. You've experienced first-hand now some of the baggage I come with. I am *completely* in if you are," I say before he can misinterpret my words, and I'm rewarded with a flicker of relief across his face. "But this wasn't how we wanted to handle the start of our relationship, and I know it's been a pill to swallow."

"I think it does suck it was taken out of our hands like that," he agrees solemnly. "Like someone else outing your sexuality. It wasn't those girls' news to share, and I really hope they learn from this."

I can't help but laugh affectionately. "You're more generous than Bryan. He wanted to slap them with an infringement of privacy suit until I reminded him that we were out in public, so it wouldn't hold. He then just wanted to sue them for being selfish dicks, but my momma sweet-talked him down from that one."

He laughs, showing off that left dimple, and I can feel the tension easing from both of us. To help that along, I pick up my drink for another sip. I get the feeling that even though we've had a couple of similar conversations over the past few days, neither of us were really trusting that the other was all in and that this relationship stood a chance.

Now…it feels like we're both operating with a little more faith and hope.

That sounds like the same page to me.

"It was always going to be a bit crazy, though, right?" Teddy continues. "No matter what we did. You coming out when you were still playing was a massive deal, and a *good* thing for a lot of people. Some considered it a scandal, but, well, fuck them." He giggles at his own daring, making me laugh.

"Damn right," I say, tapping our bottle necks together again. "Fuck those assholes."

"But," he continues, "all those people were going to have a similar reaction when you announced your first boyfriend, I reckon, no matter who he was. We just have a particularly interesting origin story, so I can see why the public would be captivated by it. None of it was *bad,* though. We didn't cheat on anyone or anything like that. So once the initial shock dies down, hopefully people might get on board with our movie-worthy meet-cute, yeah?"

I can't help but take a moment to marvel at him. "How are you so perfect?" I utter, earning myself another blush as he squirms. But I just grin and hold his hand a fraction tighter. "That's exactly what Bryan and I discussed yesterday at the hospital. And my mom, actually. She's dying to meet you, by the way."

For a second, his expression is a little goofy. "I've never been introduced to anyone's parents before."

Pride and something primally possessive curls deliciously in my chest. He might have dated and hooked up way more than me, but there are still firsts we can share together.

"She's going to love you," I promise him, lifting his hand so I can kiss the backs of his fingers. "Everyone's going to love you, Teddy. Which is why Bryan and I came up with a plan."

He raises his eyebrows. "There's an actual plan? I though you meant like…vibes going forward or whatever."

I chuckle. "Oh, there's an actual plan, a good one. But first, I need to check with you what's the best and earliest date you and your team are going to be free."

He tilts his head with curiosity. "The One-Thirteen?" I nod. "What have they got to do with it?"

"Oh, baby," I say, waggling my eyebrows playfully at him. "We're gonna have ourselves a shindig!"

CHAPTER 17

Teddy

"So your solution...is to have a house party?" I ask. It can't really be that simple, can it?

Cassius grins at me from where he's tossing a stir fry in his wok. I'd have protested him standing up to cook, but he sat down to chop all the veggies and the chicken was already diced. The nature of a stir fry is that it's ready in minutes, so I didn't push the issue when I saw how much he wanted to do this for us.

I've never had a place of my own, but I can imagine I'd also be the same with wanting to be a good host and take care of my guests.

Will there ever be a day when Cassius visits my house and I cook for him? That seems so unrealistic that I let the thought drop almost immediately. I have enough wild ideas to be entertaining in the present.

"It would be a fundraiser at my house," Cassius elaborates. We've already gone over the basics of his plan, but I can't seem to quite wrap my head around it.

"For the One-Thirteen as well as the animal shelter?"

He waves his spatula at me briefly before going back to

his animated stirring. "That's the clever part. Bryan's good at this stuff. The first phase, the house party, would be focused on the animal shelter by getting people to sponsor a pen for a year. We'd have displays of individual stories from some of the cats and dogs to draw people in and maybe even encourage some adoptions. People are more likely to sponsor more if they feel like they've adopted Spot the dog specifically. But the main focus would be giving the shelter a big bump in cash so they can clear the debt with the vets who do all their neutering and everything else. Maybe do some renovations, hire more staff, work more on marketing campaigns so they can reach more potential donors and forever homes."

"Okay, I'm with you," I say nodding and drinking a little more beer. I don't want my anxiety to spoil his excitement. I just want to make sure I understand what he's proposing. "But…what's the reason for throwing this party? Sorry, fundraiser. Other than it being a nice thing to do, obviously. I think I've missed a step."

Cassius is dishing up our dinner, so I jump up to grab the plates. That way, he can use his energy to get back to the dining table on his crutches. His good leg must be aching by now even if he was only putting his weight onto it for a little while.

When we're both sitting back down, Cassius takes my hand and squeezes it. "The reason is because the shelter is what brought us together, and this is going to be our first official outing as a couple. It's casual, but from the heart. It'll also be a great way for me to meet people from the town, sort of like a getting-to-know-you event. We'll invite the One-Thirteen because they're your friends, but they're also integral to the community. We can work on the guest list together, but I'll also invite a few guys from Seattle, maybe see who's around in LA. So it's a mix of the rich and famous as well as people who actually matter here in Redwood Bay."

"Ohhh," I say, nodding slowly. "I see what you're doing. You're breaking down barriers to encourage the idea that celebrities aren't so different from us regular folks."

"Bingo," he says with a wink.

"But...no actual reporters or anything?" I clarify.

He shakes his head and swallows a mouthful. I want to tell him to stop and eat so the food he's made us doesn't get cold, but he seems too excited to care. "We'll keep it organic, casual. Just let people post on their own accounts. We can make sure there aren't any loose cannons on the guest list, and Bryan will give everyone a brief beforehand with a few gentle guidelines of what they should avoid posting about."

I must look concerned because he reaches out and cups the side of my face, getting my full attention. "Sorry," I say sheepishly. "That just seems like so many variables."

"That's kind of the point," he admits. "By not trying to control the narrative so strictly, it gives us power. It says that we're not bothered by the TikTok livestream because we have nothing to hide."

My heart melts a little more for him. I love that he has no intention of hiding me away or acting ashamed. "But we *are* controlling the narrative to a certain extent, right?"

He grins and rubs his thumb against my cheekbone before retracting his hand to eat some more. I must admit, for a simple dish, it's really delicious. It's already making me wonder what I can cook for him next time.

Having a boyfriend is already pretty fun, I've decided.

"Oh, we're absolutely putting out a narrative that we're hoping people will latch onto," he says mischievously. "If the homophobes want to rattle their sabers about the gays shoving woke culture down their football-loving throats or whatever soapbox they're on, they'll basically be saying 'helping to rescue cute animals is bad.' Which they can, if they want." He shrugs and laughs. "Bonus for us: we'll *genuinely* be helping cute animals get rescued."

"Yeah, I love that part," I admit.

If I just think about it from that angle, all I'm really doing is working with Cassius on a charity fundraiser. And not some abstract national cause—which would still be important, of course. But the fact it's for the Redwood Bay shelter is so cool. I bet they'll be over the moon with this idea.

"The other bonus," Cassius continues, "is that the One-Thirteen will also be there, looking all glamorous. If they just *happen* to mention how having your own helicopter would benefit the people of the town, then when we announce a different fundraiser at the station in a month or two, the seeds will already have been sown in people's minds that they can give to that good cause as well." He winks at me. "That's phase two."

"You seriously think you could raise enough to get us a helicopter?" I ask, shaking my head in disbelief.

Cassius pauses and looks apprehensive. "Or whatever you guys need. I don't mean to be presumptuous of where the funds would best be spent."

I can't say as the probationary officer that I've ever thought about that or been included in any discussions on the matter. "A helicopter would probably be greatly appreciated," I say thoughtfully. "But Captain Valentine would have a far better understanding of our budget, and I'm sure whatever money we might raise would be put to extremely good use."

"Exactly," he continues. "Whatever you guys decide, it'll all be part of the same game plan. Which is to get public opinion on your side—and I mean the individual you, Teddy Foster, my boyfriend—by gently reminding anyone who might have something shitty to say about you that you and your friends *run into burning buildings* for a living."

"People will still say shitty things," I note. I might not be famous, but I've lived with the internet my whole life.

He nods. "Yeah, there's no stopping that. Some people will no doubt see through all our good intentions and say the whole thing is a publicity stunt. There's never going to be a solution that pleases everyone. But I'd rather have a charity event or two that brings the community together as the background for announcing our relationship a hundred times over than a press conference or a red carpet walk or something. We wouldn't be doing anything that we didn't mean. We're simply creating a way to confirm that you're someone incredibly special to me in the best way possible. Couples do that every day to announce their engagements and pregnancies, after all. This is just on a slightly grander scale. What?"

He's noticed I'm staring at him all silly and starry-eyed. "You said I'm incredibly special to you," I say.

With a laugh, he lifts my hand to kiss my fingers again as he beams at me, his eyes equally sparkly. "You are, Teddy."

I bite my lip and drink him in for a moment. "I might not have planned a big old party for you," I say. "But you're incredibly special to me, too, Cassius. I hope you know that."

The way he licks his lips and looks me up and down suggests he does have an inkling of how I feel. But before he can say or do anything about it, something brushes against my leg, making me almost jump out of my skin.

I snap my gaze downward, only to see a pair of bright blue eyes looking up at me from inside an opaque plastic cone.

"Kiki?" I squeak, almost too afraid to move in case I scare her off. My jolt when she bashed her shoulder into my calf didn't, but I don't want to risk it.

"I can't believe she's out here," Cassius says, equally spell-bound. "She's been terrified of everyone and everything, including me. But not you."

A lump rises in my throat as the little orange lion meows loudly at me. It's only been a couple of weeks since she was shaved. However, I can already see some of her fur growing back, which makes me very happy. I know Cassius will keep her properly groomed this time around.

Carefully, I lower my hand to let her sniff my fingers, which she does. Then she rubs her face against them…and purrs.

"Oh my god," I whisper, my eyes flicking between her and Cassius. "Do you think she remembers me?"

He scrubs his chin and swallows, his Adam's apple bobbing in his throat. It makes me think I'm not the only one feeling a little emotional from her unscheduled appearance on our date.

"I have no doubt she remembers you, baby," he says softly. "She doesn't know about TikTok or the One-Two-Two. She just knows that she was really scared, and you were there for her when she needed someone the most. Just like her daddy knows the same thing."

I blink and focus on him, and he gives me a second to let it sink in that he's right about those parallels. I've been beating myself up that I botched both their rescues by not being able to see them through to the end by myself. But in this moment, I'm looking at two souls who I gave everything I could to save…and I did just that. They're here, together, in this beautiful house.

With me.

More than anything else recently in my life, this realization is what makes me understand that I'm exactly where I'm supposed to be. This is the right place and the right time. I'm not being overlooked, dismissed or forgotten.

This is where I belong. With Cassius and Kiki. Whatever the rest of the world thinks doesn't matter.

My author knew what she was doing all along. It just took me a little time to catch up with her.

Wordlessly, I move from my seat to straddle Cassius's lap, staring into his eyes as I loop my arms around his neck. Kiki rubs against both our legs and gives a disgruntled howl, but then I feel her wander off.

That's probably for the best. Things are about to get real not safe for work around here, Miss Kitty.

Cassius leans up and captures my mouth with his, kissing me fiercely as his fingers dig into my back. He tastes of the tangy stir fry and sweet beer and his own woodsy, vanilla scent.

"I want you to know," he mumbles between kisses. "That if I wasn't so banged up, I'd be lifting you off the floor right now and carrying you to my bedroom."

I grin against his lips. "Maybe one day I'll get so big and strong I'll be the one picking you up."

He growls and nips at my lower lip, sending electric shocks directly down to my excited cock. "I'd love to see it," he says.

Maybe it's ridiculous, but even just the idea that we'd have a future like that—possibly years down the line—makes me so happy I could kick my feet with joy. Instead, I give him another lingering kiss before standing up and offering him my hand.

"Can I escort you instead?"

As he rises, he drags his hands up my sides, which has the dual purpose of steadying him and also being sexy as fuck.

"Oh, you want to go to bed already, Teddy? What on earth do you plan on doing there?"

I seize a fistful of his T-shirt and ghost my lips over his. "I thought I might start by riding that big cock of yours like a pony at the county fair."

"Jesus fucking Christ," he hisses before snagging my mouth for a truly filthy kiss. "Are you going to take care of your boyfriend, my handsome firefighter?"

"You know it," I say with a smirk.

Not wanting to waste a second more standing around here, I go to grab his crutches. But Cassius shoots his hand out and stills my arm. "Can we leave them here?"

I raise my eyebrows. "Will you be okay getting up the stairs?" I don't actually know where his bedroom is, but seeing as this whole floor is basically the open plan living, dining and kitchen area with just a small bathroom behind a door, instinct tells me we have to go up.

Turns out I'm right, but it's not a problem.

"Would you help me?" he asks, wrapping his arm around my shoulders. "I trust you to take care of me, Teddy."

I can't believe I ever thought my name might not be cool. Hearing it on his lips as he stares at me with blown pupils and kiss-swollen lips, it sounds like a prayer.

"Of course, Cassius," I assure him.

It's obvious his ankle has already improved since yesterday as we're able to maneuver much more easily across the floor to reach the staircase. He could probably have hobbled along by himself if necessary. But I much prefer how he clings to me as I use all my strength to make his short journey as easy and painless as possible.

Considering he hasn't been long in the house, his bedroom is gorgeously decorated. The large space could seem echoey, but the wooden floor and marble feature wall have been countered with fluffy rugs, cloth curtains, and soft lampshades. Shades of gray, tan, and peach make the room feel inviting, especially with the dozen or so throw pillows on the enormous bed before us.

I would have expected more sports paraphernalia from a pro athlete, but all I see is a single football displayed in a glass case under a spotlight. It must hold significance for him, and I wonder what the story behind it is. Gold frames also showcase some beautiful artwork of cityscapes, and a series of elegant bars positioned above his bed look like they might represent soundwaves.

"Is that your favorite song?" I ask, jutting my chin toward the interesting feature.

But he shakes his head. "That's my nephew's heartbeat. He's the first baby to be born in the next generation, my brother's kid. I still can't really believe I'm an uncle."

"That's so beautiful," I tell him sincerely. "The whole room is."

He smiles as I guide him to sit on the side of the bed. "Bryan helped me source everything, but I picked it all out. It was a relief to get back here yesterday after a night spent on the cold ground."

"Tell me about it," I say with an eye roll, thinking about how my bed at the station last night felt like a dream in comparison.

Then I suddenly become aware that he's on the edge of his mattress with his hands on my hips, his knees either side of mine, and he's looking up like he's just waiting for me to realize that the energy has shifted again.

My heart skips a beat as my breath hitches.

"All good?" he asks playfully.

Just like in the forest, I know he'd be totally fine if I needed a minute to collect myself or even if I had to stop all together. But between the landslide and the TikTok it feels like we've wasted enough time getting cockblocked by outside forces already, and I am more than ready to bring this fantasy to life.

"So good," I utter, yanking my T-shirt over my head and dropping it to the floor.

"Oh, baby," he says, sounding awestruck as he runs his hands up my chest, cupping my pecs and brushing my nipples with his thumbs. I shudder and bite my lip as a moan creeps up my throat. "If I had one complaint from the other night, it was not getting to see you naked."

"Happy to fix that now," I assure him sincerely.

He hums and drags his hands back down, squeezing my ass before yanking his own shirt up and discarding it carelessly on the floor. "C'mere," he murmurs, slipping his knees out from between my legs so he can lay down with his head on some of the many pillows we're already making a mess of.

I decide to skip ahead a few steps before settling on the bed with him, though. As quickly as I can manage without looking like I'm rushing, I unbuckle my belt and unzip my jeans, shoving them down and pulling them off with my socks so I'm left only in my boxer-briefs. It's clear from the bulge in my underwear how excited he's making me, and when his lustful gaze drops to it, blood only pumps harder through my veins.

He's given me more than enough reassurance that he likes it when I'm bossy, so I prop one knee on the edge of the mattress, exposing my hardening length even better as I lean over and unbuckle Cassius as well. I don't experience any of the hesitation I did when we were in the wilderness park. Already knowing how good he feels in my hand and in my mouth chases away any lingering nerves I might have had and only makes me want him again more.

As I pull down his jeans and reveal his own arousal, he lifts his hips to assist me get the job done quicker. The second I drop his clothes by mine, he's yanking me down on top of him for a messy, urgent kiss. In a reversal of our previous tryst, the only thing between us now is our underwear which does little to prevent our hard, leaking dicks from rubbing together. All the rest of his hot, glorious skin is pressing against mine as he devours my mouth with his own.

I prop myself up on the mattress as he digs his fingers into my back once more. The last time almost left bruises.

This time, I want him to try harder.

Apparently, he's way ahead of me. "There's lube and condoms in the drawer," he mumbles into my mouth.

"Is there?" I ask innocently. "What shall I do with those?"

He snorts inelegantly and tickles my sides, making me shriek. "You promised to ride my dick, hotshot. But if you'd rather snuggle up and read a book, I suppose we could—"

"Shut up," I growl before slamming my grinning lips back against his. "I need you inside me right the fuck now."

"I know, baby, I know," he groans.

Somehow, between all the kissing and groping and panting and cursing, I manage to fumble with my hand enough to drag open the top drawer of the nightstand. Luckily, the items we need are easily in reach, almost like Cassius was hoping this would happen.

The fact that he's been thinking about us fucking to the extent of setting his room up with supplies only makes me harder and hornier.

We're still in our underwear, which is just rude at this point. I realize belatedly that I've got my hands full of the lube bottle and condom packets, so for a second, I just stare helplessly down at where our covered cocks are nestled together.

"Here," Cassius says, his voice a mixture of amusement and affection. "Let me have those, then you can take care of the more important matter at hand."

He pulls the items from my fingers and waggles his eyebrows. "Right," I say breathlessly. I feel dizzy with want, and my thoughts are taking a little longer to organize than usual. "We don't need these anymore, do we? These suck?"

I snap the elastic of my boxer-briefs against my hips, making him laugh. I'm reminded in this moment that I've always treated sex as serious business, as that seemed more grown up to me. But all the laughing and silliness and messy kisses with Cassius are a thousand times better than any straight-faced seduction I've experienced in the past.

What we have right now, in this room, is authentic and joyous and heartfelt.

"Oh, there's going to be more sucking, is there?" Cassius asks, palming my cock and making my eyes roll back in my head. "You got to have all the fun last time. I think it's my turn, baby."

"You want to, um...?" I try and ask, but words are failing me.

The bastard smirks, knowing exactly what he's doing to me. "I want to taste you, yes. Tell me how you like it, Teddy. I haven't given head in about twenty years."

The idea of him being a sex-mad teenager, fooling around under the bleachers with some faceless school friend, makes me jerk in his hand. But his suggestion is even hotter, and it helps me streamline my frazzled mind.

"Uh, yeah. Yes, please. I mean, um..."

Shaking my head, I pull away from him and stop trying to use my words when actions are going to speak way louder right now. Without too much ridiculous hopping about, I free myself of my underwear and strip his down his legs in a matter of seconds. Then I'm crawling back up the bed, my naked body hovering over his as I pause and cup the side of his face, brushing my nose against his.

"How do you want to come?" he asks me boldly. "Down my throat or on my cock?"

It's my turn to grin wickedly. "Oh, Cassius," I whisper against his ear. "I'm twenty-three. I want both."

While he stares up at me with wide eyes, I crawl farther up the bed, then take myself in hand and rub the shiny tip of my cock against his lips. He nods wordlessly, gripping my ass cheeks and pulling me closer, making his consent clear.

Knowing he hasn't had much opportunity to practice this of late, I go slowly, sliding my length across his tongue as he wraps his lips around my girth.

"Oh, fuck, yes, *yes*," I hiss, letting go of the base of my shaft to grip the headboard with one hand and caress the side of his face with the other. His eyes flutter close as he draws me in more, and I love feeling the end of my cock hitting the side of his cheek with my palm.

It's not the deepest blowjob I've ever had, but it's sure as hell enthusiastic and Cassius makes the most erotic, gorgeous noises as he uses his mouth to pleasure me. I'm so busy fucking his face that I don't even notice his hands drop from my ass. I certainly feel it when he slides a cold and slippery finger down my crack and rubs my entrance enticingly.

"Holy shit, baby, yes," I cry. I'm not sure if calling him baby is an okay vibe, but it just feels right in that moment as he swallows me down and pushes against my tight entrance with his strong tip.

God, I can't wait for that to be his dick.

Before I know it, he's got two digits buried inside me, stroking my sweet spot as I ride his face, hitting the back of his throat. I'd worry I was making him gag, but he's the one not letting me ease off.

"Cassius, I'm close," I cry out in warning, but he doesn't relent until I'm throwing my head back and bellowing myself hoarse, shooting everything I've got against the back of his throat. He swallows what he can until he turns his head, and

I quickly withdraw, letting him cough and gasp for air as the rest of my load spurts onto his cheek and down his neck.

So. Fucking. Hot.

He doesn't even bother wiping his face. He just pulls out his fingers and hurriedly fumbles with a condom wrapper, ripping it open and suiting himself up as I pant and tremble, still coming down from my high. But he's got the devil in his eyes now as he pushes at my thighs, encouraging me back down the bed so I can line my entrance up with his hard, waiting cock.

"Are you going to make me come again, Cassius?" I ask, my voice shaking. I balance on my knees so I can grab the lube, squirting it all over my fingers and reaching back to coat my hole with it. Then I use both hands and pull my cheeks apart, helping him find his way. "Do you think you can?"

We both moan as he penetrates me, his dick far more intrusive and delicious than his fingers were. "You're going to come all over me," he rasps, his voice hoarse from the last time I did just that. "And you're going to scream my name, Teddy. You're going to make sure anyone in a five fucking mile radius knows who you belong to now."

I sink down further, feeling like he's already rearranging my guts and loving how it burns. "Am I really yours?" I ask, mirroring my words from the forest on purpose.

He thrusts up, his incredible abs contracting as he slams into my prostate and makes me wail. *"Mine,"* he snarls, just like last time. But everything is a hundred times more intense with him filling me up, and a sob rips through my chest. It doesn't matter that I'm still exhausted from only just coating the inside of his throat with my cream. My cock is already bouncing back to life, and when he wraps his hand around it, I lose all purchase on reality.

It's all I can do to grip his good shoulder with one hand

and the headboard again with the other, riding him hard as he hammers inside me, his fingers tight around my already sensitive length. Whatever's left in my balls is ready to shoot, but I want to make sure my boyfriend gets what he wants first.

"Cassius!" I yell. It still feels outrageous that I get to say his name in such an intimate way. But he grabs the back of my neck and drags me down for a sloppy kiss, proving I have every right to do so.

"Teddy," he utters, his thrusts aggressive and erratic as he stares into my eyes. "Teddy, Teddy, my Teddy. I need...I'm..."

"Come," I say simply.

He arches his back, his cock throbbing as he fills the rubber with his cum. A feral sound erupts from his throat as he gnashes his teeth. I squeeze myself around him, milking every last drop as my second, less impressive but equally earnest orgasm spits over his hand and his belly.

Before I can even catch my breath, he's kissing me fervently again. Then we both slowly succumb to the aftermath, our hearts racing as our dicks start to soften, and the kisses become gentler, sweeter.

"Cassius," I whisper against his lips.

He cards his fingers through my hair and gazes into my eyes. "Teddy," he says back.

I don't need to ask this time if what we just shared was good or that he enjoyed himself. It's obvious in every little laugh and reverent touch and labored breath we share.

"Mine," I say, hoping it to be true.

He rests our foreheads together. "Mine," he agrees.

CHAPTER 18
Cassius

"THIS IS TRULY AMAZING, MR. GARDA," GUS SAYS AS HE WALKS us back toward the front entrance of Redwood Bay's animal shelter. "We can't thank you enough for this opportunity."

"It's going to make such a difference!" Paisley adds tearfully.

I smile at them both and glance at Teddy. It still feels slightly risky to be holding his hand in public when we haven't officially announced anything, but I'd hope we're among friends here.

"It's our pleasure," I say sincerely. "You do amazing work here. Not only did you lead me to Kiki, but to Teddy as well."

"You're like our guardian angels," Teddy says warmly.

It's entirely possible that Paisley might combust with pride. But Gus manages to keep his composure as he holds his hand out to shake with me, Teddy, and Bryan. My PA even deigns to look up from his phone as he grips the manager's hand.

As predicted, the shelter's staff was absolutely thrilled to hear of our plans to raise money for them and highlight various pets for adoption. Bryan's just taken them through the logistics of what we're hoping for the night and locked down a date that works for everyone, including the One-Thirteen.

"I guess we'll see you at the fundraiser, then?" I say as we reach the door.

"You betcha," Gus assures us enthusiastically.

The color suddenly drains from Paisley's face. "Oh…what on earth am I going to wear? I have nothing!"

Gus laughs fondly. "I'm sure you have plenty, sweetie."

But she shakes her head. "Not for something like this! Mr. Garda said he's inviting other players from the Seahawks!"

"I might have a connection with some more high-profile guests as well," Bryan says absently, typing as he speaks. "Movie stars. Singers. The police captain apparently knows some people." He glances at Paisley with a devilish look in his eyes. "I'd say if this isn't an excuse for a new dress, when is?"

Paisley squeals and dashes off into the office where I assume she's either going to start shopping on her own phone immediately or is going to call someone to get advice on what to buy and *then* start shopping immediately.

We all laugh and smile fondly. Her enthusiasm is infectious. In fact, everyone's been excited and supportive of the fundraiser so far. Teddy's boss, Captain Valentine, couldn't believe it when I said I intended on helping his house upgrade with a helicopter of their own. It turns out that the station already has a helipad on the roof. They've just only ever used it to support other departments before now.

"So our photographer will be with you around two o'clock tomorrow," Bryan continues to organize with Gus. "He'll get the most adorable photos of the animals we've selected to showcase. If we don't halve your current occupancy numbers by the time this is all through, I'll eat my shoes."

"Those things are Italian leather, too," I inform Gus with a wink.

Gus smiles, but his eyes are also a little glassy as he rubs the back of his neck. "It gets me whenever one of our guests finds their forever home," he says thickly, nodding his head. "But if you could help a whole bunch of them at once, that sure would be something, Mr. Kallis. How's Twelve settling in with you, by the way?"

I chuckle. "Her name's Noir now and I bet there isn't a more spoiled princess in all of Southern California." Bryan gives me a cold look of betrayal, but the rest of us laugh. "And Kiki's out of her cone. She's pretty much recovered from her operation and is getting braver by the day."

Gus beams at me before turning his attention to Teddy. "And how about you, Mr. Foster? Or are your family's allergies still too much of an issue?"

"They are," Teddy says as he glances at me. "But I get to see Kiki all the time, so that's good enough for now."

Gus gives us a look that I've been getting used to over the past couple of weeks. Even though we've still been keeping things mostly private, when people see us holding hands or talking about dates we've been on, they get a bit soft and glowy. My mom practically vibrated herself into a different dimension when I finally introduced her to Teddy the other day.

For all it's complicated, people are happy for us. Really happy.

"You boys take care now," Gus says as we finally take our leave. "And thank you once again. We'll look forward to seeing you at the fundraiser!"

"Absolutely," I agree. "Who knows? Maybe Kiki might pop out and say hello."

"Stranger things have happened," Teddy says with a chuckle.

We step out into the sunshine and are greeted with a sudden wall of shrieks and chattering. It takes me a second to blink and adjust to the light enough to see that a dozen or so people have gathered by the right of the entrance, presumably waiting to meet me.

"We can just get in the car," Bryan mutters quietly, but I shake my head.

"They've been respectful staying out here. I can do a few selfies, right?"

Bryan doesn't look convinced and Teddy's immediately anxious. We've experienced a few fans approaching us since the livestream went out, but it hasn't been anything too intense, thank goodness. He's definitely on guard for the next asshole like the one we encountered at the walkway.

"Hey, everyone!" I cry as we make our way over to where they've situated themselves. "Thanks for not disturbing the animals, we appreciate that. Would anyone like a selfie or an autograph?"

"One at a time!" Bryan warns them.

The wall of noise ramps up again, but it's friendly. I see a family with kids, some teenagers and young women, and a couple of guys who seem too starstruck to speak. Hopefully they'll realize I'm just a dork underneath it all and manage a few words when I get to them.

Teddy hangs back with Bryan, but whenever I glance over at him, he's smiling warmly at me. With Bryan's media training and after many conversations between the two of us, he's getting more at ease with receiving attention. As I predicted, the online frenzy about him died down after the first few days. But I'm not foolish enough to think it'll go away, especially after we confirm our relationship and start making more public appearances.

Like she's proving my point, one of the women calls out to Teddy. "Would you want to join in our selfie?" she asks. "I just love that you guys met through that cat. I've watched so many videos of the rescue!"

Teddy looks bashful but he glances at Bryan, who shrugs at him. "Why not," my assistant says.

The young woman lets out a little squeak as Teddy walks over. "You guys make *such* a cute couple, by the way," she says before smiling for the picture.

"Thank you so much, ma'am," I tell her sincerely.

She giggles behind her hand. "Ma'am," she repeats in wonder, then dutifully moves aside for the next person to say hello.

A slim guy in a Seahawks cap sticks his phone in my face. With his scraggly goatee and thick black glasses, he gives off more of a nerd vibe than sports fan. But I've learned never to judge based on appearances alone, so I give him a friendly smile like all the others. I'm pretty sure he hung back until the end to let everyone else meet me first, so that means something.

It does. Just not what I thought it did.

"Mr. Garda, care to comment on your relationship with Mr. Foster here?"

Bryan is like a sleeper agent being activated by his code-words. He's in front of me before I can even blink. "Sorry, no. We're not here to speak to the press. Have a nice day."

"Quite the age gap, isn't it? When did you guys actually meet?"

"What do you mean?" Teddy says with a frown. "I'm twenty-three and we met about a month ago."

But Bryan is already steering me and him away. Luckily, my ankle is basically back to normal so we can make haste.

"Don't say a word, Teddy," Bryan growls under his breath. "I'm pretty sure that's Dez Starr. He's an absolute rat, blogging whatever lies he wants. Don't give him any ammunition. He'll twist anything we say."

Indeed, as we continue to head over the parking lot, Dez is following with his phone up. Presumably he's been recording since we stepped out of the shelter.

"If you haven't got anything to hide, why won't you answer a few questions? People are saying that Mr. Foster is a lifelong fan and the two of you have been corresponding since before he was eighteen. Is that true?"

Rage flies through me and I almost spin on my heels to confront him. But tiny little Bryan has a vise-like grip on me, marching us all toward the truck. Unfortunately, we parked at the end of the lot today because it was busy inside. I'm really regretting that now. Every step gives this Starr guy another second of our time.

"Is it true you're personally bankrolling the Redwood Bay fire department, Mr. Garda? Is that why you're dating him, Mr. Foster? And why are you funding a bunch of animals when there are human beings suffering in the community? Surely that money could go toward sick children or helping army veterans?"

"What the—?" Teddy starts to say.

"Zip it," Bryan warns as we reach the car.

It's pretty obvious this so-called reporter is trying to get a rise out of us whatever way he can. It's as if he's testing the fences, looking for a weak spot. His behavior is despicable, but not something I haven't had to deal with a thousand times before.

As much as we've tried, though, Teddy is unprepared.

"Mr. Foster! What do you have to say about your brother's gambling debts? Are you hoping Mr. Garda will pay those off, too? Is *that* why you're dating him?"

"What did you say?" Teddy cries, whirling out of Bryan's grip and advancing on Dez Starr. "My family has nothing to do with this!"

I try and reach for Teddy, but he's so focused on the pap.

Dez has a manic look in his eyes now he's gotten himself a reaction. "So you don't deny that your brother, Nathaniel Foster, is in over fifty grand's worth of debt?"

"That's a lie! You leave my family alone!"

"Teddy, car, *now!*" Bryan snaps. I wrap my arm around Teddy's shoulder, but he's planted himself like a tree.

Dez still has his phone recording in our faces. "So you *are* relying on your new famous boyfriend to pick up the check, hmm? How do you feel about being used for your money, Mr. Garda?"

"No comment," I say through gritted teeth.

Bryan gets between us and the camera. "One word," he tells Dez icily. "Slander."

But Dez just laughs as we finally shake Teddy lose and start maneuvering him toward the truck again. "Yeah, good luck. I get that all the time. Those lawsuits stick about as well as water off a duck's back. Besides, defamation's only a crime if what I'm saying isn't true. Sounds like you don't know your family as well as you think, Mr. Foster! And what about the accusations of domestic abuse against your colleague, Mr. Bell? Care to comment on that or shall I just go to the firehouse directly?"

I've finally gotten Teddy into the back seat, locking the door behind us. This is my car and usually I'd never let anyone else drive it. But in this case, Bryan hurtles himself into the driver's side without hesitation. Once he's adjusted the seat forward so he can reach the pedals, he fires the ignition and gets us the hell out of there.

Teddy's shaking like a leaf. I feel sick.

"Are you okay?" I ask, afraid to hear the answer. He's pale and clammy, staring at the upholstery in front of him.

"What just happened?" he whispers.

Bryan sighs and glances at us in the rearview mirror. "You just survived your first press ambush. Congratulations." He sounds tired but not angry with Teddy, which I'm very grateful for.

"I should have just gotten in the truck, like you said," Teddy utters. It's like he's slowly resurfacing and coming back to himself. I squeeze his hand, wishing I could do more to help him.

"Yes, you should have," Bryan says, but not unkindly. "Next time, you'll know. That guy is a piece of work, and there are hundreds more like him in LA alone. I'm sad to say that sometimes you just have to experience this shit to know how to deal with it moving forward."

Teddy blinks and suddenly looks at me. "Did I embarrass you? Oh my god, I'm so sorry. I was just trying to protect my family. I couldn't let him say those things!"

"I know, baby," I assure him, pulling him in for a hug. "But he's going to publish those things whether you try and stop him or not. It's not up to you to try and protect everyone at the expense of your own wellbeing."

Bryan clears his throat and when I meet his gaze in the mirror, he arches an eyebrow at me, no doubt thinking about pots calling kettles black. I roll my eyes back at him. Yeah, yeah. I should take my own advice.

"We're here to help you," I remind Teddy.

He shakes his head and draws away from me. "I should have known better. Do you think he'll really go to the station? We should head over there in case the second watch—"

"No, Teddy," I say firmly. "We can call and give them a heads up. We can also call the police and report Dez Starr for harassment and disturbing the peace. But it's not your job to save everyone all the time."

He nibbles his lower lip, looking like he's mulling my words over. "I want to protect you, though."

I cradle his face and gently kiss his lips. "I know, baby. I feel the same way. How about we go home and run a really hot bath. Then we can make whatever you want for dinner or order in. Hell, I bet my mom would come over in a flash to fix you whatever soul food you could possibly think of."

That gets a small laugh from him and that eases my nerves somewhat. He nods, which I take to mean we're okay to keep heading to my place. He was planning on staying over anyway. We can decide what he feels like doing food wise from that point.

We drive for a few more minutes in silence, all of us most likely going over the unpleasant incident in our minds. I can feel Bryan's outrage coming off him in waves, but he refrains from saying anything. I imagine that's for Teddy's sake, and I love him for that. Just as we turn into my driveway, Teddy inhales shakily.

"Do you think there's any truth to what he was saying about my brother being a gambling addict?"

My heart aches for him.

"I don't know," I tell him honestly. "The other stuff he was spouting was twisted bullshit, so I'd hope not. Do you have any reason to suspect your brother has a problem?"

Teddy's hesitation worries me immediately. "Nate likes scratchcards. He buys them without thinking whenever they're available, like a reflex. He also talks about horse racing sometimes. It's never once crossed my mind it might be a real issue, but if it is, I'm the last person who'd know. Nate can't stand me. If he gets in trouble because of me..."

"Hey, hey," I say, getting him to look at me. "Let's not get ahead of ourselves, all right?" I realize we're back in my garage and Bryan is subtly slipping out of the driver's seat. Knowing him, he'll just head home to give us the space we need. "Could you talk to your mom, maybe? Tell her what happened and carefully raise the concern."

Teddy exhales and nods, some color coming back into his cheeks. "That's a good idea."

"Right?" I say confidently before opening my door. "Once step at a time, okay?"

I kind of mean that literally as I hold his hand and guide him into the house and settle him on the sofa in the living area. Guilt gnaws around the edges of my thoughts, knowing that he wouldn't be in this position if it wasn't for me.

But this is my life. We agreed to try making this relationship work with all the complications that come with it. He's a grown man who came into this with both eyes open.

Just like he can't protect his family or friends from everything, I can't expect to do that for him, either. What I *can* do is be there for him now, as his boyfriend, as the guy who's falling for him hard and fast. I can look after him until he realizes that words might hurt but that's all they are. Words. He'll be okay after this, just like he will the next time something shitty happens to us.

Life is never smooth sailing, and no relationship is without its ups and downs. If anything, having to go through trials like this so early on is going to prove how strong we are.

I leave him to make us some tea, the way I learned to do it in London by boiling the water on the stove and serving with plenty of milk and a couple of lumps of sugar to help settle his nerves. But when I return to the sofa, I pause a second, my heart expanding about twice its usual size in my chest.

Kiki has curled herself up in Teddy's lap. She's purring loudly as he gently strokes her back.

It strikes me in that moment that this is probably what love feels like. Not like the love I have for my family or friends. A different, special, aching bond that's growing inside me. Forget everything else going on right now. I feel like I'm looking at my entire world on that sofa.

Teddy looks up at me and smiles, clearly proud of getting chosen by my scary little lion for such prestigious treatment.

I try not to let my thoughts run away with me, I really do. It's still such early days in this relationship. But it's like we're a family already, the three of us. Together, we'll take on the world, no matter what it throws at us. We've already survived so much.

That's how I know that Dez Starr can write or say whatever he wants. The internet can do its worst. Mother Nature can throw another tantrum.

We're going to be okay.

CHAPTER 19

Teddy

I'VE RUINED MY BROTHER'S LIFE.

Okay. Maybe Nate ruined his *own* life by getting into an eye-watering amount of debt with a gambling addiction that no one was aware of. Yeah, his work wouldn't know about it if some sleazy reporter hadn't dug into my family's private life because I started dating a celebrity. However, as Cassius keeps reminding me: with that amount of money, the truth would have come out anyway eventually.

But my brother is still blaming me.

Worse than that, he's got it in his head that my new boyfriend could 'fix it for him if I wasn't so selfish.'

The mental gymnastics on that one blows my mind. So, it's okay to be gay if he's filthy rich and it could help my brother out, right?

I'm so ashamed, I haven't even mentioned a word of that conversation to Cassius. It makes me feel ill to think I'd ever take advantage of him like that. My mom and dad are doing what they can to try and talk some sense into Nate, but now his work has gotten involved and they're concerned about what his problem could do to the law firm's image. He's not been fired…yet. I don't know what will happen.

All I know is that Nate is blaming me for everything. In fact, he's trying to convince us all that he doesn't even have an addiction and that we can't be mad at him for a 'bit of bad luck.' Me and him have never seen eye to eye on anything in my whole life, but my heart is still breaking for him.

Maybe now it's all out in the open he'll eventually realize he needs help and start going to meetings. For a little town, we have an impressive number of groups, and not just for gambling. There are people ready and waiting to get his life back on track. They're there to help.

Because I can't.

The incident with Dez Starr really rattled me. I was so determined to fight him off and protect everyone around me, but I just made it all worse.

Cassius and I have talked at length about how when he started earning big bucks he felt like he couldn't do anything nice for himself until he'd provided as much as possible for his family. It was his coach that stepped in and made him understand that self-care isn't selfish, and if he continued giving everything away, he was training everyone in his life that he'd bail them out, no matter what. Eventually, he came to see that by putting boundaries in place, he was actually doing them a kindness.

Is that what I'm doing now to Nate? Being kind?

It doesn't feel like it.

But at least Cassius can relate to what I'm going through, and I appreciate all the patience he's had with me as I fumble my way into this new normal. It's almost kind of funny how the relationship part of it all is the easiest. Being with him is like breathing.

I think I might even be falling in love for the first time in my life.

But since we met, it feels like the world around us has been doing its best to throw whatever obstacles it can our way. When it's just us two here in the house with Kiki, I feel like we're indestructible. But navigating real life outside these walls has felt as unstable as that landslide that tried to kill us a few weeks back.

And now we've let what feels like the whole world into the house instead.

I suppose it's fitting that it's raining again, as it has been for the past few days. Last night's shift was a crazy busy one, and I wish I'd had more chance to sleep today before having to put on a show. But that's just the way it is, and at least I'm not alone. The whole first watch is in the same boat, but they're showing their support anyway.

I really do love my work family. Even when they drive me crazy.

"Penny for your thoughts?" Lili asks, sidling up to me with a glass of Champagne dangling from her fingers. She looks stunning in an emerald-green backless jumpsuit with her hair all done up and heels high enough that she's looking down at me.

I mentally try and shake my woes away and give her my best grin. Fake it till you make it, right?

"Just thinking how you guys all owe me for getting you in on this sweet party."

She scoffs and beckons some of the rest of the crew over from where they'd been ogling one of the Seattle Seahawks, too afraid to actually go talk to him. "Probie here seems to think he's the shit now," Lili tells them with a smirk.

"Ohh, you're going to be scrubbing floors for weeks, dude," Lochlan says with a laugh.

But Anton shakes his head and looks around Cassius's living area where I'm used to cuddling up with him and Kiki as we watch TV. "I dunno, Lils. This party *is* pretty sweet."

"Gene's going to be so sorry he missed it," Yara says sadly.

Dray tilts his head. "I think he was pretty stoked to have an excuse to miss it, actually. I'm not sure posh suits and celebs are his jam. He told me he was super proud to be going to his daughter's karate graduation ceremony thing." He raises his glass my way. "Me, on the other hand? Fucking delighted to be invited. Cheers, Teds."

I laugh and tap my flute against his. "You're very welcome, man."

"Did you see Bella Dalton over there?" Anton continues. "My Rebecca's obsessed with her."

I love the warm look Anton always gets on his face when he talks about his daughter. I don't blame her for being a fan of the actress. Bella Dalton is seriously cool. This whole party is. I just hope it works out the way Cassius and I intended it to.

"Apparently," I tell my friends, "Captain Padilla knows her from when they shot the second Fallen Angels Club in the town where she used to be a detective. There was some kind of incident, I'm not sure what. Long story short, Padilla got to know the cast quite well. Sabina Max is here as well, somewhere."

"Oh, now that's someone I have to go find immediately," Lili says, licking her lips like she's going on the hunt. I'd be worried, but Sabina seems more than capable of handling horny fans.

Who knows? Maybe I won't be the only member of the One-Thirteen who ends up with a famous partner.

Although I don't really think Lili is going to settle down any time soon with anyone, let alone Sabina Max, I guess it would be nice to talk to someone who knows what it feels like to be thrown into this crazy world. My eyes drift across the throng of people, searching for Cassius. He's engrossed in conversation with a couple of people, but I can't tell who from the backs of their heads. This party is made up of a bizarre mix of people I know from around town and people I know because I've seen them regularly on my TV.

I can't blame my friends for being excited. That's how I want them to feel, in fact. The entire reasoning behind hosting a fundraiser was to break down barriers and bring the community together for a good cause. We've already raised an impressive amount for the animal shelter, and I think a couple of the dogs might even have been adopted.

Captain Valentine has been wooing all kinds of people while looking sharp as fuck in his well-cut suit. He's casually mentioning how if the One-Thirteen had their own air operations it could make a huge difference to our response times. It would also increase our ability to assist on land and sea without having to rely solely on departments from nearby towns or the naval landing field out on San Clemente Island. Navy SEALs have better things to do than rescue tourists pulled out to sea on wayward pool floats, after all.

The evening is going well. People are having fun and we're raising money. Bryan's been subtly working with some of the guests to post some photos he's approved of me and Cassius to start organically promoting us as a couple. The idea is to let people make real posts without his supervision as well, but the whole thing still feels a little off to me. It's still kind of fake.

I'm so ungrateful. I've met an incredible man and all I can focus on are the problems we're facing. It's kind of hard not to when this whole event was intended as damage control around our relationship, not to mention the drama with my brother. But it's much easier to bask in the amazingness of being with Cassius when it's simply us two. With all these people in our space, even those that are my good friends, I feel a bit like I'm in a zoo. People I don't know keep trying to talk to me and I'm ashamed to say I'm doing my best to avoid them.

Kiki has the right idea, hiding under Cassius's bed. Luckily, she got her cone off a couple of days ago, so she fits in that tight space again.

I wonder if there's room for me there as well.

"Oh, isn't this *marvelous?*"

I blink and see that my One-Thirteen buddies have been replaced by Mrs. Bloom. I'd worry how lost in my thoughts I was to drive them away, but I'm sure they'll be able to have a better time without me fretting beside them. So it's probably for the best.

And if anyone can shake me out of a funk, I'd wager it's Mrs. Sylvia Bloom.

Naturally, Miss Margot Fonteyn is at her feet, looking pristinely brushed with a teeny little tiara keeping her hair out of her eyes instead of her usual bow or sparkly broaoch.

"You're having a good time?" I ask Mrs. Bloom, grateful for the distraction, regardless if I wanted it or not.

"It's been an age since I found myself at a decent soirée," she tells me gleefully. "Your fancy man is my kind of fancy."

I laugh, feeling my shoulders relax a little. Mrs. Bloom might be intimidating, but I also know she'd never bullshit me, or anyone else for that matter. She says she's far too old for false platitudes, but I think she's still plenty young. Brutal honesty is kind of the vibe I'm feeling right now.

"So you, um, like him?"

I realize that her good approval is important to me. My own family hasn't met Cassius yet as it's all been too tense with my damn brother's troubles. Trust him to spoil my first proper Meet The Parents moment on top of everything.

I catch myself before I lose myself down that train of thought. Being unkind won't change his past behavior or do anything to improve the current situation. I always swore that I'd be better than him in that regard. When he's hurtling toward rock bottom isn't the time to sharpen my claws.

The timing just isn't the best right now. I'll be able to introduce Cassius to the rest of my family soon enough. In the meantime, I'd like to know Mrs. Bloom's first impression.

Because it seems she genuinely had never heard of him before. "Oh, darling," she'd said to me the other day when I'd invited her to this very party. "I don't have any time for watching sports, nor the inclination. It's all a little savage to me."

Back in the present moment, I look over at Cassius and so does she. "He's certainly a looker, Mr. Foster," she says in admiration. "I am enamored by his smile and by his generosity. And I don't just mean his wallet." She arches her eyebrow at me. "Money is easy to part with when one has plenty of it. But it's clear he's generous with his time, and that's not something easily bought."

It's like I can feel the sun breaking through stormy clouds inside my chest. "I think you're right," I murmur.

She gives me a little hum. "I know I'm right, dear. People of great fortune always want to spend time with others swimming in wealth. It makes for a very superficial crowd a lot of the time."

Trying not to be obvious, I glance over at her, but she's safely still watching Cassius. She doesn't often talk about her late husband, and I certainly have no idea how he came into his money. I've always thought it was through something either extremely boring or extremely illegal. I can't see how it could be anything in between.

Because she spends more of her time fussing over Miss Margot or cooking and baking for the One-Thirteen, I think I've made the mistake of underestimating her real power. But as I look at the enormous diamonds glittering around her throat and how she's analyzing the room of people like a shark, I ponder for the first time if she inherited her riches at all.

"I'm not sure if I belong here," I say before I've even consciously formed the thought. However, I guess it's true. Mrs. Bloom appears to be in her element.

I feel like a kid who's been invited to his parents' very grown-up party.

Mrs. Bloom scoffs before turning her head toward me. "That's the secret, my darling boy. Nobody belongs at events like this. They're all a fantasy. That doesn't mean they can't be fun. Their very purpose is to convey an illusion. Have you ever been to Vegas?"

"Las Vegas?" I ask before realizing how stupid that sounds. Of course that's what she means. I was just thrown by the apparent non sequitur. "Um, no. I haven't ever been."

She shakes her head. "It's a terrible place full of loud noises, flashing lights, dreadful heat, and enough glitter and sequins to destroy the whole planet." She flashes a devilish grin at me. "I *love* it."

"You do?" I ask in surprise.

"Oh, yes," she says, sipping on her drink. "The entire place is utterly false, but everyone's in on the game, and that's what makes it such a delight. You don't go to Vegas for enlightenment. You go for escape. And that's just what parties like this are all about. For one night, every person here, be they rich and famous or modest nobodies, can put on their clown make-up and join the circus. We're all dancing to the same tune, bathed in Champagne with stardust in our eyes."

"Whoa," I say, blinking and looking around the room with a slightly adjusted focus. That's basically what Cassius and I had wanted from this evening, among other things. For everyone to feel equal. But it hadn't occurred to me that the staging was actually part of how that worked. "What a beautiful way to put it."

Mrs. Bloom plucks an hors d'oeuvre from the tray of a passing waiter and bends at the waist to offer it out for Miss Margot to eat. She has the grace of a dancer, and I yet again find myself wondering what kind of life she's lived before we knew her.

"Don't you dare ever let anyone believe you don't belong in a room, Theodore," she says as she straightens up once more, brushing crumbs from her palms. "Unless you lack the necessary qualifications. Waltzing into an operating theater and demanding to be handed a scalpel is one thing. But don't ever let *money* hold you back. I've known many a buffoon who just happened to land on his feet financially."

"What about experience?" I ask, my age always on my mind.

She shrugs. "Time is the only thing that can give you that, I'm afraid. But again, don't confuse experience with wisdom. Young souls can still be wise, just as one can live a long and fruitful life, yet still be as ignorant as a pig in a palace."

I snort into my Champagne flute. "Mrs. Bloom," I say, slightly scandalized. Only she could find such a colorful way to call someone dumb as fuck.

She just smirks at me, entirely aware of how naughty she is. "I think I made my point," she says slyly. "There are some people in this room, Mr. Foster, who work tirelessly for the good of their community and get paid very little. And there are also people who happened to be in the right place at the right time with the right face who earn millions for doing very little. These can all be good people or, quite frankly, terrible people. If you judge others on their merits then hopefully they will do the same for you. If they don't..." She shrugs again, but there's a mischievous glint in her eye. "Well, forget them. Move on. When one light goes out in Vegas, they just screw another in, don't they?"

I take a moment to absorb what she's telling me. Which I

think is not to give my power away to people just because I'm assuming they're better or more important than me. We're all here playing the same game.

And this is my party just as much as Cassius's. We've both invited guests we know from our different lives, bringing them together to dance under the same twinkling lights to the same jaunty tune.

Perhaps I've convinced myself that if I protect everybody, if I save everyone in trouble, it will spare me from being judged as too young or not good enough. The exact way my brother Nate has always made me feel. Even if I rescued him from his current predicament, though, his attitude toward me wouldn't change.

There's no reason for me to be intimidated by the people in this room. They're our guests. Maybe some of them are wondering why the hell Cassius Garda would choose to be with a guy like me when he could have his pick of the elite. Maybe they'll change their minds when they meet me. Or maybe they'll continue to look down on me.

In which case…I'll let them.

There are going to be countless strangers out in the world who have nasty things to say about me, Cassius, our families and friends, the choices we make, and the things we do. The world will keep spinning regardless. Mrs. Bloom is right. I should treat stepping into Cassius's world like going to Vegas and embrace the madness and the make-believe.

Because when everyone leaves and the house is back in order, it's only Cassius and I who will still be here with Miss Kiki. That's the real world and the one I want to protect. I know my friends at the station will always have my back, and so does my family. I don't have to try and put out every fire—be it physical or metaphorical—by myself. If Nate wants to hold onto his childish resentment and prejudices toward me…well, it's his life and he can be miserable in it if that's his decision.

I am the author of my own happiness, and right now, I think I'm pretty fucking content.

"Mrs. Bloom," I say, holding out my arm for her. "Would you do me the pleasure of letting me introduce you to Cassius Garda, former all-star quarterback of the Seattle Seahawks and current very excellent boyfriend to the youngest and brightest star of the One-Thirteen firehouse?" I glance downward at the Shih Tzu on her sparkling leash. "If that's all right with Miss Margot Fonteyn, of course."

Mrs. Bloom grins, picking up her tumbler from where she placed it, and accepts my elbow gracefully.

"I thought you'd *never* ask, Mr. Foster. Lead the way!"

That's exactly what I intend to do from now on. No more holding myself back for fear of failure. Cassius is waiting for me. I'm done thinking I'm not worthy of him.

We can both be each other's heroes.

CHAPTER 20

Cassius

"I think Teddy's having a good time. Do you think he's having a good time? He looks like he's having a good time."

I look over to see Bryan glaring at me. "Noir is less needy and far more pretty," he declares, turning on his heel. "Oh thank Gaga. Captain Padilla! Are these the friends you mentioned?"

I wince, feeling bad for everything he's been putting up with from me. But this is a big deal for Teddy. Bryan made me promise not to hover and let him spread his own wings. But I feel like I've abandoned him.

Whether I like it or not, however, I am now distracted.

The police captain looks around to see who called her name, her eyebrows rising when she sees my PA. "Hey, Bryan! Mr. Garda. One hell of a shindig you've put on for us tonight, despite the rain. And, yes, these are some of my friends." She looks more than a little smug as she extends her arm to the four people with her. "Guys, this is our host, Cassius Garda, and his indestructible PA, Bryan Kallis."

"Hi, I'm Bella!" Bella Dalton cries in a beautiful English accent, like everyone in this room isn't extremely aware of who the Hollywood actress is. Her modesty is endearing, though, making me feel like we're old friends.

"Nice to meet you," I say sincerely as we shake, and she does the same with Bryan.

"This is my husband, Tony," she says proudly. "And some of my very best friends, Reyse Hickson and his husband, Corey Sheppard. We were so thrilled when Lucy invited us down from LA. We've been dying to visit her new town."

"So far, it's behaving itself just a little better than Pine Cove," Padilla says affectionately. "But it's still early days."

"Nice to meet you, man," Reyse Hickson says as we shake. "I'm a big fan, we both are."

"Oh, likewise," I tell the pop star sincerely.

Reyse glances at his husband, and they share a knowing grin that makes me almost envious. To have someone who can read you like a book and speak in a language only you both can hear...well I almost tell myself that one day I could find someone to share that with.

Then I remember I might very well have already.

"You like Below Zero's music?" Reyse asks me dubiously, referring to the boy band with whom he made his name before going solo.

Thanks to my sister, I know the five of them have been in a long-standing dispute with their former management and production company over the rights to their back catalogue. These are the same assholes that forced Reyse to stay closeted for several years to fit their 'family friendly' brand. In fact, that's how he knows the lovely Ms. Dalton. They 'dated' for a while as a cover story to maintain Sun City Records' homophobic rhetoric.

Anyway, I admire Reyse Hickson for the same reason he's probably a fan of mine. He eventually gave them the middle finger and came out anyway to be with Corey. But best of all, the Below Zero guys have done what all the cool kids seem to be doing these days and re-recorded their previous songs, so they now completely own their work. My sister has been super excited about the brand-new album they've just finished in Sweden with some hotshot producer and the upcoming tour. I tease her about being a grown woman in her thirties obsessing over a boy band, but really, we both know I think what they've done is bad ass.

"I like the funky songs," I tell Reyse truthfully. "Especially that solo album you did where you were clearly pretty mad at life."

Corey snorts and elbows his husband. "You mean you're not a 'Hearts Bound' fan?" he asks me innocently before singing, *"Oh oh oohh!"* I recognize it as the band's most famous and possibly most annoying song. I enjoy seeing that apparently the lead singer isn't even a fan of it.

Rolling his eyes, Reyse covers Corey's mouth to shut him up, despite the fact our little group is laughing hard. "I know so many divorce lawyers, darling," he says with a sigh.

Corey shakes himself free then leans over to kiss his husband on the cheek. "Sure you do, sweetheart," he drawls playfully.

"Ignore the children," Padilla says, pretending to be irked. But she then gives me a serious nod. "I'm sorry about your shoulder, man. That was a hell of an arm you had."

"You a Seahawks fan?" I ask.

She blows a raspberry at me. "Sorry, dude. 49ers for life. But game recognizes game, you know?"

I laugh and hold out my beer bottle so she can clink hers against mine.

"May I ask what are your plans now?" Bella smiles at me and I curse inwardly. I've been so focused on Teddy's role at this fundraiser that I forgot to rehearse my own bland answers for questions like this. I know she means well, but it's my Achilles' heel right now.

"Still figuring things out," I tell her honestly.

Bryan springs back to life, having been stoically observing the conversation as well as constantly scanning the room to make certain nothing is amiss. Aside from the fact we had to add an umbrella bin to the cloakroom and a second doormat to minimize how much rain the guests were trailing in, it all seems to be going very well from what I can tell.

"Cassius has been focusing on recovery and settling here in Redwood Bay," Bryan says smoothly with a bright smile. "But we've had fun filming some commercials recently. The one with that guy from New Zealand was pure art."

"And *hilarious*," I agree wholeheartedly. "Rangi is a genius. He can make you feel so cool one minute, laugh your ass off the next, then suddenly you're crying and you're not even sure why." I shake my head. "Damn. Shooting that silly underwear commercial was probably the best I've felt since I had to retire from the field."

Bella gives her friends a knowing look. "It's funny you should say that. Would you chaps mind if I stole our gentle giant away for a moment? And chappette," she adds for Padilla. But the cop just gives her starlet friend a shove on her arm.

"You know I enjoy being one of the chaps," she says with a grin. "Speaking of which: chaps? How about we go and find some insanely hot football players for this single lady to embarrass herself in front of?"

Corey and Bella's husband, Tony, laugh, but Bryan manages to slip behind me and vanish rather subject himself to such an ordeal. Bless his heart, he really does suffer for me at times.

"It was awesome to meet you, Cassius," Reyse says as he catches my hand for another shake. He pulls me in and lowers his voice. "Listen, uh…Corey works for a housing organization that helps LGBT youth in tough situations. I know you didn't get to enjoy it long before you had to retire, but what you did…coming out at that moment? I'm sure you already know, but holy shit that meant so much to so many people. Corey and his guys saw it firsthand. It was a gutsy, once in a generation kind of play. I just wanted to say that I might not follow football as much as the other guys in my family. But that kind of bravery made me a fan for life. If you ever need anything, even if you just want to hang, just hit us up." He juts his head, and I realize he's indicating Teddy. My heart swoops. "You and your cutie pie."

He winks, and in a flash, he's let me go to take his husband's hand again, heading off with the others to go help Padilla lust after some of my guys.

"Well, that was interesting," I say as Bella slips her arm through mine. She has this uncanny way of making me feel like we're besties at a slumber party and I can spill all my secrets to her. I wonder if she has that effect on everyone.

"Hopefully, it's about to get even more interesting," she says in a conspiratorial tone. "Did you enjoy acting?"

I frown and think about it. I didn't really consider those commercials we did 'acting' in a real sense. That's when you have a character and a plot and all that.

"Uh, well…I really loved working with Rangi," I say honestly. "He had a vision, and him picking me to see that through was a rush. His directing was dope. He just knew how to talk to everyone and get the best final cut, even if it took several takes. It reminded me of some of the best coaches I've played under."

Bella spins, pressing a glass of Champagne into my hand. I'm not sure where she got it from, but we've been gliding through the party, so I guess a server passed us with a tray? She's also got one in hand and holds it up, looking like she's about to cry with excitement.

"What if I told you that Rangi has already been signed to direct the next Fallen Angels Club installment…and he floated your name for a part."

A good few seconds go by before I realize I'm staring at her with a slack jaw. I snap it shut, then open it again to take a gulp of Champagne. I'm not sure how well it'll mix with the beer, but right now—fuck it. "You guys want me…for an action film?"

She shimmies and sips from her own glass, positively buzzing.

Because of me. That's pretty damn cool.

"He told me after I mentioned I was heading down here to meet you. He made me promise to give you the hard, rugged, take no prisoners sale pitch." She bats her eyelids and pouts before putting on a twee American accent, turning her knee inward and pressing a finger to her chin. "Pwease be in my moobie, Mister Cassius, sir!"

I laugh and wave her off. "Okay, never do that again. But…seriously? Me?"

She straightens up and returns to her regular English rose self. "Rangi loved your energy. He *basically* wrote this role for you. You'd be a rival secret agent who eventually sees sense and helps the girls save the world. But the real kicker? We'd spend the whole movie playing you up as this Casanova, the hot muscle man who gets the job done, you know? A real man's man. Then at the end we reveal he *is* a man's man—with a super hot boyfriend."

My eyebrows shoot up. "You'd…as in…are…the character would be *gay?*"

She shrugs. "If that works for you? He could equally be bi. The point is to take what Hollywood loves about action stars and prove anyone can be a hero." She places her hand over my heart. "Isn't that why *you* came out? To prove that anyone can play football? Black or white, rich or poor, gay or straight? Everyone should be welcome on the team so long as they can kick the ball."

"I mostly threw the ball," I tease her.

She looks at me deadpan. "Yes, well, in *real* football, that's against the rules." She cackles and pokes my chest. "What do you say? Would you like to come in and read a scene or two? Basically, the part is yours to reject."

I shake my head. "I don't know what to say." I've been so lost. It feels incredible jarring to suddenly have a direction in which to steer my rudder.

"Say yes!" she cries, then downs the rest of her Champagne. "Oh, we'll have such fun, I promise. The world is your oyster, Cassius. Don't let anyone convince you that you've stagnated. The truth is that you're in your prime and there's a whole new legion of fans simply waiting to discover you."

I turn and scan the room again, only looking for one man. I feel like I want to burst with excitement, and I know exactly who I want to tell my news to first. I see him deep in conversation with an elegant lady, who I guess from context to be his neighbor, Mrs. Bloom. I get the impression he's in good hands for the time being.

"Yes," I say as I whip my head back around to grin at Bella. "I say yes! Let's give it a try. Unless I totally suck and you guys want to fire me, I'm saying right now that I want to give this my best shot. Even if it's just for a good time. It beats moping around my house wondering what the hell to do with my time."

She smirks wickedly and quirks a perfectly penciled eyebrow. "Well…I would assume you're doing *that* delectable beauty whom you keep looking at over there. Am I wrong?"

My cheeks heat and I'm grateful my blushes aren't as visible as Teddy's. "A gentleman would never kiss and tell," I say politely.

"Which means you're fucking like rabbits." She beams and

seizes my biceps with surprising strength. "I'm so very happy for you, Cassius. I know we don't know each other—at least not yet—but I'm jolly well going to go ahead and tell you that you deserve this anyway. Congratulations. Everyone should find someone who puts a look on their face like you have now."

I swallow and nod, not expecting such enthusiasm from a Brit. Aren't they renowned for being demure?

I prefer her unbridled joy.

"Is that what you found with your fella?" I ask her.

She grins. "Minus the fucking, yes." She moves a lock of blonde hair and holds a finger behind one of her earrings. I realize with pride that I recognize the colors of the dangling gems are the same as the ace flag. I've been studying them all, but I haven't had many opportunities to see many in the wild until now.

"Hell yeah," I say sincerely, clinking our almost empty Champagne flutes together.

"It takes some getting used to," Bella says more seriously, indicating the room with her glass. "The rules and the politics of all this nonsense. It left Tony feeling quite hollow at the beginning. If your sweet young man ever wants to chat with someone who's been through it, I know Tony would love to pass on any wisdom he's gleaned over the years of putting up with me."

I give her a sincere smile. "Wow, yeah. I'm sure Teddy would appreciate that, thank you. Did you guys have a hard time going public as well then?"

"Oh, the press put my poor darling through the ringer," she says, a frown darkening her usually happy features. "They were convinced I'd left Reyse for him or, worse, *cheated* on Reyse with him. They constantly compared the two of them even though there wasn't anything of substance behind it."

I shake my head. "I'm sorry. I don't remember any of that."

She bumps her shoulder against mine. With her long legs in those high heels, she's very nearly as tall as me. "*Exactly.* I know this all seems like the end of the world right now, but people will get used to it. The scandal will fade and leave you in peace." She rolls her eyes. "Mostly. Honestly, I'll never understand why reporters are so interested in us when there are real crises going on around the world."

"Because people like to think they know us," I say with a rueful laugh. "That we're their friends. It's kind of sweet that millions of people genuinely just want to see what we're up to and know we're okay."

"And then there are those who would gleefully strike a match and set us on fire just to watch us burn." Her scowl turns to a playful smile and a wink. "Luckily, you've found yourself a man who specializes in putting out fires. And it looks like he's making his way over here. I'll give you guys a moment."

She leans in and kisses my cheek before melting into the crowd just as Teddy appears. "Was that Bella Dalton?" he asks me in awe.

"Now that *is* someone I know," Mrs. Bloom says happily. "She's a plucky one." Her dog wags her tail from where she's standing by her mom's feet, well behaved on her leash.

I chuckle and reach for Teddy's hand that isn't supporting his neighbor's elbow. "That was Bella, and she was lovely. I think she'd like to meet you if we get a chance later."

"Me?" Teddy asks incredulously.

Mrs. Bloom nudges him. "I said you belonged here, didn't I?"

Teddy blushes. "You did," he mumbles.

I kiss the top of his head, beaming. "Of course you do,

baby. Now, are you going to introduce me to your charming friend?"

"Oh, sorry!" he cries. "Cassius Garda, this is the One-Thirteen's very glamorous and very awesome neighbor, Mrs. Sylvia Bloom." His gaze drops to the dog. "And this is Miss Margot Fonteyn. Mrs. Bloom, this is Cassius, my, um, boyfriend." His voice is a little shaky, but he grins with confident pride as I lean in to gently kiss Mrs. Bloom on each cheek.

"Teddy's told me so much about you, ma'am," I tell her truthfully.

"Likewise," she says as I draw back. "Apparently, you play football?"

Every now and again it does me a lot of good to be reminded that there are people in this world who know nothing about my sport and have never even heard of me. I like that Teddy's neighbor doesn't feel like she has to pretend in order to impress me.

"I used to play quarterback, yes," I say, not feeling the same pang of regret as usual. Bella's offer is still fresh in my mind and I'm tingling with anticipation about talking it through with Teddy. "I hear you make a mean rhubarb crumble. I'm sure my mom would love to trade notes. She's here somewhere, no doubt forcing my dad to talk to the mayor about litter picking or congestion."

Mrs. Bloom raises her nose in the air. "Oh, I have a few stern thoughts myself about the parking situation outside of the library. Perhaps Miss Margot and I shall go join them."

"No doubt my mom would love that," I say with a laugh. "It was nice to meet you, ma'am."

"And you, Mr. Garda." She gives me an approving nod. "You look after my Theodore, now."

"So long as he looks after me right back," I tell her with a wink, wrapping my arm around my man's waist, loving how he feels pressed against me.

"Oh, there's no worry about that, I'm sure," she says as she and her pup wander off.

For a second, I simply turn and face Teddy, inhaling his unique scent and beaming as I hold him in my arms. "I'm so proud of you."

He blinks in surprise. "What did I do?"

I shrug and press a quick kiss onto his lips. "Just being yourself. This is a lot, and having you here is the best feeling."

He relaxes against me and smiles. "I think I finally convinced myself that this isn't all a dream I'm going to cruelly wake up from one day."

"Yeah?" I ask, trying not to get my hopes up. "I'm your dream?" My biggest fear is still that he's going to realize that this is too much and I'm not worth the effort. But he nods and squeezes my arms.

"You are," he murmurs, his gaze not wavering from mine. "One I'm never waking up from. I belong wherever you are."

My heart explodes in my chest. "Damn right, baby. And now the whole world knows it, too."

I lean down to kiss him, but after only a couple of seconds I hear jeering and wolf whistling. "Oh, guys! Get a room!"

Teddy and I part to see most of the One-Thirteen advancing on us, all big grins and thumbs up. I laugh, loving how they're not intimidated enough by me not to tease their friend. I know most of them from when they rescued us after the landslide, but we haven't really met properly. Teddy helped me retrospectively put names to faces.

Lili and Yara are easy enough to distinguish from the guys, Lili in a bold jumpsuit and Yara in a long, light pink strapless dress. The men are almost all in black suits, except the jokester who I'm pretty sure is Sawyer. He's paired a silk shirt with skintight leather pants and knee-high stiletto boots. The all-black feminine ensemble on his muscular frame is a daring look of which I very much approve. Simply by being himself, he's defying stereotypes.

Just like me and Reyse, I suppose.

"So are you guys officially dating now?" the red-head guy, Lochlan, asks us excitedly. No wonder his nickname is 'Beast' with how built he is, but I feel the golden retriever vibes rolling off him.

"Um, yeah," Teddy admits shyly, looking up at me.

"Definitely," I confirm.

Yara coos and Sawyer high fives his best friend, Anton. The more sensible one of the gang, Lieutenant Rico Flores, reaches out to shake my hand. "Welcome to the family, man," he says sincerely. "Teddy's a great guy."

From the way Teddy tenses beside me, I think both he and I expected Rico to say that Teddy was the lucky one to be with me. I appreciate that this guy has gotten it the correct way round.

Unfortunately, I don't get any longer to enjoy being properly introduced to the One-Thirteen.

"Uh…guys?" Drayton says, the Australian who's temporarily filing in for the guy on honeymoon in Japan. "That's not normal, right?"

I follow his gaze, as does the rest of the team. The conversational tone around the room is shifting to alarm. People are moving away from the front of the house, and it's not until I look down that I realize why.

Water is spreading across the floor. Fast. It's sloshing in from the entrance hall like someone emptied a bathtub.

"What the—?" I say in horror.

But the words die in my throat.

An almighty crash rips through the air closely followed by several terrified screams. I try and move to see what's happening, not quite processing what I'm witnessing. A car—a whole *car*—has plowed through the wall, taking out the front door with it. Several feet of water surges inside, knocking people off their feet with shrieks and splashes, sweeping furniture up that further slams into my guests, and shorting out the sound system, killing the music with a pathetic fizzle that seems inappropriate for the magnitude of the situation.

A flash flood is tearing through my home, heading straight for me and Teddy. My last thought before the water hits us is that I have to protect him. I have to protect *everyone*.

That's when the lights go out, plunging us into darkness.

CHAPTER 21

Teddy

It all happens so fast.

One second I'm basking in the glorious feeling of hanging with my friends as they rib on Cassius, his arm wrapped deliciously around me.

Then people are screaming. Windows are shattering. Dirty, freezing water is gushing inside the house, knocking us off our feet as the power goes out. Instinctively I grab onto Cassius, trying to keep him with me as chaos unfurls.

As quickly as I go under, slamming on my ass, I'm resurfacing, gasping and wiping my eyes so I can do my best to look around in the gloom. "Guys?" I yell.

"One-Thirteen, sound out!" Lieutenant Flores shouts. I can just about see him as he struggles to his feet. The brown water is swirling around us, like it's circling a drain.

I suppose it is. Cassius's house is on a steep slope, and the water has to go somewhere. It wasn't meant to be in a flood zone, though. That was something he mentioned he'd specifically checked with the contractors before they even broke ground.

Fucking global warming.

"Foster, here!" I reply to Flores before turning to Cassius. "Are you okay?"

"My house," he utters, sounding completely dazed. "All these people. Teddy, we have to—"

"We're going to get everybody to safety, I promise." I might not have been prepared to go to work tonight, but this is what me and my friends do.

As we heave ourselves back up to standing, fighting the water to keep our balance, I see my team doing the same as they all shout their names at the lieutenant. Earlier, I was worried Gene was missing out. Now, I'm extremely glad our oldest squad member hasn't been thrown into the thick of it with the rest of us.

Everyone appears to be okay, so now it's up to us to manage the situation. Even without our gear, these people are lucky to have a whole squad of firefighters at their party.

Anton and Sawyer have been able to switch on their phone flashlights, and I hurry to copy them. All around us people are shouting and crying and splashing through the rapidly moving flood water, shocked and disoriented.

"Flores!" Captain Valentine's voice booms through the cacophony. "Call Dispatch and alert them to the situation, let them know we're on scene. The rest of you, we need to evacuate the building *immediately!*"

"Mom!" Cassius yells, but everyone's yelling. Everyone's trying to get out even if they can't tell which way to go. I think of Mrs. Bloom and Miss Margot, and my heart wants to shatter. But I can't lose my head. I have to do the opposite.

"We should split into groups to clear the house," I shout at my colleagues, most of whom have also been able to switch their flashlights on. Thank goodness for modern day waterproofing.

"I can help!" Captain Padilla cries, wading her way toward us. Her hair is bedraggled, and her sequin dress is ripped, but she has a grim look of determination on her face. "I hope you don't mind, Garda, but I already got your Seahawk buddies in a line, helping people get out around that Camaro."

"Good thinking, Captain," Valentine says. "And Foster is right. We need to divide into teams and—"

The floor gives a horrifying lurch underneath us.

"OUT!" Valentine bellows to the crowd. "Everybody out RIGHT NOW!" He whips back around to address us. "Bell, haul ass to the biggest exit point at the front and direct people toward you. Kwon, you follow him and help anyone you can along the way. Nelson and Quick, you go right with Captain Padilla. Ortiz and Hendrix, you stick with me, and we'll go left. Lieutenant Flores, you work with Foster to clear the room behind us. Mr. Garda, I need you to evacuate as quickly as possible."

"No, this is my house," Cassius tells the captain defiantly. "I know it better than anyone. It makes sense for me to stick with Teddy. Please, get everyone else out." He looks at Padilla. "Make sure Bryan is okay, will you? And my parents, he'll know what they look like."

"Consider it done," the police captain tells him firmly.

Cassius squeezes my hand as he looks around distraught, and I can imagine what he's going through. Seeing people regularly come to terms with losing all their possessions in house fires is heartbreaking, but all that really matters is that everyone gets out alive.

The other levels of the house were off limits, so I really hope nobody snuck downstairs to look at Cassius's car collection or upstairs to...

Upstairs.

I grab Cassius's shirt.

"Kiki," I rasp. "She was in your bedroom."

His eyes go wide. "Fuck!" he cries as he pulls away from me, trying to head for the stairs.

"Wait!" I shout, pulling him back.

I won't lie. My first instinct was also to run off with a half-cocked plan. But I can't do that anymore. Not when I have an amazing team right here beside me and I need to start relying on them more. I don't have to rescue everyone all on my own.

But I *am* going to rescue Miss Tequila Sunrise.

Again.

"Flores!" I shout back at the lieutenant. "We think Cassius's cat is in the next floor up, but there could be civilians as well. I want to do a sweep."

The house is groaning all around us, but I can also detect the wail of sirens coming from outside.

Reinforcements, thank god.

Flores looks around the party area, seeing that at least half of the guests have already managed to get outside and hopefully onto higher ground. Our teammates are directing people and helping some of the walking wounded. Across the room from us, Lochlan has a very disgruntled looking Mrs. Bloom in a bridal carry and Miss Margot Fonteyn is drenched but safely in Lili's arms. We're not out of the woods yet, but the situation seems to be under control.

Flores turns back to me with a nod. "Let's do it, but make it fast. Mr. Garda—"

"I ain't leaving without my damn cat!" he yells, already forging his way toward the stairs through the now waist deep water. It's brutally cold and the strong current is swirling around us, doing its best to drag us back.

It won't succeed, though.

Flores gives me a resigned look and then we're surging forward ourselves, heading after Cassius in the opposite direction to everyone else.

It's a relief to get out of the water, but as we run up the steps in our sodden clothes, it's easier to feel the building shifting all around us. My heart is in my throat as Flores follows me down the hall and into the bedroom. I don't want Cassius's house to collapse. But I *really* don't want to collapse with us still inside it.

"Fire department, call out!" I yell as we pass the other rooms, but no one answers, so Flores and I continue into the bedroom.

"I can't find her!" Cassius cries as soon as he sees me, clutching either side of his head. "Kiki! Kiki!"

I dash over and grab his shoulders, giving him a firm squeeze. "We'll find her," I promise. "She's going to be terrified, though. We need to keep our cool so we don't scare her any more than she already is. Take a breath for me, baby. Can you do that?" He blinks at me and shakily inhales. "Good, that's good. Now, we're going to need something to get her out in. Where's her carry case?"

He frowns then shakes his head. "Downstairs in the utility room by the garage. If there even is still a utility room. How is this happening? None of this was supposed to happen!"

"I know, I know," I tell him. "But it is, and we are *going* to get through it."

This is why we run our drills so vigorously. The only reason I'm staying calm right now is thanks to hours and hours of training my muscle memory to just react and my brain not to succumb to panic. Out of the corner of my eye, I see Flores scouring the room for our ginger menace, but I can tell he's had no luck yet.

"What else could we use to keep Kiki safe?" I ask Cassius.

He bites his lip as he concentrates before his face lights up. "I have a duffle bag in the wardrobe."

"Perfect," I say as we run over. "She'll hate it, but I can strap her across my body in that." Who knows what I might need my hands for to get us out of here.

It's a free-standing antique and I wonder if it—like so

many of Cassius's possessions—is going to survive this ordeal. But that's something to worry about later when we're in the clear. If anyone can replace a bunch of stuff, it's Cassius Garda.

Kiki is irreplaceable.

He pulls a navy Seahawks bag from the bottom of the closet, upending it to dump its contents on the floor. Flores jogs over to us, shaking his head.

"Are you sure she was in here?"

My gut wrenches. There's no way I saved her from that river only to lose her now.

Cassius balls the duffle up in his hand. "I guess she could have run anywhere," he says, his voice tight. "But this is where she spends most of her time. Under the bed is her favorite hiding spot if she's scared, but I couldn't find her."

I drop onto my belly and shine my flashlight to check for myself, but aside from a few sneaker boxes, I can't see anything. If she isn't in here…she could be anywhere in the whole house. She could have gotten outside and been swept away by the flood…

Logically, I know at some point Flores and I are going to have to call it in order to get the human beings to safety. But the idea of leaving without Kiki feels like ripping my heart out of my chest.

I think of Lochlan Bell, defying Captain Valentine's orders in order to rescue puppy Rocky from the burning warehouse coming down around their heads. I know I'm not supposed to look up to examples like that, but that's who the One-Thirteen are, it's what we do.

If I abandon Kiki, I'll never be able to live with myself. I wouldn't be able to ever look Cassius in the eye again. They're now my family, and I have to protect them.

I just don't have to do it alone.

"Lieutenant, help me sweep the other rooms on this

floor," I tell him despite being the lower ranking firefighter on the scene.

But Flores is already running out of the room to do as I asked. "Anyone else here?" he shouts as he does. "Fire department, call out!"

I turn back to my man. "Cassius, have you got any of those chicken treats she loves in here?"

"I do!" he cries, launching himself at his nightstand. The fact that the big tough football player has kitty nibbles by his bed makes my heart melt.

"Shake them and call for her," I tell him. "I'll go help the lieutenant. Remember, keep calm—"

"And carry on," he finishes, giving the packet a hearty jiggle.

The tiniest meow comes from above our heads.

I hold my breath as Cassius and I look at each other, our eyes wide as we strain our ears over everything else going on around us. I absolutely did not expect that to work so fast, or even at all. I just wanted to give Cassius a job to do to stop him freaking out.

"Do it again," I whisper.

He does.

The meow is louder this time.

I snap my head up as my heart summersaults in my chest. "The wardrobe!" I cry. I'd go weak at the knees from relief, but my legs have got a lot of work to do yet. "Rico!" I shout down the hall. "We found her, but I need a boost!"

"I can—" Cassius begins, but I cup my hand against his cheek.

"Not with your shoulder," I say firmly. Lieutenant Flores is already back in the room with us, ready to assist. "You be ready with the bag. She's going to fight."

"That's my girl," he grits out, hurriedly giving me the

treats and unscrunching the duffle, ready to catch an irate ball of fluff and claws.

"Up there," I say to Flores, pointing to the top of the wardrobe.

"Gotcha, Probie," he says, linking his fingers to scoop up my foot.

I bounce up the few extra feet I needed and cling to the side of the wardrobe.

Kiki is curled up against the wall, trembling and looking at me with enormous blue eyes.

"It's okay, baby girl," I say softly, tipping out a few bits of freeze-dried chicken in front of her. Luckily, it isn't dusty as Cassius hasn't been here that long, but that's really the least of my issues.

A bloody-chilling screech tears through the house, most likely metal twisting, followed by other snapping and crumbling sounds. The window near us shatters as the frame warps, making us all flinch and Kiki try and scramble away from me.

We haven't got time to do this as gently as I'd like. But even if she never trusts me again, she'll be alive. So I lurch forward, and Flores automatically boosts me higher. I wrap my hand around Kiki's chest and yank her to me. She howls and flails, but I just hug her tighter as gravity brings me back down again. I slip from Flores's grip, but he grabs my thighs to slow my fall. We both stumble on our feet, and I tip Kiki into the duffle bag. Cassius had it half closed already, and he zips up the rest, quick as a flash.

"You did it," he says breathlessly.

"We did it," I assure him.

"*We* need to get the fuck out of here, right now!" Flores shouts, already running for the door. "Anyone else here? This is your last chance! Fire department, call out!"

Mercifully, there doesn't seem to be anyone else up

here, so it's just ourselves we have to worry about. Cassius hands me the squirming, yowling bag, and I throw the strap over my shoulder, making sure that Kiki is secured across my body. Then I hold my hand out for Cassius to take.

"Let's go," I say. He nods, and we sprint toward the stairs.

It's only then do I realize that the floor is way more uneven than I appreciated. My heart hammers in my chest as we turn the corner and rush down the steps back into the flood water.

I suppose the good news is that the level has receded by a couple of feet. Also, once we get low enough, I can see the One-Thirteen second watch near the front of the house in full gear. The civilians look to have all been cleared out.

That's where the good news ends, though.

The central supporting beam has huge cracks in its center where it's buckled. It's like the entire house is folding in on itself.

There's really no telling if the worst of the damage has been done already, or if the whole building could still come down around our ears.

"Lieutenant!" Captain Valentine bellows from across what's left of Cassius's kitchen-dining-living area. "Stay where you are, it's not stable! Is there anyone else with you?"

He shakes his head. "Just us three and the cat. What's our exit strategy?"

"Can you reach a window at the front of the property?" Cap asks.

We look at each other. "Back to the bedroom?" I suggest. "We can climb out."

Flores nods. But before he can reply to the captain, the supporting beam contorts, raining drywall and chunks of concrete and metal into the swirling brown water.

"Go, go, go!" the lieutenant yells, and we bolt back the

way we came with him leading the charge and me bringing up the rear.

Kiki is like a tornado made of knives inside the duffle bag. But I know as long as she's inside, I can keep her safe, even if she's terrified.

She's right to be.

The whole house lurches as we scramble down the corridor. Without warning, Cassius goes flying, tumbling to the floor in front of me with a yell. Flores whirls around, and we both dash to him.

"My fucking ankle," Cassius cries in dismay.

"We've got you," I promise him despite the fear gripping my heart. How's he going to climb down now? Hopefully it's a mild sprain like before, but still—when are we going to catch a break?

I only just got Kiki out of the river and Cassius out of the landslide in one piece. How many of our nine lives have we already used up?

Do we have just one more to get us out of this crumbling house alive?

"Rico, can you…" I say to my lieutenant, not quite sure what I'm asking, only knowing that the corridor is too narrow to fit three people side-by-side and that I've already got Kiki to protect.

"It's okay, Teddy," Flores says, looping Cassius's arm around his neck. "We'll go first, all right?"

In a flash, he has Cassius up on his feet and limping back toward the bedroom. But the entire building is shaking and I'm struggling to find stable footing.

I think the lower floors might finally be giving up.

"Teddy!" Cassius yells, looking over his shoulder at me.

"Get to the window!" I scream. "Rico, get him out! Don't look back, Cassius, I'm right behind you!"

Except I'm not. I'm pinwheeling backward, flailing my arms to grab at the banister to give me some purchase.

And that's when the floor in front of me begins to disintegrate.

Debris is raining all around me as the hole appears, growing rapidly between me and the bedroom. Flores glances back, his eyes widening as he realizing how much trouble I'm in.

"Get Cassius out!" I shout. "Don't stop! I'm right behind you."

I can't think about how there might not be a wall for them to scale in a matter of moments. I can't think about how unstable the floor is. Every second we waste could be our last. So I back myself up as the house rattles around me and pause only long enough to hug Kiki through the bag. She's stopped thrashing, like she knows this shit has gotten really real. "Come on, Miss Kitty," I tell her. "We've got this."

With a deep breath, my legs erupt, and I vault the two of us over the gaping space. My foot almost hits dead air, but I fumble and roll forward, cradling Kiki protectively to my chest.

We've made it, but a structural beam crashes through the ceiling in the bedroom, causing me to scramble back toward the closet where we started. At least there's no sign of Cassius or Flores. They must have made it out the window.

Now it's our turn.

But it's like the whole house is in a trash compactor, the space getting smaller around me. Walls crack, metal squeals, glass shatters, wood snaps, and water is dripping and spraying from everywhere.

I just have to make it to the window. Even if I have to jump, that feels like a better option than staying here.

My whole body is trembling as I haul myself back onto my feet, clinging to the closet for support. I'm probably better off crawling over the bed than trying to go around it and under the fallen beam. It's covered in shit, so I yank the duvet toward me to expose the mattress underneath. Cassius and I have made love here so many times.

How was I to know that the last time would be, well, the last?

"No, we're getting out of here," I growl to myself.

At least I thought it was to myself.

"Damn right you are, Probie!" Lili yells, her scowling face suddenly appearing at the window. "What are you playing at?"

She's barefooted as she swings her legs around and drops into the room. She's still in her green jumpsuit with streaks of mud all over her exposed skin. "How the...what?" I stammer as I crawl over the bed.

She grabs my arm and hurries me back to the window. "You really thought we'd just leave you hanging, dumb ass? You're stuck with the One-Thirteen now. Live with it, emphasis on *live!*"

As she shoves me forward...I see the ladder from the rig lined up outside. "What? I didn't think the truck would have room—"

"Escape first, explain later!" she yells as the house gives another sickening groan.

She has a point.

I throw myself out into the night, spinning to face the ladder so I can climb down it quicker. Glancing up, I see Lili shimmying after me. The house continues to crumble and sag, but all that's left inside are things. Kiki and I were the last two souls to make it out.

We're safe. We made it.

A sob racks through my chest, but I breathe through it, focusing on getting back on solid ground. There are people shouting and cheering from behind me, but I can't make sense of any of it. My trembling limbs don't stop until I stumble off the ladder.

And straight into Cassius's arms.

"You're all right!" he yells between peppering kisses all over my face. "Holy fuck, you're all right! Teddy, god, Teddy, I—"

I cut him off with a kiss to his lips, hard and full of life, tears spilling down my cheeks. "I love you," I blurt out, not wanting to waste a single second more without saying what's in my heart. "I love you so much, Cassius."

He grips either side of my face, looking earnestly into my eyes. "I love you, too, baby. You and Kiki are my whole world. I don't care about the house, only that you're both okay."

"Jesus, Probie!" Lochlan's voice rings out, making me look around. "Way to scare the shit outta us."

"That cat has a serious death wish," Dray says as my team converge, throwing their arms around us in a slightly claustrophobic group hug.

"So don't squish her!" I cry out with a laugh from under several pairs of arms. "She's used up enough of her nine lives already."

"Okay, ease up," Valentine says. The One-Thirteen step back enough for Cassius and I to breathe. But they're all reaching out and touching my back and arms still, Cassius's as well. It gives us enough space to unzip the duffle bag just a little so we can see Kiki curled up inside, safe and sound. The captain squeezes my shoulder, pulling my attention back to him. "You showed good instincts in there, kid. Hell of a job."

Lili ruffles my hair. "Not really a kid anymore, is he?"

"I suppose not," Cap says with a relieved grin.

"Well done, Foster," Lieutenant Flores says sincerely.

But I shake my head. "Thank you for getting Cassius out."

I turn to my boyfriend, not quite believing we're all standing here in one piece. Mostly. "How's your ankle?"

"Hurting like a bitch," he says cheerfully. "But there are about a hundred EMTs around here, so I'll get one of them to patch me up, don't worry."

I kiss his smiling lips, my heart finally starting to slow down. "And Lili! Thank you for pulling my ass out. I can't believe the second watch let you go up instead of them."

She grins wickedly. "Oh, they tried to stop me."

"The emphasis being on *tried*," Sawyer adds, making everyone laugh.

"Gee, I can't wait to write up this report," the captain gripes.

I suddenly realize that even though there's still several inches of water around our ankles, the rain has stopped. The flood is draining, leaving the crooked, broken house just about standing. I dread to think what the inside will look like when it's dried out or whether anything is salvageable, but that's definitely a problem to deal with in the morning.

Maybe next week.

"Did everyone else get out all right?" I ask. "Mrs. Bloom?"

"She and Miss Margot are keeping Cassius's parents company right over there," Yara assures me, pointing them out.

"No casualties as far as we can tell," Flores assures me. "Just some minor injuries and a lot of people in shock. Captain Padilla is already organizing transportation out of here for those that don't need to go to hospital."

"And Bryan?" Cassius asks urgently. "Did anyone see where—*oomf.*"

The small cannonball comes out of nowhere, smashing into Cassius's side in a fierce hug.

"I was waiting for the firefighters to be done with you," Bryan's muffled voice comes from where his face is buried against Cassius's chest. "Stop fucking giving me heart attacks, okay? I'm far too young and pretty to let your early death kill me, too."

Cassius laughs and strokes his hair. "I'm fine, I promise. Just think of it this way. You'll either get to decorate this house all over again, or another one from scratch."

Bryan blinks and sniffs, pulling away from Cassius's torso. "Good observation." He turns sharply and promptly engulfs me in a hug of my own, careful of Kiki in the bag at my hip. "Thank you," he says stiffly. "For everything."

Once I'm over the initial shock, I laugh and pat his back. "Of course. I'm sorry the weather sabotaged the party. Not exactly the narrative we were hoping for, huh?"

That yanks Bryan out of whatever pesky emotions he might have been feeling. He jerks back and grins at me, a little glitter still lingering around his eyes behind his smudged glasses.

"Are you kidding?" he says, sounding slightly manic. "You can't *buy* publicity like this. Let Dez Starr try and tell people now that you're with the big man here for his money. There are already about twenty videos blowing up online showing you and your buddies saving the day." He looks around at the One-Thirteen. "And the award for the Best Supporting Cast goes to…"

"Yeah, yeah," Flores says, waving him off with a tired laugh. "I'd settle for a hot shower over a trophy right now. Can we get cleared to go home already?"

I look sadly at Cassius's ruined house. "I'm not sure what we're going to do," I murmur to him.

But he surprises me by grinning before kissing me sweetly. "I have a feeling we'll work something out, baby. You, me, and this very brave kitty cat. I've got my whole world right here in my arms. Everything else will fall into place."

Ignoring all the hustle and bustle around us, I lean in and hug him tightly, cradling Kiki against us. "My world," I repeat.

I've spent my whole life feeling like I wasn't important to anyone. Yet somehow, I've managed to find friends who fling themselves into helicopters and collapsing buildings for me, and a boyfriend who looks at me like nothing else matters to him.

I still find it hard to believe this isn't fiction. But I guess even in real life, people do sometimes get their happily ever afters if they're lucky enough.

Despite all these disasters that have been plaguing us, I think I might be the luckiest man of all.

CHAPTER 22

Cassius

WHAT A NIGHT.

At least an EMT was able to bandage up my traitorous ankle again and give me a cold pack. I had some naproxen in my Longhorn to help calm down the inflammation, and seeing as it's apparently not just a truck but also a *submarine,* Teddy and I were able to sit in the dry while the aftermath of the flash flood unfolded, wrapped in more emergency blankets to not only keep us warm but the seats protected. Thank goodness I keep this vehicle parked out front.

I dread to think about the Ferrari and the Lambo that were in the garage. Teddy's car, too.

When I feel able to hobble, I leave a dozing Teddy there with the doors shut so Kiki can be left to roam out of the duffle bag without my supervision. I'm sure the poor little thing is going to be horribly traumatized by all of this on top of everything else she's been through, but I'm not going to give up on her.

One day, she'll trust that her home is safe and she's not going to find herself getting swept out to sea.

Unlike the rest of my stuff.

Most of it I don't care about. But seeing as the building didn't totally collapse, I'm really hoping I might be able to retrieve some nostalgic items once it's been made structurally safe to enter again.

That won't be for a while, though, and all that really matters is that there was miraculously no loss of life. That's why I left Teddy to sleep in the car with Kiki. I want to make the rounds and speak to as many of my guests and staff as possible to personally ensure they're physically okay and not too rattled.

This never should have happened. The flood risk was minimal. But according to Captain Valentine, several other properties were caught up in the same flood that should have been totally safe. Like the landslide Teddy and I also survived, this was allegedly a combination of baked dry ground reacting to an onslaught of rain in a short period of time.

But climate change isn't real, right?

Whatever. I'll have plenty of time to be furious later. Tonight, I spend the next hour or two speaking to who I can before they're cleared to go by both the police and the medics.

Paisley seems more upset about her dress and my house than anything she suffered, mostly because before Mother Nature hijacked the night, we already raised enough money to clear the shelter's rather large debt with the veterinarian. Not only that, they've got credit that should last them at least six months, if not a year, so they can focus on simply housing, feeding, and marketing for all their fur babies for the next several months. Gus is choked with emotion as he tries to thank me for the tenth time.

You'd think Mrs. Bloom coordinated disaster relief efforts every day from the way she puts herself in charge of the station handing out emergency blankets, hot chocolate and protein bars. Poor Miss Margot looks like she's been electrocuted by how wild her long coat is. She's currently just a pair of black eyes and a little black nose in a tumbleweed off fluff. But seeing as she's wrapped in a Seahawks hoodie with a bowl of milk in front of her, she doesn't seem to be feeling too sorry for herself.

My former teammates all give me thorough back slaps in condolence for my house, offering to help any way they can. I assure them I'll be just fine but point out that the other households affected tonight in Redwood Bay might not be so fortunate. My friends assure me they'll take care of it.

When tragedies like this strike, I'm sure the victims usually have to face a battle with their insurance company on top of everything they've lost. I already know mine is going to be difficult because *this never should have happened.* But I'm lucky to have considerable savings and assets at my disposal. I want to do everything in my power to ensure the other households who suffered tonight have that same peace of mind. The fact that my buddies want to help with that even though I'm not even on the team anymore warms my heart.

Speaking of rich and famous friends, I'm surprised to find my new LA posse still hanging around. Although in shock like most everyone else, Bella, Reyse and their husbands are all pretty calm about the whole incident. I guess when you live adventurous lives like they do, they have a higher threshold for freaking out.

"Cassius!" Bella cries when she sees me approaching. "Are you okay?"

The four of them are waiting by a sleek black car that I assume someone called to take them back to the city. The roads are apparently all clear now. It's crazy how much damage a flood can do in a matter or minutes before the water just washes away, like nothing ever happened. Well, aside from all the silt I'm sure was left behind inside my house. Damn, that's going to be disgusting once it dries out.

"Yeah, I'm fine," I tell her as I let everyone in the group give me a hug.

"You're limping," Reyse says dubiously.

I shrug. "I'll live. Are *you* guys all right? I still can't believe this happened."

"Spoken like a true action hero," Bella says proudly, swatting my arm. "You'll be wanting to do your own stunts, I'm sure."

Her job offer had gone clean out of my head, and I laugh, feeling excited all over again. "We'll see," I tell her. It's going to be nice to have something else to focus on aside from getting back on my feet.

Again.

"Are you heading off?" I ask the group.

Bella sighs. "We *were* waiting for Sebby, but I think she might have a different plan for the rest of her night."

She points to her co-star, and I spy Lili Kwon taking *very* good care of Sabina Max by flirting with her outrageously. From a distance, it looks like the feeling is entirely mutual.

Good for them.

After swapping numbers, I leave the rest of them with well wishes for an uneventful drive back to LA. Then I head back into what's left of the triage center outside of my destroyed house.

I marvel at the rest of Teddy's squad. They came out for a party, yet when they were needed, they sprang into action without a moment's hesitation. And now, even when the actual team on duty is here, they're doing what they can to help while still in their bedraggled evening wear.

I already knew Teddy was brave and selfless, but if I was to go off that old adage about seeing who a man is by the company he keeps, it's safe to say that Teddy is the best of men.

Again, I already knew that, but it's nice to be proved right.

I'm completely oblivious as to how much time has passed until my phone rings in my pocket. I'd already made sure my folks were fine before sending them home in a cab and spoken to both my brother and sister, so I'm not entirely surprised that it's Bryan's name that flashes up with the time. It's not even one in the morning, which feels early. But I suppose the flood hit almost three hours ago.

As I answer, I realize I can't remember when I actually saw Bryan last. "Where are you?" I ask instead of saying hello. But my PA is used to me and just laughs at my bluntness.

"Doing what I do best, remember?"

"Damage control?" I say, peering through the crowd of people still left outside the ruins of my home. The many flood lights mean visibility isn't a problem, but I still can't see where Bryan's calling me from.

"Quit looking for me," he says, and I can hear him eyeroll. "I left ninety minutes ago, thanks for noticing." I'd feel bad, except I know he'll be proud of himself for that. "I'm texting you the address of where you're staying tonight. After that horrendous shit show, your guardian angel, aka me, has found you something adorable and I have just stocked it up personally with some goodies. So all you have to do is drive your lil' tush over there with your man and your cat and I will call and let you know when you need to resurface. I booked three nights just in case."

We've been closely working together for several months now but even still I'm struck dumb by his above and beyond approach. "Bryan, I..."

"Don't get mushy," he snaps. "You know I used your credit card. I also bought myself some ridiculously expensive wine because Jesus, Mary and *Joseph*, I'm going to need it when I get home. So be a good boy and drop off the grid until I summon you back, okay?"

I chuckle weakly, too tired to argue, especially when I'm so impressed. "Bryan, *thank you*," manage to tell him before he can wriggle out of my heartfelt gratitude.

He hums. "Well…thank you for not dying…I guess," he mumbles before ending the call abruptly.

I laugh again, already on my way back to my car, but not before catching Captain Padilla to let her know that Teddy and I will be heading off.

She claps me on the shoulder and sighs. "Hell of a shindig, Garda. But if you're thinking of doing anything for New Year's…maybe scratch my name off the list. I'm not sure I could handle the excitement."

"Sure thing," I assure her good-naturedly. "See you around."

She gives me a salute then gets back to business.

As promised, Bryan has messaged me a what3words location. I can't see anything like a hotel on the map, but I trust him and I'm too exhausted to double check his math, so I simply program it into my phone to guide us there. When I arrive back at my truck, I peer inside the window before opening the door. What I see makes my heart melt.

Teddy is still asleep, but now Kiki is curled up in his lap.

Maybe she won't be so traumatized, after all.

I clamber inside and give him a gentle shake. "Hey, baby. We're going to go somewhere to spend the night, okay? Do you want to say goodbye to your friends before we leave?"

He blinks owlishly at me and yawns. "I'll message the group chat," he mumbles, getting his phone from his pocket.

The drive isn't long, but I still charge my phone as we go. Who knows the next time I'll be able to. Teddy dozes, leaving me to navigate, which I don't mind. I feel like my body is still trying to flush out the adrenaline so my hands are ever so shaky on the wheel, but my mind appreciates the quiet to process everything that happened.

I'm sure at some point the loss is going to hit me like a truck...but at the same time, maybe not. Bryan will absolutely revel in sorting out all the logistics. My things will either have survived or not. The only thing I really care about is having Teddy and Kiki here with me.

Tonight could have been a devastating tragedy. Instead, everyone made it out of the flood, and I became even closer with the man I'm falling in...

No. The man I love. And he loves me.

We might have had extremely bad luck with the weather, but it feels like destiny that we found each other in this crazy world of billions.

Bryan's coordinates take us down a suspiciously dark dirt track. But just as I'm getting worried, a small light appears in the distance. As we approach, I see a sign that reads 'Aurora Glamping Pods.'

"Oh, Bryan," I mutter in apprehension, having had just about enough of the great outdoors for the time being. "What have you gotten us into?"

I should never have doubted him.

The turn-off leads me down another track where we eventually happen upon a lake. As we drive around, I start seeing arched wooden huts, all nicely lit with warm glowing lights and spaced a decent amount apart. I don't want to risk taking my eyes off the road for too long, but I think each one also has a hot tub out front.

So...maybe this won't be terrible. Bryan did say 'adorable,' and with his standards I should never have assumed that meant camping.

Not long after that, I find our number, parking the car up and killing the ignition.

"Baby," I say softly, squeezing Teddy's knee. "We're here. Wake up."

He inhales and snaps his eyes open. "Sorry, fell asleep again."

"Don't apologize for that," I say sincerely as I unbuckle my seatbelt. "Did you message your friends, though?"

He frowns and pulls his phone from his pocket, careful not to disturb Kiki. "I have now," he says with a guilty laugh.

We don't have any bags with us other than the duffle we used to transport Kiki out of the house. I grab it just in case, but she's so pliant, Teddy's able to simply carry her to the front of the little pod that's apparently going to be our home for the next day or two.

The key is in a code box that of course Bryan sent me the digits for. After I retrieve it, I unlock the door and let us inside.

"Oh, wow," Teddy says as he stops at the threshold. "This is…"

"Adorable," I say affectionately. "You can thank Bryan."

"I will," he says. We step farther in, and he places Kiki down as I close the door, shutting out the rest of the world. "What's all this? Oh, Cassius. Look!"

I take in the grocery bags on the kitchen counter to our left in the first half of the pod. A small sofa stands to our right, facing a TV mounted on the wall. A bathroom is built into the back left quarter with a king-sized bed wedged in the remaining space on the back right.

And that's it. But there are fairy lights strung everywhere, illuminating the pod rather than the built in downlighters and giving the place an ethereal, cozy feel. As well as the bags of food, Bryan has left a bunch of flowers in a vase. On the bed is a basket of items he looks to have supplied himself, chiefly phone chargers, a simple selection of underwear, sweatpants, T-shirts and a fresh Seattle Seahawks hoodie each. By the sofa is a filled litter box for Kiki along with wet and dry food, and a scratching post that I'm guessing came from his own apartment. On closer inspection, the grocery bags have sensible items like bread and coffee, but he's also included all kinds of sweet and savory snacks. The fridge has some cheese, meats, and milk, as well as juice and beer.

It's our own little bubble of heaven.

"Take a shower with me?" I ask Teddy, crowding into his space, suddenly needing to feel every inch of him pressed against me.

"Will we fit?" he asks dubiously.

"I'm sure we'll manage," I tell him with a grin.

Of course, Bryan's also provided us with toothpaste and brushes, hair and body products, and the brand of facial moisturizer I use. I'm not entirely sure how he was able to source all of this so fast in the middle of the night, but I've decided if it's witchcraft, that's okay by me.

The corner shower unit is bigger than I might have assumed at first glance, but it's still a bit of a squeeze to get us both inside. However, neither of us seem to care as all our relief comes crashing out after such an unbelievable, intense night. Before long we're soaped up, kissing messily as he strokes my cock and I finger his hole. I wish we could do more, but without lube or condoms, I enjoy the simplicity of getting each other off under the blissfully hot water.

Yet again, I shouldn't have underestimated my other-worldly PA.

"Oh, shit," I say with a laugh as I'm unpacking the basket of goodies on the bed. I was intending to plug my phone in then wear some boxers to sleep in. But nestled underneath everything else is exactly what I was wishing for. Lube and condoms. I'm torn between embarrassment that Bryan would buy those for us and horniness for what I really wanted to do to Teddy back in the little shower cubicle.

Who am I kidding? Horniness wins out almost immediately.

"What's—*oh*." Teddy blushes, and it only makes me need him more. He's just set out some food for Kiki, and she's curled up peacefully on the sofa after her ordeal. Bryan gave us explicit instructions not to resurface until he reached out to us.

What else have we got to do while we're here? Crossword puzzles?

We're both still naked, so despite the recent fumble as we cleaned up, it's obvious that I'm interested once again. Of course Teddy is. He's still in his early twenties, for crying out loud.

But as he approaches me, he slides the condom box from my fingers and looks at me seriously. "Do we really need these?" he whispers.

My eyebrows creep up my face. "I guess I don't...if you don't?"

He looks at them and bites his lip. "We have regular physicals, and I know I'm negative for anything we might worry about."

"Me, too," I say quickly. "Not to sound like a complete amateur, but I've never, ah, done that with anyone."

His mouth drops into a cute little 'O' shape. "I get to be your first bareback ride?"

My heart stutters in my chest. "If that's what the kids are calling it these days, then, yeah."

Teddy snorts, tossing the condoms aside and getting in my face, his lips ghosting over mine. "That's what *I'm* calling it. Cassius, what do you want? To fuck me or to get fucked?"

I'm lost in his green eyes, having trouble concentrating on words when all my blood is rushing south. "Uh, both?" I croak.

Teddy snorts, then leans in and catches my lower lip between his teeth before letting it slide free. "Which do you want *first*, then?"

"You," I say automatically. "Uh, you. I want to fuck you. Please, baby. I want everything. I, uh…"

"Shh," he tells me kindly before treating me to a longer, more sensual kiss. His fingers skim up my sides, and I rest my hands on his hips. "Make love to me, Cassius," he murmurs against my mouth. "Get me ready with your tongue."

I moan and nod, prompting him to draw away from me, which I'm not a fan of. But then he turns and crawls up the bed, showing off his peachy ass, and I'm a big fan of that.

He lies on his stomach, hugs a pillow under his head, and spreads his knees, making his hole open and inviting for me. I grab the bottle of lubricant, leaving it at the foot of the mattress so it'll be in reach when I need it. But then I waste no time in pulling apart his plump cheeks and burying my face against his most intimate area.

"Fuck, fuck, *fuck*," he gasps as I lick and kiss his fluttering hole, loving how he humps the duvet, seeking friction on his dick as I pleasure him. I'd already fingered him quite thoroughly in the shower, so this is more for fun than practicality.

Oh, and *what* fun.

He mewls and squirms and pants and every other delicious little thing. I turn my gorgeous man into a puddle beneath me. And just when he seems like he's going to combust, I pull my slightly numb face away, douse my cock in sweet smelling, shiny lube, then yank his hips up so I can line myself up and ease my way inside.

"Oh, Cassius, yes, *yes*," he babbles. His face is turned to the side as his upper half presses into the mattress, his skin flushed and damp. We're going to need another shower after this.

I don't care. In fact, I can't wait.

"That's it, baby," I grunt, his channel unbelievably hot and tight around my bare, throbbing cock. "You feel so amazing. Do you like that?"

"Love it, Cassius!" he wails. "Love you. Oh, Christ, yes, yes!"

After all that prep, it doesn't take me long to bottom out. Then at Teddy's insistence, I start thrusting, claiming him over and over as he howls my name.

I almost wish the neighbors were closer so someone could witness this monumental moment, but I wouldn't actually want to disturb them.

Because I think we'd be disturbing them a *lot* over the next few days.

"Teddy, I'm close," I warn him, feeling my insides burning up like a rocket ready to take off.

"Come in me, Cassius," he begs, wrapping his hand around his leaking cock and stroking vigorously. "I'm yours, I'm *yours!*"

He starts shooting over the bedspread and that's all I need to drop my head back and let go, stars bursting behind my eyelids as my orgasm rips through my body, tearing me apart and piecing me back together all at once.

We collapse in a heap, and I smother his body with mine, tangling our limbs as I plant sloppy kisses anywhere my lips can reach. "Teddy," I say with a sigh. "Mine, all mine."

I know we need to clean up soon or we'll regret it. And I really hope there's clean bedding stored under the mattress, otherwise we're going to find ourselves in an uncomfortable situation by the morning, if not earlier.

But we're both boneless and beyond tired as we take a second to catch our breath. I'm fighting off passing out, but I *swear* I hear him whisper, "Forever."

Could he really be mine forever?

I guess I'll find out eventually, won't I?

"Do you think it's going to rain?" Cassius asks me.

"Oh, don't," I groan, elbowing him playfully in the ribs then pointing up at the perfectly blue sky. "I think we're probably going to be okay."

He chuckles and wraps his arms around me from behind, pressing our temples together and sighing as we watch the busy goings on outside of the One-Thirteen firehouse. Our helicopter fundraiser event is in full swing, and it feels like half the town has come out in support on this gorgeous Sunday afternoon.

"I don't know," Cassius counters. "Good things happen when it rains."

I can't help but laugh incredulously. "Your house practically got *destroyed* the last time we had a big storm here."

He shrugs. "Yeah, but we're rebuilding that. I'm talking about how you agreed to be my boyfriend in the rain. And how you told me you loved me for the first time in the rain. Not to mention that you saved my cat's *life* in the rain."

"Our cat," I correct, attempting to frown, but the smile creeps out anyway as I look back over my shoulder at him.

He matches me with a grin. "Oh, my apologies. *Our* cat. And *our* house will be better than ever when it's finished."

"Our house," I say, squirming against him, happiness humming through my veins.

After the events of the previous shelter fundraiser, Cassius began renting an apartment in town as a temporary measure while he sorted out what was salvageable. It wasn't just about recovering his possessions, although we were able to rescue a surprising amount of his stuff. He and the surveyors had to determine whether or not he'd have to start from scratch after the disastrous flood damage. No one was all that surprised when he was told he'd be better off razing the property to the ground to make absolutely sure it would be structurally sound, but he went a step further and picked an entirely new location so construction could begin right away.

And this plot hopefully really *does* have a zero risk of flooding.

I didn't want to rush anything, but as it became clear that I was spending all my time at his place when I wasn't here at work, he was the one to suggest we try living together and see how that went. The situation at home with my parents was okay as it was mostly just the three of us. But Nate is still refusing to get help, and whenever he came around the tension was unbearable. That combined with the desire to finally spread my wings at twenty-three were the push I needed to at least try living with my boyfriend.

The logical side of me was worried that by jumping in too deep, too fast, we'd ruin what we were building. But another side of me recognized that perhaps subconsciously I didn't think I deserved to be this lucky or happy, and wanted to sabotage it.

Cassius and I have suffered through enough forces in the universe trying to tear us down without me doing it as well.

So much like the time I jumped into a swollen river because I knew with all my heart it was the right thing to do, I took the leap.

And never looked back.

I love waking up beside him. I love cooking dinner together and washing the dishes. I love watching TV and sharing closet space and bickering about who took the trash out last and all the other million tiny little things that come from being a couple and living together.

I love him so much. There are days where I still step back and wonder how the hell this became my life. But I trust now that it's better than fiction could have ever been.

I am the author of my own destiny.

The fame issue has mostly faded into the background, which is kind of crazy. I never thought I'd get used to strangers approaching us, asking for selfies and autographs. But here in Redwood Bay, I do think the novelty of having our golden boy home again has worn off a little. People aren't so shocked to see him around anymore. He's not Cassius Garda, former NFL player and Seahawks superstar. He's just Cassius.

Teddy's boyfriend.

It's different when we're in LA, which has been fairly often these days. Between visiting our new friends Bella, Tony, Reyse and Corey, as well as Cassius having pre-production meetings, readings, wardrobe fittings and every-thing else for his new Fallen Angels Club role, we find ourselves making the drive pretty regularly. I'm so proud of him for pursuing a new career that he's excited about, I find it's easier putting up with the fans, especially as most of them are very sweet. Even the rude ones bother me less now.

If this is the metaphorical price I have to pay to be with Cassius, I'll gladly pay it.

Sometimes, it's still a tightrope walk to make sure that

literal finances don't create a chasm between us. It makes sense for him to be responsible for the house, seeing as it's going to be a multi-million-dollar mansion that he'll be paying cash for up front. My firefighter salary isn't going to contribute much toward that.

But I'm paying a percentage of rent on the temporary place, and we've agreed that I'm going to be investing in furnishing and decorating the new place alongside him. Cassius wants this to feel as much of my home as his, not like I'm a guest.

The truth is...my home is wherever he is. Although I'm also still very much not interested in being his sugar baby. So we'll have to wait and see how it all shakes out. But so far, I think we're doing okay with juggling the various different factors.

Cassius has also reassured me by not throwing his money around to solve everybody else's problems. There's a fine line between donating generously to charity and being taken for a ride. I never mentioned my brother's demands that Cassius should help him clear his debt, but because my boyfriend is so amazingly thoughtful and observant, he worked out that was the main source of conflict between us anyway. I was mortified, but he made me feel better by assuring me that after a lifetime of bullying me, Nate could absolutely clean up his own damn mess.

The One-Thirteen was a different matter altogether, though. After the way my team sprung into action and saved everyone from the flood at his house, even though they were off duty, left Cassius wanting to throw caution to the wind and simply buy us our new helicopter outright. Luckily, Bryan and I were able to talk him into paying half, which is still insanely generous. But he has to make sure his own house is in order first, literally.

However, that's why we're here today. Hosting a community day at the firehouse like we originally planned, engaging with the people of Redwood Bay who we devote our lives to protecting. Technically, the second watch are on call, ready to go if the tones sound with the rigs parked out on the road, clear of all the festivities. But Dispatch is routing all minor calls to the One-Two-Two, so unless disaster strikes, they should be able to stay with us and the third watch to have some fun over the next few hours.

I glance up at the blue sky again, daring the universe to give us another crisis. But I think it knows not to cross me anymore.

My mom said she'd try and swing by later with my dad, and if they do, that's cool. They and my other brothers will always be my family. But so long as Nate is causing trouble, I'm not going to feel guilty about keeping my distance. I'm not a little kid anymore and I've got my own life to live with the family I've chosen.

That's Cassius and Kiki. That's the One-Thirteen. And it's also probably going to be several more cats and dogs from the shelter once the house gets finished being built. Kiki might be outraged to begin with, but I'm sure she'll adapt. She's gone from a violent little lion to a fluffy lap cat in a matter of months. Of course, she still growls at herself at three o'clock in the morning and tries to drink running water by licking the top of the faucet. She might be friendlier, but that doesn't stop her from being orange, after all.

That's what so special about choosing your family. It isn't blood that obliges you to stand by their side through thick and thin or sheer dumbassery.

It's love.

Although, nobody says you have to love them *all* the time.

"Hey, Probie!" Lili yells from where she and Rico are manning the barbecue. "We need more ribs from the kitchen!"

I laugh and squeeze Cassius's arms around me. "Not your probie anymore, so that sounds like a you problem, Kwon!"

She glares at me while Rico just laughs.

It's funny, but now I'm a regular firefighter like the rest of my team, I feel it's okay to think of Lieutenant Flores by his first name. I guess seeing as I'm less preoccupied with how much younger and inexperienced I am compared to everyone else, his rank is less intimidating. It also helps that he's been spending more time with us all lately, almost like he's avoiding being at home. I wouldn't ever pry, but I hope everything's okay with him.

Yara waves her hands and puts her beer down. "Don't worry, I'll get it!" She pauses and points at her eighteen-year-old brother, Fabian. "Be good."

He rolls his eyes. "No, I'm going to down some tequila and steal your ambulance in the thirty seconds you're gone."

Bless Yara. She actually hesitates a second before realizing he's obviously joking. It must be hard having to raise your younger sibling like she has. They seem to have come through the worst years since their parents passed, though, and I only hope it gets easier as Fabian starts navigating adulthood.

A transition I know a thing or two about.

When I look back to the summer, it feels like I was a different person. And it's not just that I've now qualified from being a probationary officer to becoming a fully-fledged firefighter. It's not that I have a boyfriend and I've moved out of my parents' place.

It's that I know myself well enough now to realize being an adult isn't about constantly proving I can do everything by myself. It's trusting that I'm stronger when I work with those I love. It was childish to think it was weak to ask for help, especially when I've committed my life to aiding others. I see that now.

If I can, I try and look in the mirror every single day and simply tell myself, "I'm grateful." Because what kind of insane life is it that I lead? I'm dating the guy I grew up crushing on. There are still pictures of Cassius inside my locker, it's just now they're photos of us we took at the beach instead of magazine cut outs. And most people probably tolerate their work colleagues or make casual friends with them, but I'm lucky enough that these misfits really are my family.

I look around for my friends at all the stalls and activities our community has pulled together. We're hoping to raise some of the funds needed to not only get us that helicopter but pay to train whoever's going to be flying the thing.

It's a shame Drayton isn't with us permanently. Rumor has it he was a pilot with the Australian Maritime Border Command before he moved to America. But of course he was off as soon as Del got back from his honeymoon, moving onto his next assignment. Last we heard, he was somewhere up in Oregon, enjoying the much colder winter surfing. For someone who's only subbed for us a short while, I do miss him. He fits in well with the team. If he was here, I wonder what he'd be doing.

As Christmas is only a couple of weeks away, Captain Valentine made the sacrifice to sweat his ass off in a Santa Claus outfit so all the little kids can tell him if they've been good this year. He's so patient and attentive with them, it makes me wonder if he's ever going to be interested in having children of his own someday.

Gene's here with his whole family. Him and his wife have set up a station making Hanukkah latkes for people while the four older kids run around exploring all the games and activities.

Del's new husband, Colt, has the youngest Haskell bouncing on his hip as he chats with his friend, Elizabeth. Her two kids are currently waiting in line for Del to paint their faces with bright colors and glitter. Honestly, I had no idea he was such a talented artist.

Lochlan and his boyfriend Dario are currently in charge of the bobbing for apples game. Their dogs, Rocky and Queenie, are helpfully chasing any fruit that goes astray.

Anton is with his ex-wife, Meagan, and her new husband, Brent, as they talk to Gus and Paisley at the shelter's information booth. I have a sneaking suspicion that Anton and Meagan's daughter, Becca, is going to be getting a four-legged surprise under the tree this December twenty-fifth. She's currently the one in Del's chair, and he's making her face look like a zombie's, much to her friends' delight.

I love that when Anton came out, Meagan was his number one supporter and that Anton was the best man at hers and Brent's wedding. They all co-parent Becca Bean together in what I think is a fantastic example of a modern family, especially when 'Uncle' Sawyer is in her life almost as much as they are.

In fact, it's unusual that he isn't by Anton's side as well, involved in such a big decision as adopting a pet. I look around the front lot of the firehouse through the crowd of people, wondering if he's just inside the house or perhaps helping Mrs. Bloom with her cake stall.

Eventually, I see him slightly away from the hustle and bustle of the crowd. He's leaning against one of the rigs, a beer bottle dangling between his fingers, simply looking in Anton's direction.

I swear his expression is one of absolute heartbreak.

But then it's as if he senses my attention on him, and he smiles my way so fast I wonder if I even really saw what I thought I saw. He was probably just lost in thought or tired from a night with one of his countless paramours. Nothing to worry about, I'm sure.

"Probie!" he cries in delight as he practically skips over to us. "Shouldn't you be litter picking or something?"

"Not the probie anymore," Cassius and I say together in amusement. By the way Sawyer cackles, I assume that was exactly the reaction he was hoping for.

"Hey, dude," he says, giving my boyfriend a salute. "Where's that cute PA of yours?"

"Washing his hair," Cassius says automatically, making me laugh again. "Also, calm down, Casanova. Bryan's off limits, all right?"

Sawyer holds his hands up, attempting to look innocent. "I didn't say a thing," he assures us with a devilish smirk. Cassius hums, not entirely convinced.

"He loves organizing these things," I explain to my Lothario colleague. I doubt he's actually interested in Bryan. However, he has an image to maintain. "But he doesn't attend them unless he really has to. I promised I'd take care of Cassius, and Padilla swore she'd make sure no one got into trouble, so he's probably home with a book." I love how close the two of them have become in a slightly unlikely friend-ship. But the fact he's branching out by himself shows that this is Bryan's home just as much as Cassius's now.

We wave at the police captain where she's handing out leaflets for a self-defense class that's starting in the new year. Klaus, the sniffer dog, is sitting patiently by her feet, a hundred times better behaved than Rocky or Queenie. Apparently, he's going to be retiring soon. I wonder if he's got a home lined up to go to or if the shelter will help with that.

"Okay, real talk, then," Sawyer says, frowning at Cassius. "Now…this is an important question, so I need you to give it actual thought before you answer."

I groan, knowing almost certainly what's about to

happen. But Cassius looks at my colleague seriously. "Fire away."

Sawyer snaps his fingers and points at Cassius with a grin. "Favorite dinosaur, go!"

"You don't have to answer that," I assure him with a laugh.

But I haven't even finished speaking when Cassius says, "Compsognathus!" with confidence.

Sawyer and I both blink at him. "Deep cut, man," Sawyer says respectfully.

"What's a comp…"

"Compsognathus," Cassius says again proudly. "Thought to be one of the smallest yet fastest dinosaurs to have ever existed."

"Like anything about you is small," I mutter into Cassius's ear, making him snort.

"Carnivore, too," Sawyer says obliviously with a nod. "Speaking of which, I need to get me some ribs. I'll catch you guys later!"

He scampers off toward Lili and Rico, leaving me with Cassius.

Just the way I like it.

"What's your favorite dinosaur, baby?" Cassius asks, kissing my cheek.

"Brontosaurus," I tell him, not needing to think about my answer, having played this game with Sawyer many times. "Sturdy, dependable, majestic."

Cassius hums and nibbles my ear. "I can see that. Long neck, too. Good for *swallowing*."

I groan and wonder if we can possibly sneak off without anyone noticing. It's doubtful, but I catalogue all the ways I plan on driving my boyfriend wild when we get home later.

My boyfriend. My home. My life.

This really is my reality. On paper, it looks like a

complete fantasy. My dad always says to be careful what you wish for, but now I know better.

Sometimes when you wish upon a star, all your wildest dreams come true.

————

Thank you so much for reading Teddy and Cassius's story! Next up in **Redwood Bay Fire**, we have Rico Flores, our stoic lieutenant, and his best friend's down-on-his-luck younger brother. If you don't want to miss out on their hard-earned romance, pre-order **Up In Smoke** today!

Want to discover Reyse's story in **Homecoming Hearts #5?** And see what Bella got up to when filming in **Pine Cove #5?** Turn the page to discover box sets of more heart-warming small town and found family series from HJ Welch, and contemporary fairy tale adaptations from Helen Juliet!

————

Thank you to my team!

Cover Designer: Jacqueline Sweet

Editor: Meg Cooper

Love, Support & Inspiration: Ed, AK, Sarah, Hubby & our kitty cats

Extra special thanks go out to Charlie Novak on this one! I couldn't have made it across the finish line without your cheerleading and encouragement to eat chocolate mwahaha

REDWOOD BAY FIRE #1: IGNITING HIS FLAME BY HJ WELCH

Love makes us all brave

DARIO

After escaping my controlling ex-boyfriend and moving to Redwood Bay, I swear off men for good. The only company I need is my new rescue dog, Queenie. Meeting gorgeous firefighter Lochlan Bell at puppy training class doesn't count because he's straight, yet for some bizarre reason he's decided to become my friend. When he suggests *pretending* to be my boyfriend for Thanksgiving to stop my concerned family from worrying about me, the lines start to blur. Even if Lochlan suddenly realizes he likes men, though, he'd never be into a nerd like me. Right?

LOCHLAN

Who knew that pulling a trembling puppy from a burning building would lead to meeting my new best friend? Dario Garcia-Perez is so cool and smart, I'm surprised he puts up with a dumb jock like me. But I can tell he's running from something that hurt him real bad. Or some*one*. It takes me way too long to realize that all these protective feelings I have for him might mean something else. Something more. Something amazing. Just as we start getting closer, though, Dario's past comes back to haunt him. The difference now is that he has me, and I'm not going anywhere.

__Igniting His Flame__ is a red-hot, standalone MM romance. It's the first book in the found family __Redwood Bay Fire__ series. Join the members of the One-Thirteen house as the heat turns up and they find true love! This book features a completely oblivious bisexual himbo, two four-legged best friends, a childhood bedroom with only one bed, a shared obsession with all things sci-fi, a disaster at the amusement park, an ex with a dangerous vendetta, and a guaranteed HEA with absolutely no cliffhanger.

Content Warning: This book deals with a past domestic abuse situation between Dario and his ex. No violence occurs on page.

Click here to get the Igniting His Flame eBook

REDWOOD BAY FIRE #2: FROM THE ASHES BY HJ WELCH

Love is never lost

COLT

Walking away from Zahir Delacroix was the worst mistake I ever made. Over the years, I've tried to convince myself it was just a high school fling that wasn't worth coming out for. My father was always clear that I was expected to follow in his footsteps, which meant becoming a hotshot lawyer and finding an appropriate high-society wife. Except I never did marry, and my legal career has brought me right back to Redwood Bay to take over his practice. Of course the first person I run into is Zahir, and it's like the last fifteen years never happened. I still love him. Always have, always will. But I know he can never forgive me for what I did, nor love me when my family will never accept him. This time, it looks like I'm going to be the one left with a shattered heart.

ZAHIR

After ghosting me the moment we graduated high school, I never expected to see Colton Ross again. Coming face to face with him on a call is completely unexpected, and now he's back in Redwood Bay, our paths refuse to stop crossing. I'd be a fool to let him into my life again, but my fragile heart can't seem to resist my first love, my only true love. It might feel like destiny has reunited us, but nothing has really changed. I'm still never going to fit into his world, and I refuse to be his secret once more. But am I strong enough to let him go a second time?

From the Ashes is a red-hot, standalone MM romance. It's the second book in the found family **Redwood Bay Fire** series. Join the members of the One-Thirteen house as the heat turns up and they find true love! This book features a second chance at first love, tattered hearts that need to learn to trust again, an intimate portrait painting session, surfing lessons, a grandma who suffers no fools, earth shattering revelations, and a guaranteed HEA with absolutely no cliffhanger.

Click here to get the From the Ashes eBook

boyfriend Dair when he gets home from work. Hold on to your horses, Marine!

————

Troubled Waters

Bodyguard Scout Duffy doesn't know what's worse: the fact that his scorching one-night-stand, Emery Klein, is his bratty new client, or the fact that he doesn't even remember Scout. But Emery's life is in danger thanks to his out and proud charity work, and once he finally recognizes Scout, their chemistry in undeniable.

————

Homeward Bound

Swift Coal just found out he's a father, and his daughter (and her cranky cat) are coming to stay. His best friend's younger brother, Micha Perkins, has nowhere to go and a wrongfully tattered reputation. He's relieved when Swift asks him to be a live-in babysitter. He just has to hide his lifelong crush. Easy, because Swift is straight—right?

————

Bright Horizon

With sixteen years between them, baker Ben Turner and lawyer Elias Solomon have no idea their crush is mutual. But when Ben inherits his long-lost family's estate and becomes an overnight millionaire, Elias swears to protect the innocent younger man from the vultures circling him. To unravel the mystery of the inheritance, they must go to England to confront Ben's estranged relatives...and their feelings for each other.

————

Crossed Paths

Raj Bhat is done living in the shadows. It's time for him to take charge of his own destiny and tell the man he's fallen for how he really feels.

———

Midnight Sky

It's the night before New Year's Eve. Taylan Demir is all alone, and he's just lost his dog. Except when his handsome customer, Hudson Perkins, comes to his rescue, Taylan doesn't just get his dog back. He's suddenly got a hot date, and maybe someone to kiss when the clock strikes midnight.

———

Memory Lane

Angel Shields saved Jay Coal's life in high school, and Jay has secretly loved his straight best friend ever since. Now Angel's back in town with amnesia after a suspicious work accident and it's Jay's turn to rescue him. He pretends to be Angel's fiancé to see him in the hospital, but with his scrambled-up memory, Angel's not sure it's fictional after all. He just knows he loves Jay more than ever.

———

Thin Ice

Kamran's ex broke his heart, tricked him into aiding a bank robbery, and now he wants him to do one last job. There's only one way to say no: seek the protective custody of the biggest, grumpiest FBI agent ever, Lee Marshall. And pretend to be his boyfriend for a week-long family reunion in their giant mansion. Wait, what?

———

Calm Shores

Gorgeous, sophisticated Dante walks into Oliver's bar and orders…a boyfriend?! Dante needs a man to keep his mother from setting him back up with his awful, cheating ex, and Oliver is up for the challenge.

———

Fresh Snow

Emery Klein is throwing the best Christmas party ever, but his fiancé, Scout Duffy, and all their friends have something more exciting in mind.

———

Each Pine Cove book can be read as a stand alone and has its own happy ever after. But if you read the whole series, you'll see a lot of familiar faces!

Click here to get the Pine Cove eBook bundle

Click here to get the Pine Cove audio bundle

Spark

The last thing Joey Sullivan wants is to go back to his homophobic family, but he's penniless and has no choice. Recently single and heartbroken Gabe Robinson loves the town Joey hates. As a librarian and voluntary firefighter, he's used to helping people. When Joey gets a lucky break out of state, Gabe doesn't hesitate to take him on a road trip. The sparks that fly between them have to be just temporary, though. Joey can't wait to leave town and his family are eager to kick him out the door. Can Gabe's love save him from ending up on the streets? *Contains bonus epilogue.*

Burn

Songwriter Raiden Jones never thought he'd need a bodyguard. But when a malicious hacker starts destroying his career and threatening his life, he finds himself desperately in need of protection. That means ex-Marine Levi Patterson is stuck on tour with the bratty Raiden, their friction quickly turning sexual. Bisexual Levi is firmly in the closet and Raiden's never thought of being with a man before, but the chemistry is too fierce to ignore. Will the hacker ruin everything before they can work through their differences? *Contains bonus epilogue.*

Steam

Bad boy movie star Trent Charles is in need of an image makeover. Ashby Wilcott wants some peace and quiet after his ex-boyfriend cheated on him. They both find themselves in a remote ski resort, but Ashby refuses to fall for hot-as-hell Trent. Good thing Trent is straight, because Ashby is done with trouble makers. Except when Trent rescues Ashby from a sleaze, they find themselves pretending to be boyfriends for a wedding weekend. Ashby awakes a longing in Trent he's never felt before, and Ashby realizes Trent has a heart of gold. But can this fling last longer than the melting snow when there's a creep determined to tear them apart?

Blaze

Reyse Hickson might be an international pop sensation, but he's also forced to remain in the closet thanks to his homophobic record label. When gorgeous Corey Sheppard saves Reyse from a mugging, Reyse can't resist falling into his bed, if only for one night. However, a family emergency calls Reyse home, and it seems like the perfect chance for him and Corey to steal some secret time together. But it can't last. Reyse's label would never allow it. Can Reyse and Corey walk away from the best thing that's ever happened to either of them? Or is this love worth going down in a blaze of glory? *Contains bonus epilogue.*

Each Homecoming Hearts book can be read as a stand alone and has its own happy ever after. But if you read the whole series, you'll see familiar faces returning, and enjoy the spectacular ending of Blaze even more!

Click here to get the Homecoming Hearts eBook bundle

door, will Joshua and Darius's blossoming love be strong enough to save each other?

———

A Right Royal Affair

Nobody knows that Prince James of the United Kingdom is bisexual, and as he's sixth in line to the throne, it needs to stay that way. But when he meets the cheeky, outrageously gay Essex boy, Theo Glass, everything could change. Against his better judgement, James asks Theo to help him put on a royal charity ball to remember. Can they resist their mutual attraction for a whole week alone in a picturesque castle, or will true love bloom?

———

Hair Out of Place

Raphael d'Oro is a secret prince who has spent his entire life exiled in a London penthouse. But now he's in a race against time to get back to his tiny European nation to claim the throne that's rightfully his and save his people. Good thing he has his insanely hot older bodyguard to take care of him. But Griff Thompson would never want someone as inexperienced as Raphie, would he? Even *if* they keep finding themselves in places with only one bed…

Click here for the Fairy Tale Collection eBook

Click here for the Fairy Tale Collection audio

About the Author

HJ Welch is an author of contemporary MM romance series, including the international bestselling Pine Cove series. She lives just outside of London with her husband and three balls of fluff that occasionally pretend to be cats. She began writing at an early age, later honing her craft online in the world of fanfiction on sites like Wattpad. Fifteen years and over half a million words later, she sought out original MM novels to read. By the end of 2016 she had written her first book of her own, and in 2017 she achieved her lifelong dream of becoming a full-time author. When she's not writing she's usually dancing, singing, filming music videos, taking long walks, working on jigsaw puzzles, drinking prosecco, or talking about Taylor Swift.

She also writes contemporary British MM fairy tale adaptations as Helen Juliet.

You can contact Helen via the following:
Newsletter: https://www.subscribepage.com/helenjuliet
Website – www.hjwelch.com
Facebook Group – Helen's Jewels
Instagram – @helenjwrites
BlueSky – @helenjuliet.bsky.social
Book Bub – @HJWelchAuthor
Facebook Page – @HJWelchAuthor